For Blood or Money

Other Titles by Nathan Everett

The Volunteer

Journey inside the head of G2, a chronically homeless man that in a less politically correct age we'd have called a hobo. This dystopian literary fiction takes the reader into G2's concept of the present and his memories of a time before he volunteered to trade places with a homeless man.

For Money or Mayhem

Computer forensics detective Dag Hamar is pulled from behind the safety of his computer and takes to the streets when he discovers a link between an online predator and real life kidnappings around Seattle. His fledgling romance is threatened when his girlfriend's daughter is suddenly among the missing.

The Gutenberg Rubric

Two rare book librarians race across three continents to find and preserve a legendary book printed by Johannes Gutenberg. Behind them, a trail of bombed libraries draws Homeland Security to launch a worldwide search for biblio-terrorists. Keith and Maddie find love along the way, but will they survive to enjoy it?

Steven George & The Dragon

Steven has always known he was a dragonslayer, but on the day his village sends him to slay the fearsome beast he realizes he doesn't know what a dragon looks like, where it lives, or how to kill it. His quest is facilitated by the exchange of "once-upon-a-times" with the people he meets on the endless road. Think Grimm. For young adults, not children.

For Blood or Money

Nathan Everett

ELDER ROAD LLC
BELLEVUE WA

Second Edition

Requests for permission to make copies of any part of the work should be submitted via email at ElderRoad@comcast.net or mailed to:
Permissions Department,
Elder Road LLC
15600 NE 8th St, Suite B1 PMB#392,
Bellevue, WA, 98008.

ISBN 978-1-939275-21-9

ElderRoad@comcast.net

Contents

For Blood or Money

Biting the Big One

I PICKED UP A TAIL at the start of display Aisle 200 and she was sticking to me like cat hair on a blue suit. I didn't really mind. She was the only thing I'd seen in a skirt all week. Cocktail waitresses don't really count.

I was in Vegas for the annual Geek Convention, also called SpyCon. A lot of private dicks, investigators, cops, and undercover geeks get together to view the latest in high tech toys, hear improbable tales of law enforcement, and act like they are on covert missions. Basically fun, and the only reason I drive from Seattle to Vegas once each year.

I'm Dag Hamar, PI. And I'm a tech geek.

I dallied in front of a display of long-range listening devices, guaranteed to filter individual voices out of a crowd at a hundred feet. She either had to stop in front of a display of interrogation techniques or move on to join me. She chose the latter.

"Do those things really work?" she asked. "They seem too small to be effective. You really need a tripod to steady it if you are going to pick out an individual, don't you?"

Good technique. A tail would never actually approach her quarry. Doing so would call attention to her and therefore disqualify her as an effective tail. Unless she thought you'd invite her to join you. That would make the job of tailing you a lot easier. Well, it was a good ploy. I'd play along for a while.

"You're right, a nice big mic on a tripod would be best, but it's an interesting technology. Supposedly you can even bounce off any solid surface. It has possibilities." We walked on to the next booth and she asked the exhibitor a detailed and intelligent question about miniaturized transmitters. The exhibitor was all too thrilled to give her an equally detailed response, just to be in her presence. She was tall and slender, and the kind of natural honey blonde whose hair stuck out in all directions. And cute. She had no end of cute.

I decided to hang around and wait for her instead of losing her at just that moment.

We chatted as we walked down the display aisle that included everything from night vision glasses, to telephone bugs, to high-resolution miniature digital cameras. This was really toy heaven. I'd already selected a miniaturized homing device in the top of an innocuous looking ballpoint pen. It was the kind of thing you could give to a mark or slip onto him without his ever knowing you were tracking him. I do like gadgets.

For her part, my tail was proving herself charming, funny, and flirtatious—sure signs she was not what she appeared to be. It's been years since young women have been charming, funny, and flirtatious around me. I'm not only a PI, I'm a retread.

We turned into Aisle 500 and she turned more abruptly than she intended and stumbled into me. I caught her and she leaned into me and said breathlessly, "What would you say if I asked if you'd like to get lucky?" She looked up at me with teasing eyes that held a hundred unspoken promises.

Okay. I'm flattered, even if I know this is a pro job. What's a man to say?

"Well, hypothetically speaking," I said, "I'd have to consider that you are a very beautiful young woman making an obvious pass at an older and distinguished gentleman. Then I'd have to say, no." She looked up at me startled.

"No?"

"No."

"Why not? Don't you like me?"

"Oh, I like you very much. I think you're delightful company."

"Then why?" I couldn't tell if she was acting hurt or insulted, or a little of both. It was the first crack I'd seen in her act.

"First of all, I try to never get involved with anyone less than half my age," I said. Plus seven, I added silently to myself. How true. Unfortunately I'm pretty successful at it. She did not seem impressed.

"Okay, do you remember that long distance mic that could pick a single voice out of a crowd?" I asked.

"Yes."

"They have one over on that balcony, considerably less than a hundred feet away, that's been following us ever since we left that booth, meaning every word has been recorded." She appeared startled and turned to look.

"Third," I continued, "you are a woman of exquisite taste, but the buttons of your blouse don't match. That tells me that the one in the middle is a fisheye camera that you are using to record our interaction." She clapped a hand over the offending button.

"And finally, judging by your Olympic University lapel pin, I'd have to say that Lars Andersen is standing around here someplace laughing at us for all he's worth," I concluded.

"Wow," she said. "He told me you were good."

"The best I ever trained," Lars interjected walking up behind me. "How you doing, Dag?" I greeted my old friend and mentor warmly. "It's good to see you haven't forgotten everything I ever taught you," he said. "I was worried about your skills going downhill stuck in that office all the time. No field work, no fun."

"Oh it's not that bad," I said. "I accomplish a bit here and there."

"Like what?" Lars asked.

"Like three embezzlement cases, two bank fraud cases, six child porn cases, three industrial espionage cases, and fifteen identity theft cases," said Jordan Grant walking up next to Lars. It was turning into old home week. I shook Jordan's hand.

"Sixteen if you count John Doe," I said. Damnedest case we'd ever had. He had stolen over twenty identities, but we never could identify who he really was, even after he was in custody. He had completely erased his own identity in the process.

."So you guys all know each other," my tail said. "Anybody want to introduce me?"

"Dag," Lars said, "Let me introduce you to the finest student I've had since you and Jordan. This is Miss Deborah Riley." I reached out to shake her hand.

"I'm glad to meet you D…" I broke off as she squeezed my hand in vise-like fingers.

"If you call me Debbie, it will be the last time you ever use your tongue," she intoned lowly.

"Geez, Riley," I said, "why don't you say what you mean?"

"Riley," she repeated lightening her grip. "I like that. Nice to meet you Mr. Hamar."

"Now what I want to know, Lars, is why you think she's so good? I picked up on her right away."

"Yes," Lars winked at Riley. "I figured you'd made her back at the long-range mics. What do you have to say for yourself Riley?"

"Dagget Hamar. Arrived in Las Vegas Tuesday afternoon at 3:00 driving a yellow 1983 Mustang in mint condition. Accompanied by a small dog named Maizie, checked into the Capricorn Motel just off the Strip. Dogs accommodated. Conservative tastes. Even wears a suit to a geek convention. Spent a lonely evening last night in the third row of "Cavalcade" enjoying an adult circus show. Plays in the casino for no more than half an hour at a time with modest bets—mostly Blackjack."

"You compiled quite a dossier," I said.

"I've been following you for three days," she answered. "Lars told me I had to get caught today or we'd never get together."

"Now I am impressed," I laughed. "It's always good to welcome another one of Lars's protégés."

"He said there's a lot I could learn from you," Riley said, winking at me. "I'd like to find out."

"Dag," Lars interrupted, "we've got reservations for four at the Monte Vista Room at 7:00. Why don't we pick up the conversation there. We all need to get out of this den of spies and get cleaned up before dinner."

It was arranged, that fast. When I got to the Monte Vista Room, Lars, Jordan, and Riley were already there waiting for me. The first thing I noticed was that even though Lars and Jordan were well into a martini, Riley was sipping tonic. My kind of girl. I ordered one as well and shortly thereafter we were seated.

It's always a lively conversation when Lars, Jordan, and I get together as we do most years at this convention. Even though he's a good bit younger than I am, Jordan and I studied criminal justice under Lars at the same time. I went into private business and Jordan eventually joined the Feds. Our paths keep crossing, though, since I do so much computer forensics work for his department, FinCEN—the Financial Crimes Enforcement Network. We've got along great for years.

Riley, it turned out, had done her undergraduate work in computer science and went into a graduate program in criminal justice under Lars. I have to admit: even when she wasn't being a vamp, she was bright and beautiful, and just plain fun to be around. As of the end of May she would be all but thesis for her Master's Degree and Lars wanted her to apprentice in a working agency. He'd chosen mine.

I usually work alone, but lately I'd had a lot of smaller projects that could easily have been handled by an assistant. It sounded like it might be workable. I suggested that she come to interview when we got back to Seattle.

When dinner was over, I stood to leave while Lars and Jordan had another drink. Riley stood and walked out of the restaurant with me.

The casino we were in was an aging beauty of the old Strip, not likely to last much longer against the modern megaplexes that now dominated Las Vegas. It had a gold rush theme from the 1840s. The waitresses were dressed in old-time cancan skirts with the hem pulled up and tucked in the waistband.

I estimated some of them to be the original owners.

Riley put her hand through my arm as we walked through the casino, maybe as much for protection as from any sense of attraction.

The tall, elegant blonde was dressed in a black cocktail dress that exposed about fifty not so very square inches of flawless flesh to the harsh casino lights.

"So, Dag Hamar," she said looking up at me. "You wanna get lucky?"

"I thought we'd covered that point, Riley," I said.

"I mean in the casino," she said laughing. "Teach me how to play roulette."

"That's easy," I said. We stepped up to an opening at a table and I asked the croupier for four $5 chips. I handed one to Riley and said, "The best way to play roulette is to lay your first bet on your age. If the ball rolls into that slot it pays 35 to 1." She pushed her chip onto the 29 square. I looked at her with one eyebrow raised. She moved the chip to 28, glanced at me and sighed, then moved it to 27. I reached out and dropped the remaining chips on 26 just before the dealer called "No more bets."

When the ball came to rest, he reached over and put the pip on top of my chips as he called out "Black 26." He scooped off the other players' chips and paid my three red chips with five black, and a green. I left the red and green chips on the table for him, scooped up the five hundred, shoved four in my pocket and handed one to Riley.

"You are supposed to be honest when you bet your age," I smiled. It was the first time I'd seen her less than fully composed.

"How did you know?" she asked. "My birthday is in two weeks!"

I suddenly found that I couldn't answer her. My smile was still on my face and I was looking at her, but I couldn't see her. She faded in and out. There was a pain in my chest and my right leg was crumpling under me. A roaring sound deafened my ears. I reached toward her and she held my hand as I sank to the floor in the middle of the casino.

"Call 911!" I heard her yell. It was going to be too late. I knew that. I'd never had a heart attack, but there was no mistaking what was happening. Then she was shoving something into my mouth and forcing me to chew it. I tasted the bitter flavor of aspirin.

I was sure a heart attack in the company of a beautiful young woman was supposed to be under different circumstances.

Eight Months Later

TROUBLE BLEW INTO MY OFFICE with the scent of lilacs on a spring breeze. A tear collected in the corner of my eye.

I sneezed.

Damn allergies.

"Are you Dag Hamar?" she snapped, turning toward me.

"Yes ma'am," I responded, standing. There were still tears in my eyes. Floral scents really kill me.

"I liked you better with long hair and a beard." I wiped my eyes and looked at her—above the spike heels, tight skirt and ample bosom. The bubble burst. What she meant was she liked me better 30 years ago.

"You found your way in, I assume you can find your way out," I growled as I sat back down.

"I want to hire you," she said. "I need a private investigator."

I was about to tell her to have her privates investigated elsewhere when Maizie came to the rescue. She slipped up behind my unwanted guest and stuck her cold wet nose in the back of her right knee. The lady gave a short screech, tottered on her high heels and fell over backward into the chair behind her. I couldn't help it. I laughed.

"What the hell is that?" she asked indignantly, clamping her knees together to block Maizie's assault on her next target.

"My dog," I said. "Maizie, here! No personal sniffing." Maizie came scrabbling around the corner of my desk with all four feet skidding to gain purchase on the hardwood floor. She leaped up into my lap and began licking my ear.

"I can see it's a dog, but what is it?"

"She's a mix," I said. Then I went ahead, "A Pit Bull and Dachsund mix." I could see the wheels start turning.

"Which was…?" she started. "Never mind," she finished, shaking her head. She started again. "I need your help. Not some other detective. It has to be you. Please treat me as you would any client."

Any client? Not likely. This woman was one of Seattle's most prominent women. Her picture was in the paper at least once a month shaking hands with the mayor, the governor, or the president of a major corporation. Rumor had it that she had a finger or some other body part in any arts, politics, or business plan in the city. There weren't many reasons I could think of for her to want me on an investigation, and those I could think of weren't good.

"Okay, Mrs. Barnett" I said. "Let's suppose you just came in here to hire me. If the job interests me, won't interfere with my other work, and if I like the client, I might take it. So spill."

"Simon is missing," she plunged in. "I haven't heard from him since he left Sunday before last. I need you to find him."

Simon Barnett was the president and majority owner of a privately held conglomerate with revenues in nine or ten figures and a net measured in billions. His office was on the top floor of the Washington Building, but for all the space, I'd heard he employed relatively few people there.

The Simon Barnett that I knew was more than a corporate bigwig—and much less. If I were in his position, I'd probably disappear too. One reason was sitting right in front of me. I stared fixedly at Brenda Barnett. As much as Simon shunned publicity, Brenda lived for newspaper photographers and famous handshakes. While she smiled for the cameras, he quietly bought and sold people in the form of stocks and corporations.

"That's only ten days," I said at last. "Surely it can't be that unusual for your husband to go away for a while. He probably has a mistress."

"Yes, well…" She paused. "This is different," she sniffed.

"Did you go to the police?" I asked.

"No. Simon wouldn't want it."

"And you think he'd want you to come to *me*?" Something was fishy here and it wasn't just the smell of Puget Sound lapping up against the pier where my office was located. "I don't do missing persons. I'm a computer pathologist." Computer forensics is actually the field. Most of the time, I try to recover data erased from hard drives. Sometimes the job includes extracting evidence of computer crime for the police. I don't do missing persons.

"That's why I've brought you this," she said. She reached into her bag and pulled out a sizable laptop computer. Not the latest model by any means, but a good little computer. I held up both hands to stop her from putting the thing on my desk.

"Hang on," I said. "Keep that in your lap and not on my desk. I want to know more before it leaves your hands." She sat back with the laptop on her knees. "Why are you coming to me? I'm not the only one in this business anymore."

"Simon says," she answered.

"So we're playing that game again," I sighed. Simon Says. The very phrase transported me back to college days with two friends I thought would be with me for the rest of my life. I was older by a couple of years because of my military service, but Simon and Brenda were my constant companions from Freshman Orientation on. Most of the time we agreed on what we were doing, where we were going, and when we were doing things. We were tight. But whenever there was a question, we always yielded to Simon. He was clever about things, knew where things were happening, how to get in, and which direction to take to avoid the campus cops if we were out past curfew. (Yeah, we still had curfews back then.) We started calling it "Simon Says." If there was a question, we waited for what Simon said, and that's what we did. Now Brenda was telling me that Simon says he wants me on the case, in spite of the bad blood that had kept us apart for decades.

"Look," Brenda sighed. "*I* wouldn't come to you. Simon left instructions. We have uh… an open relationship. Hell, he's probably slept with more women than Wilt Chamberlain. And I've… Never mind. But there's always been a code. Check in at least once a week. If he doesn't check in within the week, open the envelope."

"A week was three days ago," I said.

"I didn't want to open it. I didn't want to know what was in it. I was afraid that it might be a farewell note; that he'd left me. I stared at it all day Monday. When I opened it Tuesday, I couldn't believe what he said." A tear gathered in a corner of one of her eyes and she dabbed at it with a tissue. I reminded myself that I was dealing with Brenda Barnett.

"What was in the envelope?" She handed me an envelope that had been torn open along one end. I shook the sheet of notepaper out and unfolded it on my desk. The writing was clear. Simon always printed in block letters. Something about having studied drafting way back when. The note was short and simple:

"If you are opening this, I've been gone for at least a week without a word. Take my laptop to Dag Hamar. Dag, Simon says, FIND ME."

I was going to be plunged into the regretful past whether I wanted or not. "Simon says." Old habits die hard. I found myself unable to say "no."

"Brenda, presumably you're holding Simon's laptop. Do you know what's on it?"

"I don't care what's on it. I'm interested in finding Simon. He says give it to you."

"You need to know that if I have that laptop, I have all the information that is on it. If he does on-line banking, I will know your bank accounts. I'll be able to read his e-mail. I'll know if he visits pornographic websites. In essence, I will have his entire identity at my disposal, and probably yours. Are you ready to trust *me* with that?"

"Are you saying you'd steal my identity?" she asked, coyly, as if it were a great compliment.

"No. I like my own identity, thank you." I reached in a desk drawer and took out a blanket release form and pushed it across the desk toward her. The form gives me permission to access any and all information on a hard drive and affirms my confidentiality. She signed it without reading.

"I'll need a $5,000 advance," I said nonchalantly. "I charge $1,000 a day plus expenses. I'll bill you weekly for everything I'm working on. I won't bill you time that I'm working on other cases." She didn't even blink as she wrote out the check and pushed it across the desk to me.

"You said you'd have access to all my banking information," she smiled. "Just deduct your expenses from it." The smugness in her voice made me cringe as she set the laptop on the desk and stood to leave as my assistant, Riley, burst into the office.

"Dag, I'm sorry I'm late. It's time for your pills," Riley said as she rushed in pulling off her jacket. "Oh, I'm sorry. I didn't know you had a…" she looked at Brenda and then at me, "client?" she finished.

"Oh, your new squeeze, Dag?" Brenda asked with a smirk. "I'd heard you grew out of your juvenile phase. I see I heard wrong."

"Riley's my assistant," I said, irritably.

"Then she won't mind if you have dinner with me tonight," Brenda said. I thought better of what I'd just said.

"Sorry, no can do. It's employee appreciation week and I'm taking Riley to dinner tonight. I promised." Poor Riley was standing staring open-mouthed, but her eyes went wide when I said I was taking her to dinner.

"Well, I'm sure the invitation will still be open when you get tired of her," Brenda said. "Tomorrow?"

"I think we've finished for today, Mrs. Barnett. If you want results on this case, I should get to work. Now as I said before, I assume since you found your way in you can find your way out. Good day."

I turned my attention away and Maizie jumped down from my lap to run around and greet Riley. Brenda saw the dog move and took the hint to leave.

"Sorry, Dag," Riley said. "I didn't mean to interrupt. I just realized that I hadn't gotten back to get you your pills and I knew you'd forget. So who was the muffin-top?"

11

"It's okay, Riley. It didn't make a difference. You could have been Mother Teresa and Brenda Barnett would have thought the same thing and said the same thing. It's just the way she is." I took the pills that Riley shoved at me and pulled the laptop closer to me.

"What's a muffin-top?" I asked absently. Riley laughed.

"It's a size 12 woman stuffed in a size 10 dress... and bra," she answered. "Come on, now. Don't tell me you didn't notice. Her cups overfloweth." Riley is pretty blunt about some things. I had to chuckle.

"That's our new client, Riley: Brenda Barnett. Her husband is missing and she wants us to find him."

"Probably ran away. And it's only you she wants, not us."

I looked up. Riley was sitting on the front edge of my desk with her feet propped up drinking a cup of coffee. Maizie sat on her lap licking the breath she exhaled. I envied her. This heart dictates that I lay off the caffeine.

"Well, she gets the pair, whether she wants it or not. Brenda has a very low opinion of women. She has already dismissed you and expects that you will be gone before she ever sees me again. That's a big advantage for us. She doesn't know you will be investigating."

"Really, what do I get to do?" Riley asked excitedly.

"Number one, rush this check to the bank. I don't want to invest a minute on this case without cash in hand."

"You think she'd cheat you?" Bad choice of words. Would she cheat on me? I guess that's not what she was asking.

"She wouldn't even recognize it as cheating. She'd be reckless. She might not have the funds in her account. She might assume that I won't cash it for a couple of weeks and not be concerned, or that the bank would cover it if there was a problem. She might figure that I'll just forget about it and it won't make a difference. But there's really only one reason that I'd take a case like this."

"What would that be?" Riley said shoving her limited cleavage together and then dropping the check down her front.

I swear, I wasn't watching that.

"Money." I said. "She and Simon can pay more than any client we've ever had."

"There's another reason," Riley probed seriously. "You don't do missing persons and it would take more than money to get you into this."

"Yes, that's what Simon says," I mumbled. She didn't probe anymore which is good because I really wasn't ready to say anything else.

"You're really taking me to dinner tonight, though, aren't you? Say to the Ninety-Nine?"

"Look Riley, you know I'd like to, but I need to get home. I've got Maizie and this laptop to start tearing down."

"You said. And besides I'll take Maizie home on the way to the bank. Then I'll go home and get changed and pick you up at 7:30. That gives you another four hours this afternoon to stare at the outside of that computer case and then hide it before I get back."

"Okay, but I want you to do some real work while you are at it. We are looking for Simon Barnett, CEO of Barnett, Keane, and Lamb. I want you to start compiling dossiers on Simon, Brenda, and the business. What are his patterns? Where does he go? Who does he see? There are probably some public records, but BKL is privately held, so there won't be anything in the way of stockholder filings and such. You'll have to use those pretty little legs of yours to do some old fashioned investigating. Got it?"

"Really? For fun!" She swung her gams off my desk and headed for the door grabbing Maizie's leash off the hat rack. I'm not sure if she was more excited about dinner tonight or getting to dig into Brenda Barnett's affairs.

She bolted out the door with Maizie in tow, and I had the promised four hours to stare at Simon's laptop. With Simon, you never could tell. The clue he was trying to get to me could literally be on the laptop, not in the data. What I understood from the moment I read the note was that Simon wasn't missing.

He was hiding.

I've Got a Secret

SIX O'CLOCK GETS EARLIER EVERY MORNING. If it weren't for the wet nose stuck in my face and the demands of having a pet that needs to be walked, I'd have rolled over and stayed warm and comfy in my bed. But Maizie was insistent.

I hauled myself out of the sack and headed for the john. Aging sucks. A back injury from when I was in the Navy keeps acting up on me, especially when the weather changes from dry to wet like it did this morning. I count it a good day if I can stand up straight by the time I get from bed to bath. This morning I was all the way to the kitchen before the last spasm subsided.

The clouds hung heavy around Queen Anne giving the Space Needle that strange other-worldly appearance that makes you think aliens have landed and are taking over downtown. With Maizie on her leash and an umbrella over our heads we set off through the cold mist for the office. Lower Queen Anne is a great place to live. I can walk to the Waterfront with only a couple of stops to rest. Thankfully, Riley drives me home at night. I'd never make it back up the hill with my breath as short as it's been lately.

My first stop was at a coffee shop on Broad. It's one of the few independents that were left in the city that spawned coffee-love throughout the world. But big name brands are the lowest common denominator for anything that wants to be called espresso. The little independents were where you got a cup that opened your eyes and put a smile on

14

your face. Tavoni's was just that kind of shop.

Maizie and I stepped through the front door at 7:00 and both shook the water off. At that hour, when they open, there is never a question of standing in line, or even ordering. Jackie came out from around the counter and brought me my espresso and Maizie's biscuit.

Yeah. Espresso with my heart. There are a few pleasures in life that are worth dying for.

Jackie brings me an Americano—two shots of espresso pulled on top of two shots of hot water. I'd drink the espresso straight, but it cools off too quickly.

Espresso is an art, both in creation and consumption. I held the cup in both hands and absorbed the warmth through my fingers as the aroma tickled at the edges of my nose. I never drink fast. If I dove in and took a drink I'd just burn my tongue. I just hold it there and breathe. Then slowly bring it closer—about four inches from my face— and inhale deeply. A properly-made espresso will pick me up from that distance and jumpstart my heart. I could feel it working before the cup actually touched my lips. The first sip was mostly crème. That's the oily foam that rests on top of a freshly-pulled shot of espresso. Just beneath the silky foam comes the first taste of heaven. The coffee was strong enough to dry my mouth out. The flavor washed across the sides of my tongue first then swept up to meet in the middle. As soon as the black liquid hit my throat, I inhaled again, sucking air down with the coffee until my lungs felt like they would explode. Lowering the cup so not to cool it, I expelled the air out through my mouth in a long sigh.

The cup at Tavoni's was the only cup in the day that I got any-more, and I savored every last drop without thinking of anything else. I didn't read. I didn't talk. I didn't listen. I coffeed.

After my coffee was finished, I checked the headlines of the newspaper and looked through the business section. When Maizie had finished her biscuit, we took our refreshed selves on to the office.

Riley was doing research at the library and then at the court-house to look up all relevant records on BKL. I figured I had about six hours before she got back to the office. She tried to get me up and dancing after dinner last night, but I just couldn't do that. Of course, there wasn't a man in the club who didn't want to wrap his arms around her dressed the way she was. She didn't really like people to be that close to her, though. What a real contradiction in terms.

I unlocked the vault and checked the status of my drive set-up.

The vault was a special room I had built in this office when I first moved here years ago. I don't show it to anyone who doesn't need to know. The vault was located behind a wall next to the bathroom. A remote control sat on my desk for the wide-screen television on the wall opposite. If you knew the codes it would also unlock the vault. The wall slid open and a small room was revealed. The room was temperature controlled to keep the heat from my servers at bay. I had my own network and web servers so I didn't have to use an ISP for connection to the Internet. The room was small, if only because one wall was lined with servers. It took a lot of power, but kept me independent from third parties.

Before I left last night, I wired Simon's laptop into the system behind a firewall and a write-blocker. Then I spun the disk up and did a full spectrum analysis of the hard drive, including making two copies of the disk on new drives. I disconnected the laptop from the system and locked it and one backup in the safe in the vault. I wouldn't touch the subject hardware unless I discovered there was a hardware key needed for security override. There was no more than one computer in a hundred thousand that required a hardware key. I wired the other backup drive into my network, protected by a firewall. Once that was done, I closed and locked the vault.

I didn't work on computers in the vault, I kept them safe there. I worked on an ultra-portable laptop. It weighed less than three pounds and could connect to the Internet from just about anywhere in the world. I connected through a cellular connection so there wasn't a wireless network in the office that anyone else could detect. I used a virtual private network to connect to the real power that was safely locked up in the vault.

I was paranoid about security, which is why I was so good at getting around other people's.

If Simon wanted me to find him, he wouldn't have made it too hard to do, but that assumption could trip me up. Simon would set things up in such a way that he thought only I could get the clues. That meant he probably tried to be cleverer than he actually was which could backfire and get a person into trouble. And I couldn't rule out the possibility that the laptop itself might only be a hook to get me involved in the case.

If Simon was hiding more than himself, I thought, there might even be information on the computer that he didn't want me to find. He would use obvious clues to get me looking in one direction and obfuscate what he didn't want me to know. I fully expected his calendar would show only appointments he wanted me to know about.

I wanted to know why. Why after over thirty years did Simon send Brenda to me? Why did he want to play "Simon Says?"

For the rest of the day, I examined the results of my various searches of the hard drive. I stopped only twice. The first time was when Maizie insisted that it was time to go out again, which was a good reminder to take my pills and eat some lunch. The second time was when Riley came bursting through the door about 3:00 and proceeded to give her report.

Riley was in quite the mood. She paced up and down in front of the window of my office creating a striking silhouette against the light of the window. The setting sun lit her blonde hair and visually set it on fire. She was thin for five feet and nine inches tall. She moved like a cat and once told me she's a "brown belt," but I don't know in what discipline. Truth was I wouldn't test her. Riley was as sharp as Lars had promised and understood computers as well as she did the finer points of criminal justice. She didn't know it yet, but I planned to bring her into full partnership someday soon. Her apprenticeship days were about over.

"BKL is a kind of holding company. That's why there are so few people who work there. All the actual work is done in the companies that they hold. It's hard to tell exactly how many of those there are, as they only have to file if they own more than 20% of a publically-held company. But if they own 100%, it's not publically traded and they don't have to file SEC papers at all. The original business was a consulting firm, mostly accounting and high finance. They were significant in restructuring Allied Materials about nine years ago. That was just before Allied went private. Turns out BKL bought it out for pennies on the dollar. Allied had it rough for a while but made a killing in the aftermath of Katrina. They pulled down mega-contracts for supplying building materials and rumor has it that BKL is ready to take them public again."

She barely paused for breath before she was off on the next of BKL's acquisitions. They were into import/export, financial consulting, travel planning, and even owned a small brokerage. Two local car dealerships listed wholly-owned subsidiaries of BKL as owners. Simon had spread a wide net and was raking in cash hand over proverbial fist.

"And then there's our over-endowed client," Riley continued, making sure I understood she was punning. "Seattle Arts Council, Board of Directors of the Art Institute, Mayor's Council for the Homeless, Governor's Task Force on Public Transportation, Board of Directors of Cornerstone Bank, Board of Directors of Livermore Mortgage, Symphony Patrons Club, Seattle Athletic Club, President of the Homeowners Association of Madison Park, the list goes on and on. Her picture has shown up in the newspaper with governors back to Booth Gardner and nearly everyone who is anyone in the Financial 500. But there is nothing about anything she's actually done. She's just there."

"I suspected as much," I said, causing Riley to pause. "Tell me Watson, what does it all spell out? What do all these interests of Simon and Brenda Barnett say?"

"They are all over the map," she answered. "There doesn't seem to be any sense to any of it. One minute she's glad-handing a Republican, the next she's donated $5,000 to a Democrat. There's no common thread among the businesses that BKL invests in. You'd think they were all different businesses entirely. I don't see anything."

"Money," I answered myself. "Money and influence. And if you have money and influence, you have power."

"And if you have power," Riley continued, "you have enemies."

"You think?" I said. "Don't you think Simon and Brenda Barnett are beloved by everyone with whom they do business?" She looked at me blankly, as though I'd just spoken to her in Swedish. "I'm being sarcastic, Riley," I said. "Don't make me explain."

She laughed and plopped down on my sofa in a very unladylike pose.

"Do all Swedes have such a dry sense of humor?" she asked. "After eight months, I still can't tell when you are joking. I thought you were defending them."

"Not likely, Miss," I snapped. "But it never hurts to look past the obvious. Are they beloved benefactors or feared powers? Or does it make any difference at all? Get your shoes off the furniture." She kicked her shoes off onto the floor and continued to lie draped over the sofa like a knitted afghan. Maizie came over and licked Riley's fingers, then finding no resistance, jumped up on the sofa with her. She absently scratched the dog's ears and I could all but hear the wheels turning in her head.

"Dag, how do you get your fingers into so many pies? It's one thing to be in the right place at the right time to make a good investment, but so many? How do they get their leads? How do they know what to buy?"

"That is the question," I repeated. "Where do they make the contacts that keep Brenda so publicly involved and Simon so positioned to make big purchases? Do they entertain a lot? Do they go to the same club? Do they co-own a timeshare? And then you have to ask if Brenda's participation on so many committees is the lead generator and Simon is the closer?"

When I leased this office thirteen years ago, the owners were in the middle of a pier renovation project to try to bring new life to the Waterfront. They thought they would encourage businesses to take space and thus drive more traffic to the Waterfront. But Chameleon Imports had taken up one entire end of the facility three floors high and had it filled with the kind of faux artifacts you'd find in a cheap hotel. Nearly all their business was shipping and receiving, with very little retail or foot traffic. The rest of us who rented space on Pier 61 had few walk-in clients as well. So much for generating a lot of consumer traffic. It was a long way from my little two-person office to the mega-conglomerate that Simon ruled over at BKL

It was full dark when I turned around and saw that Maizie had fallen asleep next to Riley and that Riley was struggling to keep her eyes open. I grinned at the two of them.

"Think you can get me home before you start snoring?" I asked.

"I don't snore, Dag," she said indignantly getting up and putting her shoes back on. "As if you'd know."

We headed for the door and I turned out the last light and locked up my office. When she dropped Maizie and me off at our house, she asked me a curious question. "Dag, where does the money go? Do they just spend it? They've owned the same house for thirty years. What do they do with it all?" She had a point.

Maybe there was more missing than Simon.

Gone Fishing—With $ for Bait

THERE'S AN OLD ADAGE in detective work: follow the money. Riley's question about where the money goes got me thinking, and it kept gnawing at me all night. In that odd way that the mind works, I found myself in a very hot dream with an unidentified model-quality date. But at every "important" point in the dream, my date would vanish and a sign would pop up that said "please deposit fifty cents more." Most of the dream was occupied with trying to get fifty cents to deposit.

When I woke up, it was crystal clear to me that I had been looking for the wrong kind of clues on Simon's computer. I resolved to start checking bank and financial records and find out where the money was going.

Riley had Friday off to meet with Lars on her thesis, so I had the day to myself in the office. I gave her time for her thesis work and didn't require her to make it up. It was part of our agreement. Nonetheless, I knew that she would drive me to my appointments on Saturday even without asking.

I'd told Brenda that with the computer in my possession I would have access to all the personal information that was on it. That was only partly true. In order to get into bank records, I needed not only the computer's password, but the bank password. That could have been a real problem unless the user had stored the password on the computer, like Simon did. It was a pretty common mistake people made with their computers. They entered a user name and password and the operating system popped up a window that asked if they'd like to remember the password. Well, who wouldn't? Remembering passwords was a pain in the ass. Creating and remembering *secure* passwords was even harder.

Of course, when they selected the option to remember their password they got a little warning that anyone using this computer might be able to access the information they were saving. But who ever thought of anyone else using their personal computer in their home. Of course no one else had access to their computer—unless their spouse brought it to a computer forensics geek and told him to have a go at it. Getting into Simon's bank accounts was as easy as looking up his Web history of places visited and revisiting them. Auto-sign-in and remembered passwords took care of the rest.

I didn't know what I expected to find, but it wasn't this. His bank account was a model of accounting perfection. It showed regular paychecks from the firm, normal utilities, and a mortgage payment. Groceries were bought. In general, it indicated a couple living within their generous but not extravagant means. There was a satisfactory balance in the account and the check Brenda wrote to me was already posted. I scanned the checks that had been paid and noted that most of them were signed by Brenda. Simon didn't seem to do much with this family account.

The bank account led to credit cards and these, too, seemed in perfect order. But they showed a lot of different locations. Simon and Brenda traveled a lot. Dinner in New York, shopping, theater in DC. The next day, a hotel in Vegas. Did they ever stay home?

One account led to another and I discovered that there were often charges made in geographically different locations on the same day. A hotel in Orlando on the same night that one was paid in Acapulco. They traveled a lot, but not necessarily together. Finally, I came across the first of what I'd call Simon's personal accounts. This account showed mainly cash deposits and cash withdrawals. Normally, if there aren't checks you don't know where the money goes, but with ATM records, you can tell the route it went to get there. It was obvious that Simon had some favorite spots to get money. That could only mean that he visited those places regularly. And that he used a lot of cash.

As I continued to investigate the accounts that the laptop was revealing to me, it was like finding little piles of virtual cash stuck in nooks and crannies all over the house. The diversity in business that Riley had spotted yesterday seemed to be reflected in the diversity of Simon's accounts as well.

I found myself having pulled on a pair of surgical gloves that I wore when pulling apart a computer. But I wasn't doing more than reading the private accounts of a one-time friend. It was like handling his dirty underwear. I didn't really want to touch any of it.

It was still drizzling in Seattle, a gray, cold, wetness that felt like it had settled in for the season. It gets down into my bones and I decided there was no remedy but a bowl of Phó from a Vietnamese shop up at the Market. Maizie and I wound our way through the maze of tunnels and elevators that would get us from the Waterfront up to the Market and I ordered at the outdoor counter. At least they had an awning over the street so customers who sat on the outdoor stools were sheltered. Unfortunately, I couldn't go inside with Maizie.

I sat there eating the hot soup and stirring bean sprouts and hot sauce into it, still caught up in the puzzle of Simon's accounts. One of the cash machines that he frequented was located right here near Pike and First. I looked around, trying to picture him coming down from his penthouse office a few blocks away to get cash, lots of cash, near the Market. What kind of business was around here that he would want cash for? He certainly didn't buy that many groceries.

The lights changed and, in the fashion peculiar to that intersection in Seattle, all traffic stopped and pedestrians crossed from every corner at once, some straight across the street and some diagonally between the corners. That was when I realized that one of those corners was still occupied by one of the older strip clubs in town. A block away was another.

Suddenly I wished I was still wearing those latex gloves. Was that where Simon's money was going? I couldn't imagine Simon going into a strip club—too many people might recognize him—but he'd always had an appetite for women. He had to be sating it somewhere.

They say that the only people who understand the national debt are billionaire entrepreneurs and mathematicians. Billionaires because sums of money in the billions and trillions are real to them. Mathematicians because a billion is as real a number as a hundred. I fell into the latter group. I could theoretically spend thousands of dollars a week, but I had no idea how Simon would do it. And his ATM withdrawals mysteriously stopped about ten months ago. Didn't he use cash anymore?

I decided to start tracking down the major vices to see if there was one that might have gotten Simon hooked: women, gambling, and drugs.

Back at the office, I kept sifting through the files on Simon's computer, but this time with a purpose. I plotted his cash transactions back for over two years. In addition to the ATM transactions near the market, there were two other locations that came up repeatedly early on, then suddenly stopped appearing in the records about ten months earlier. I looked up the addresses and found my first big clue. The two addresses were for Indian casinos within thirty miles of Seattle. This was something I knew a little bit about.

I've always liked games, even though I've never been a big gambler. Still, I knew both of the casinos that were on the list. Several months ago, I was called by the operations manager of the Sammamish Casino and Bingo Hall. His records had undergone a tribal audit and came up short over half a million dollars. He called me in to sift through his computer system for the leak. Finding the leak and getting a conviction on the embezzler saved Frank Deep Water Johnson his job. He always felt he owed me and was careful to be sure I earned complimentary meals and show tickets at the casino slightly faster than my play level merited. I called Frank to see if he could help me.

"Dag Hamar!" he exclaimed when he picked up the phone. "You must come out this weekend and I will get you a ticket to see Serendipity. In fact, bring your lovely assistant and I will get two tickets."

"Frank, it sounds like a great idea," I responded. "I wanted to come out this evening anyway to ask a couple of questions. I need a little deep information about a player."

"Dag, you know that player information is confidential. I have to be careful," he answered.

"I'm going to try not to put you on the spot," I reassured him. "I'm on a missing person case and my records show that up until about ten months ago he was a regular out there. I was hoping you could tell me where he moved his action to."

"Oh, that shouldn't be a problem. If he is no longer a customer, then I'm not so picky about keeping information from you," he laughed. "Are you suspecting foul play?"

"Not yet," I answered. "I'm just looking for a place where a very rich man could drop a few thousand dollars and not be conspicuous. Maybe because he was playing with other very rich men like himself."

"Dag," he lowered his voice, "forgive me, but the game you want isn't in your league. Technically, it doesn't exist. This is Washington State, remember."

"I understand, Frank," I said. "Let's just say that a businessman from the East is coming into town tonight and he wants to play where someone might be interested in a company he is selling."

"I see," Frank said. "What would this businessman's name be?" I took a moment to do a mental inventory of identities that I could use and not get in trouble. Back at Gumshoe U under Lars, each of us were taught the fine art of creating a false identity that looked real enough to get us through a credit check. I seldom pulled a set of identity papers out of my safe except to keep them up to date, but I had some good ones.

"Sorry," I said after a moment. "I was lost in thought for a moment. The businessman's name is Jeremy Brett. He's a business broker from New York representing a high tech startup in Minnesota looking for venture capital or outright sale. Funny, but he looks a lot like me."

"Yes, well, I'll be watching for Mr. Brett when he comes in this evening at, oh, about 9:00. I'll have a couple of tickets available for him in your honor, but he should come alone," Frank continued. "And he should bring money. There's a thousand dollar minimum buy-in for the game he wants to play."

"I'll let him know," I said. "I'll… I mean, he'll see you tonight."

So, there was a high stakes poker game at the Sammamish Casino. Strictly speaking, that wasn't legal. Poker tables were typically $25 or $100 limit. Frank was alluding to a no-limit game. Well, I figured Brenda could afford to front me a thousand dollars to find out information on Simon. I'd bill her for it.

I printed business cards that looked official enough and stopped by a local phone store to pick up a new cell phone and activate service in Jeremy Brett's name. Maizie and I then caught a cab for home.

Friday night is Maizie's sleep-over with Mrs. Prior, my landlady. I swear those two were made for each other and I was barely tolerated at times. We live in the top half of a duplex on lower Queen Anne. In her part, Mrs. Prior lives with an assortment of animals—birds, rabbits, and even a snake. She says that Maizie loves all the animals, but I think Maizie would love to eat all the animals. She absolutely drips saliva when I ask her if she wants to see Mrs. Prior.

Mrs. Prior was a pet psychic—excuse me—communicator. That portion of her day that was not taken up in caring for her own animals was spent caring for or communicating with others. She greeted us at the door and carried on a conversation with Maizie that completely excluded me. Finally, Mrs. Prior turned to me and said, "Maizie says she worries about you because you aren't eating right. She says you need to have more fish in your diet and less red meat. And you should sleep more." A large pink feather stuck through the back of Mrs. Prior's tied up gray hair bobbed up and down with each sentence like a huge exclamation point. I told her that I would definitely have fish for dinner and not to worry. "Salmon," Mrs. Prior called after me as I mounted the stairs to my unit.

I went into my apartment to get dressed. Since I was going to the Eastside and had promised Maizie I would eat fish, it seemed like a good idea to eat at the Front Street Fish House in Issaquah. I changed into a dark suit with a clean shirt and tie and pulled twelve crisp hundreds out of my emergency safe. I thought a moment and pulled out a couple more. I pulled Jeremy Brett's wallet out of the safe and checked the contents to be sure they were current. New York driver's license, credit cards, a couple of photos of people who looked like they could be related or just friends. Then I walked down stairs to the tuck-under garage where my yellow Mustang spends most of its time and headed east.

I walked into the casino and wandered casually through the slot area toward the cashier cage. Frank intercepted me before I was halfway across the casino. He called me by the name of Jeremy Brett. He had already prepared a player's card and established a line of credit for me. I glanced over his shoulder at one of the security cameras in a bubble over the floor.

"I wouldn't do this for anyone else, Mr. Brett. I owe your friend a debt of gratitude. I trust you will not make me regret my hospitality." We crossed the floor and bypassed the cashier's cage. Behind it there was a door with a keypad lock on it which Frank keyed quickly. I'd always supposed that door led to the counting room, but instead it opened into a small and elegant poker room. There were only three tables and a bar. A few spectator chairs held attractive young women, relaxing and talking among themselves. The mistresses? I wondered.

Frank introduced me to the room at large and indicated that the other players would introduce themselves if they saw fit. I played dumb, but there were only a few faces that I didn't recognize from the newspapers as executives of major Seattle area businesses. These were the type of people that you wouldn't see in public together unless it was at a charity fundraiser or an SEC hearing. I was pretty sure that given a little time I'd be able to identify the rest. No one volunteered his name, but one man I recognized as the founder of one of the few dotcoms in Seattle that survived the '01 bubble bursting motioned me to an empty chair at his table.

"Thousand dollar buy-in," the dealer said as I sat down. I passed the credit chit Frank had given me to him and he handed out an incredibly small stack of chips. Values on them were $100 and $25. People didn't bet smaller than that. I noticed a few silver coins and $5 chips scattered among the other players and assumed there had been some split pots during the game so far. There were a few comments about fresh meat at the table and chuckles, then we got down to playing table stakes, no limit Texas Hold'em.

I was on the button for the first hand, meaning I was the figurative dealer and got the last card. I also got the last bet of the first round. I thought I saw a look and a nod pass among the players. By the time it was my turn to bet, the bet was up to $900 and all six other players were in. I understood. They were going to see if they could put me out on the first hand. I looked at my cards and saw pocket 10s. Not my favorite hand, but not bad either. The question in my mind was whether they really wanted me gone from the table or if it was just a test of my guts.

"Well," I said, "it looks like it might be a short night. All in." I pushed my entire thousand dollars onto the table and there was a general nodding of heads as if I'd passed a major test—like whether I was worthy of playing in their league. I wasn't, but I wouldn't let them know it.

Five players were still in for the flop and it didn't look like help for anybody. I was relieved not to see a face card turn up in the first three cards. So, in order for me to be beaten, someone had to have a bigger pair in the hole than what I had, or they'd need to pair up twice on board.

Fourth Street was a Jack. That hurt and one of the players came out aggressively with a bet that folded all but one of the other players. A pair of Jacks, I had to assume, but for the first time I saw another possibility. There was a mix of suits showing on the table so no flush would win this hand. With a 2, 7, 8, and Jack showing, the highest hand possible was three of a kind—unless the dealer turned a nine on the River. It was really too much to hope for and I prepared mentally to buy-in for another thousand. Then the dealer turned another 10. The two remaining players made their final bets and showed their hands—a pair of Jacks for one and two pair, 7s over 2s, for the other. The dealer paid the side bet and asked for my cards. Three 10s. The dealer pushed close to five thousand in chips toward me. With careful playing, it took me nearly two hours to lose them back to the others.

When I was near my break-even I excused myself from the table to go to the bar for a tonic. I was exhausted and aside from enjoying playing cards, I hadn't really gotten anything out of the game. This was a table where no one talked business. They were just rich men playing Friday night poker.

I was surprised to be joined at the bar by one of the lovely women who had been waiting and observing the game. What a boring night they must be having. She introduced herself as Cinnamon and spoke admiringly of my poker skills. I laughed and we shared small talk. I hadn't gotten anything from the poker players, so when I found out that Cinnamon often came to the game to watch I decided to probe her for information.

"I'm a little disappointed," I said. "I was hoping to see an old friend here tonight. He set up the arrangement for me to join the game."

"I know just about everyone who plays," Cinnamon said. "Who were you looking for?"

"Simon Barnett," I answered casually.

She turned her stool and mine to face the bar away from the game.

"Shhh." She cautioned me. "We should go someplace else to talk. You game?"

"Won't your boyfriend mind?" I asked. I hadn't actually identified anyone she seemed to be attached to, but I couldn't imagine why a young woman would be here if it wasn't as a girlfriend.

"Oh, I'm just a hostess. Some of us come around in the evenings and get drinks for the guys and flirt. They give us good tips." What an interesting concept. I had seen the young women get drinks for guys, but I wasn't paying enough attention to them to notice that they were treating everyone pretty much equally. I went back to the table and cashed in my chips.

"I've got tickets for the 11:30 show tonight and this charming young woman has consented to join me," I announced. "I hope I'll see you all again on my next trip."

"Friday nights," one of the men answered. "Welcome anytime."

"You behave, Cinnamon," said another sternly.

"Yes, Papa," she replied with a giggle. There was a general round of laughter. We slipped out the door as the game resumed.

"That was your father?" I asked, unable to believe it.

"No," Cinnamon replied. "He was just acting like it. He's really my boss."

"Is that why you didn't want to talk about Simon in there?"

"Him and all the others. Mr. S. has been mysteriously missing the past few days and it has all of them nervous. Do you know where he is?" Cinnamon asked.

"No. In fact I was hoping to find him here. I'd heard he wasn't seeing anyone lately."

"No one except Angel," Cinnamon answered.

"Who is Angel?" I asked.

"She's his special friend," Cinnamon replied. "You know. They're like a couple, except he's married."

"Hmmm. Sounds like I should meet this Angel. We might share some common interests."

"Don't you like me?" Cinnamon asked, pulling my arm around her waist and melding her lithe body into my side.

"Ummm, yes. Of course," I said. "I didn't mean it like that. I mean…" I stammered, "I don't mean anything like that." Cinnamon laughed at my discomfiture.

"Of course you didn't," she smiled. "Do you live here in Seattle?"

"Part of the time," I said, remembering my cover just in time. "I'm bi-coastal."

"That's okay," she said sitting beside me in the theater. "I like both boys and girls, too."

"No, no," I hastened. "I mean I live on both coasts—part of the time in New York and part of the time here in Seattle." Cinnamon laughed at me and I realized she'd been playing on words and I'd taken her literally. I was blushing.

"Aw. I bet that makes it hard to hold down a relationship, doesn't it?" she said.

"Not so much," I said. She kept throwing me curve balls, but I was beginning to warm to the game. I felt a sudden need to appear worldlier than my last few comments had seemed. "I have a wife in New York and a girlfriend in Seattle. They both maintain pretty well."

"Are you rich?" she asked bluntly.

"Well enough. I live on other people."

"Like expense accounts?"

"Yes, like that."

"Are you on an expense account now?"

"Mmm hmm." Damn. Her fingers had found a particularly nasty knot in my neck and I was enjoying this entirely too much.

"I like men on expense accounts," she said leaning forward and brushing my ear with her lips. I was prevented from responding aloud by the start of the concert. For me it was like being transferred back to the music of my youth. They played mostly sixties and seventies hits. I'm sure that to Cinnamon it was campy rather than nostalgic. But she kept herself glued to my side, holding my hand and rocking to the music. When we filed out of the theater at 1:00 she asked if I was going to go back to play cards.

"No," I responded. "I'm still jet-lagged and am ready to head home. I'd love to meet Angel, though, if you could arrange an introduction for me sometime soon."

"Will your girlfriend get jealous if you have another date tomorrow night?" she asked turning to me with wide eyes. I'd had enough experience parrying Riley's casual flirtation to be able to resist this, but damn! And this girl didn't even work for me.

"What did you have in mind?" I asked.

"Well, we've got a kind of private party we go to on weekends. I'm pretty sure Angel will be there tomorrow night. I'd be happy to get you in, and if your girlfriend is nice, you can bring her, too. Pick me up at

8:00 and I'll take you to the party. Maybe she and I will hit it off as well as you and I have. That could be fun!"

"Give me your number and I'll call tomorrow as soon as I set it up with Deb," I started. Damn, I should have used a different name for her.

"I'll look forward to meeting her," she said. "I'll trade you my number for… oh, say ten percent."

"Ten percent of what?" I asked.

"Of your winnings tonight," she smiled. "Remember? We are here for tips."

"Uh, you know I didn't win that much," I answered fishing in my pocket.

"Yeah, but you took me to a show. That counts," she answered. I pushed two hundred dollar bills into her hand, figuring that it wouldn't seem too much and wouldn't be insulting either. "Mmmmm. You did better than I thought," she said, then pulled my face to her and kissed me.

Damn! That girl can kiss.

All right. Deep breath. I extracted myself from Cinnamon after a long hug that resembled a dance. She let go of me in small stages as if she were pulling herself from a sticky taffy. Regain my composure. This was not what I came here for.

"I'll call you tomorrow and pick you up at 8:00," I said accepting the card with her phone number on it. I'm not sure where she pulled it from.

"It's a date, Mr. Jeremy," she cooed and waved a kiss my direction as the valet brought up my car. I didn't look back as I drove away.

I didn't know where the money was going, but I was pretty sure some of it had passed this way.

Dark Angel

IT MUST HAVE BEEN AT LEAST 7:00 when I got out of bed this morning. By the time I'd put myself together, I could see Riley on the front walk talking to Mrs. Prior. Maizie was dancing around them, ready to go to the spa to have her nails done and get a shampoo. Mrs. Prior says that Maizie loves to get pretty at the spa.

She's supposed to be my guard dog, damn it! Pink ribbons ruin the whole effect.

I went downstairs before Riley could push the doorbell and got in her car for the ride to the office. Riley often swaps days when she has class or an advisor meeting with Lars. I really wouldn't mind if she just took the time off, but she's got a work ethic that is uncompromising (unless there is a video game that just has to be tried at the office). I told her from the beginning that I'd pay her while she was in school or working on her thesis. But today I was thankful that she was making up the time.

"It's approved," she yelled, dancing in her seat. "Lars says it is a good thesis and the evidence is well and carefully planned out. It's a good thing, too, since I've got over half of it written. Another month and I'll be able to finish this. In January it should be all edited and ready to submit to committee."

"I'm really proud of you, Riley," I said. "You've worked hard for this and you deserve to get your degree." I paused for a moment before I plunged ahead. "How would you like to be my girlfriend?" I thought she was going to drive off the road.

33

"Dag!" she exclaimed in shock. "Are you serious? What about all that *quid pro quo* stuff you keep spouting at me?"

"I think we can suspend that in the interest of our investigation. I got a lead last night that might take us to a shortcut in finding Simon. I just don't want to go in without backup, and the only way I can get you in is as my girlfriend."

"You had me for a minute. I should just have said 'Yes.' I've had enough of academia and research the past two days. What's next?" she asked.

"Well…" I hesitated. I'd never sent Riley out on this particular type of assignment before. I'd asked her to keep an eye on someone and given her a couple of interviews to do, but this was going to require a lot more of her than she'd done before.

"You're not sending me to the library again, are you, Dag?" she moaned to me. I laughed. Okay, she wants field work.

"No, Sweetcheeks. No library for you today," I laughed. "I want you to go to a party with me tonight—a very exclusive party. We are going in the company of another attractive young woman who gets tips for flirting with corporate executives. We need information about how the place works and who she works for."

"I'm always up for a party. What's the scoop?"

I told her in detail what I'd learned last night, without including any reference to the kiss. I filled her in on the whole scenario and the identity that I'd used, the cover story, and what I wanted her to interview Cinnamon about.

"Let me get this straight," she said at last. "You want me to meet this escort, pretend to be your West Coast girlfriend… Wait, do I know you are married to a woman on the East Coast? Okay, so it's an amicable arrangement. I'm used to sharing you around. So I pretend to be interested in the party scene for my own purposes so I'll have something to do while you are out East. Do I have a job or am I simply a kept woman? I find out how she got into this, who invites her, who owns the place, and what she knows about the Missing Man." Riley paused.

"Yes, but there is one other thing that I want you to be sure of," I said. "Don't make any arrangements for a threesome."

Riley turned in her seat as she pulled up in front of the office and stared at me. Then she shocked me.

"Believe me, Sweetcheeks," she threw back at me, "if I thought there was any chance, I wouldn't be sharing."

"So, while you are occupying Cinnamon, I'm going to try to interview Angel and maybe ask questions of some of the other partiers."

"Well, this will be fun," she said. "But just one other thing…" I paused half out of the car and turned back to her. "Was she good?" she asked with a raised eyebrow.

"No personal sniffing, Riley," I said with a wink.

She parked and came into the office a few minutes later. By the time she got in, I had the laptop out of the vault and sitting on my desk. We were going to launch a two-pronged attack on the computer this morning, but first I had to call Cinnamon. I reached for the phone only to have Riley push my hand down on the receiver.

"Not yet," she said.

"I told her I'd call this morning, Riley," I replied trying to get the phone out from under her grip.

"You are so obviously not a party girl," Riley went on. I sat back. "When a party girl says tomorrow morning, she means sometime after noon—preferably not too soon after."

"This from a party girl?" I asked, raising an eyebrow.

"Not me, but I've got friends. Weekends you don't call them before noon. You don't know if she's even gotten to bed yet. Or at least to sleep."

I couldn't argue with that and let her sway my enthusiasm for setting things up right away. Instead we turned to the computer.

"How come you've got the laptop out?" Riley asked.

"I need you to do some work on it," I answered. She was definitely surprised. "I want you to do a data recovery routine on it. It struck me, as I was looking at the files, that there were things missing. I think Simon, or someone who knew I was going to look at his computer, took a day to delete information she thought might be too personal.

"The bee-atch!" Riley exclaimed. "Do you really think she would do that?"

"In a word, yes," I answered. Riley took the laptop gingerly and went to her desk in the outer office. I knew she would be careful, and that the rewards would be high.

I spent until 2:00, digging into more of Simon's financial statements. It had occurred to me to check the disk for fuzzed files. File fuzzing is one of the easiest ways to conceal information on your hard drive. Frankly, I use it myself. I figure that if my computer was in the hands of someone with my talents, my secrets wouldn't be safe for long regardless of what I did. But my worry isn't about people with my talents. It's people I work for who would be likely to think that they could walk off with my computer and have all the information on my clients that they want. For them, file fuzzing is as effective as any means of protecting unencrypted data other than not keeping it on your computer in the first place.

It's a pretty simple technique—just a matter of changing the file extension. The most common would be to rename a word processing file—say it's a .doc file—to an image file like .jpg. If you try to open the file, you get a message back that says it is not a valid .jpg file. It looks like it's been damaged.

Most applications leave a code in the file's header that identifies the file type. So I have a program that examines every file on the computer to see if the file type in the hash matches the extension. If they don't match, I've got a fuzzed file. I also know what to open it with. The process of examining every file, however, is a lengthy one. I set it up to run while I was gone and figured I'd pick it up on Sunday. While I was at it, I set up a file content search for "Angel." If she was Simon's mistress, chances are there were e-mail messages, account records, checks, or some odd bit that listed her name.

We called Cinnamon just before we closed up shop at 2:00 and a very sleepy voice answered the phone. She was instantly awake, however, and was happy we would pick her up for the party at 8:00. She gave us an address on Capitol Hill. I asked what Riley should wear and

Cinnamon said sexy party clothes. Riley motioned that she knew what to wear and I rang off.

Riley dropped me off at the Swedish American Center in Ballard and then went home to get ready for our date. She was getting into character like an actor ready to go on stage. She leaned over and gave me a peck on the cheek when she pulled to the curb in front of the Center and said sweetly, "Bye, Honey. See you later." Off she drove leaving me on the curb wondering what I'd gotten myself into.

Even though they never allowed me to speak Swedish or to hear them speak it, my mother and father were very firm about keeping in touch with other Swedes. I started coming to the Swedish American Center in the fifties. Barring a few years when I was in my twenties and "knew better," I've been coming back for special occasions ever since. In the past couple of years I've found that I'm coming back more and more frequently. These are the people who make me feel like family.

Saturday afternoons I play cribbage with all comers and drink water since I can't take any more of the black Swedish coffee. There is always a Saturday evening dinner social where everybody brings what they can to share. My stop at the deli for *knäckerbröd* and herring each week is winked at and deemed an acceptable contribution. Surprisingly, it seems to always be eaten.

Today I was filling time before I could get on with the evening's investigation. Even though I was going to the party on official business, I couldn't help but feel squeamish about people possibly finding out that I was "going out" with my assistant. All these kind mother substitutes that I surround myself with on Saturday afternoons would be shocked. Finally, at 7:30, I walked out of the Center and Riley's car pulled up in front. She waited for me in the car and I worried she was having second thoughts.

When I got in the car I was shocked with what I saw.

It was only her car that convinced me that it was Riley sitting in the seat next to me. She wore a straight black wig with bangs cut straight across her eyebrows. The plunging neckline on her silk blouse drew the eye downward to the skin-tight shiny black pants she was wearing. Over this was a waist-length jacket with three-quarter length sleeves. Her makeup accented her eyes and lips. She could easily have been one of the women I saw in the private room at the casino last night. I was staring, I confess.

"Don't you think you took the get-up a little far? You don't actually have to go to work there. I just wanted you to interview the hostess."

"I need to look like I *could* go to work there. How else are we going to find out what is going on?" I handed her $200, much to her surprise.

"These girls expect to get tipped for their time," I explained. "Don't be afraid to be nice to them… within limits." I tried not to watch as the money disappeared into her outfit. I swear I don't know how women do that. There was no room there for a pocket.

Cinnamon greeted us warmly and after taking one good assessing look at Riley, hugged her and gushed, "Debbie! I'm so glad you came! This is going to be so much fun!"

Before I slipped into the back seat behind Riley she leaned over and whispered in my ear, "You told her my name was Debbie?"

"Well, you look like a Debbie tonight," I laughed. There was definitely vengeance in her eyes when she responded.

"I hope you like the threesome then." I nearly swallowed my tongue as she closed the door behind me.

We parked a block away from a Seattle high-rise and walked parallel to the hill. In Seattle a Waterfront high-rise is all of twelve stories. The elevator took us to the entryway of the penthouse where it opened up to a burly security guard who blocked our paths.

"This party is by invitation only," the guard said folding his arms across his chest.

"Back off, Davy," Cinnamon said pushing him gently aside. "They are my date tonight—approved by Mr. Jonathan."

"All right," Davy said. "But I'll need your electronics, please," he said, holding out an envelope for us to drop our cell phones into. After signing a receipt and getting a claim ticket, we were allowed to pass through a metal detector and into the main part of the condo.

Inside, the mood was relaxed and we were greeted by a hostess to whom Cinnamon introduced us. I started to give her my name and she put a finger to my lips and said "First names only in here, Jeremy. Cinnamon will show you around." Cinnamon ushered us first to the bar. Riley and I both ordered a tonic and lime, and Cinnamon had a glass of white wine. I was digging in my pocket for some cash, but Cinnamon pushed my hand down and said, "Just leave a nice tip before you go, Jeremy. Okay?"

Hmmm. I remembered my tip to her last night and wondered how nice you had to be for a glass of water. I wasn't sure I'd given Riley enough money.

After we got our drinks, she took us on a grand tour of the condo. It was hard to judge how many people were there. At 9:00 the evening was still young. Soft music played throughout the apartment, just loud enough that it was difficult to hear anyone who was more than a few feet away, but not so loud that you had to shout at your companion. The penthouse was immense, occupying the entire top floor of the building. The living room was set up with several intimate seating areas, each of which by nature of its high-backed furniture provided a modicum of privacy. The kitchen provided the bar area. A variety of cold hors d' oeuvres and finger food were displayed where they were easily accessible.

Various bedrooms were set up with more intimate settings and had locks on the doors. Finally there was a rooftop deck that was complete with walking paths through a garden and a hot tub that was currently unoccupied in the drizzling rain. A canopy kept the falling water separate from the whirling water.

I wasn't sure how to go about getting the answers we needed, or how to bring up the idea of meeting Angel. Trust Riley to jump into the breach.

"So what do you get out of being here?" Riley asked bluntly. "It looks like a pretty quiet party."

"It's fun," she said. "I get to come to a really nice place, meet nice guys who are very rich, learn all sorts of interesting things about their businesses, and go home with spending money for the week."

"Spend a lot during the week?" Riley asked. I was afraid she might have crossed over a line, but Cinnamon didn't pause.

"Oh, around a thousand a week," she said. "And who knows, maybe I'll meet Mr. Right up here. That's why most of us come here. These are some of the best catches in Seattle."

I looked around. It didn't seem like much of a future for a young woman. Compared to most of the geezers here, I was looking young. Maybe the ladies planned to marry rich and old, hoping he'd die soon. Well, I was a perfect candidate, I thought grimly. Except for the rich part.

"Over here," Cinnamon said. "I know Jeremy wants to meet Angel, and I'm dying to get to know you better, Debbie." She pulled us down the hall to a game room in which several young women were playing pool with two older men "helping" them with their shots. There was a great deal of wiggling and giggling going on. Sitting on a stool with a glass of wine and a sour look on her face, it was evident that one lady at least was not having fun. Before we got around the table to approach, Cinnamon whispered in my ear. "By the way, I think Debbie is just adorable. We're going to have so much fun! I'm sure we could all three have a good time together. Don't throw away my phone number." Then we were next to Angel and Cinnamon was bubbling.

"Angel sweetie, I want to introduce you to Jeremy. He's quiet and shy, but really nice." Angel groaned almost audibly and Cinnamon dropped her voice. "He's also a friend of a friend of yours. You might have a lot in common." Angel's attention sharpened and focused at those words. "Well, toodles!" And then Cinnamon was off around the table to coach another girl on what shot to make. Riley kissed me on the cheek and said, "Have fun!" She wiggled herself around the pool table to join Cinnamon.

"Hi Angel," I said. "Can we sit and talk for a while?"

"I don't know, QuietandShy. Maybe we should go someplace where we can lock a door behind us. I don't want to be interrupted by your girlfriend. What did you want to talk about?" She might have been angry or depressed a minute ago, but she was every bit a professional when she took my arm and smiled. She led me out of the game room. At 6'2", there are not too many women who look me in the eye, but when Angel stood up, I looked up at her. I guessed her heels were three or four inches high, but she was still at least six feet tall. She was bottle blonde, and I figured other parts of her were artificially enhanced as well. Her face was so perfect that I guessed she'd had a nose job at one point. When we crossed the room together conversations paused as people watched.

"I'm looking for Simon."

The expressions washed across her face like water, one after another. But the one I caught most was fear. Her eyes darted around the room and it was clear she was deliberately not looking at the overhead security camera concealed in a casino-like bubble.

"Shhhh." She said placing a finger on my lips and letting a smile fill her face as if I'd made a perfectly naughty suggestion. "Not here. Let's get our coats." She ushered me to the door and we retrieved our coats and I signed for my cell phone. "Mr. Jeremy wants to take me dancing at the Colorbox, Davy. We'll be back in a couple of hours," she said to the security guard who stood in front of the elevator. He looked angry, but held his tongue as he stared at me before stepping aside to allow us to enter the elevator.

We didn't speak until we were out the massive front doors of the condo building.

"There's an all-night coffee shop two blocks from here on Olive," I offered. "Unless you were serious about going dancing at the Colorbox."

"The coffee shop will be just fine," she answered. "I just don't want to talk about Simon up there. You can't tell who is listening."

I'd forgotten that the designated coffee shop was uphill from the Condo, so I was unable to carry much of a conversation while we walked. Angel was polite and concerned, but not much help. It was all she could do to make the climb herself in those ridiculous shoes. Once there, however, we settled into a pair of chairs next to the window and sipped our beverages. Then she launched in before I was able to start.

"Where is he?" she began. "He was supposed to call me Monday with instructions on where and when to meet him. And nothing.

41

Nothing all week. I've been worried sick."

"I was hoping you would be able to help me on that front, Angel," I said. "I'm looking for him, but this is as fresh a trail as I could find."

"Why do you want to find him?" she asked, suddenly defensive.

"Because he asked me to find him," I answered. "It's an old game we used to play called 'Simon Says.' I got a note along with his laptop computer that said, 'Simon Says Find me.' If I can, that is exactly what I'll do. When did you last see him?"

"Simon Says?" Angel asked.

"Simon Says," I confirmed. She visibly relaxed. If Simon Says, then it must be okay. That's the way it has been for as long as I can remember.

"He spent part of the night with me on Saturday two weeks ago. He had to leave and go home to his bitchy wife half way through the night. He was going to fly to Singapore on Sunday and then he'd send me instructions on where to meet him. Since then nothing."

"Are you his mistress?" I don't know any way to ask these questions subtly.

"I'm his soul-mate, his inspiration, his conscience, and his guardian angel," she said.

"Sounds like a tall order."

"I'm a tall woman. Or didn't you notice? You're pretty tall yourself."

"Not many women can look me straight in the eye, I confess," I said. She really didn't answer my question. I was going to have to figure another way to ask it.

"Yes, I'm his mistress," she supplied bluntly, catching me off-guard. "I hate the word. It does absolutely nothing to describe our relationship. I rescued Simon at a time of moral crisis," she continued. "He didn't know what to do and I helped him."

"With sex?" I asked. "That's always an effective resolution to a moral crisis." Okay, I was being a little judgmental.

"You've got a lot of gall, don't you?" she said flatly. My cheeks were stinging as if she'd slapped me. And I'd have deserved it. I needed to recover the situation fast.

"Sorry," I said. "That's not about you. I've known Simon in situations of moral crisis before. Somehow his solution always seems to be the same. I'm sorry I reacted like an ass. I haven't spoken to Simon in thirty years. I'm still trying to figure out why he contacted me to find him."

"Simon discovered that a lot of his wealth was not particularly legitimate," Angel continued after a pause to acknowledge my apology. "His partner has been making unauthorized investments. The whole thing stinks. Simon wants out."

"And you believe Simon is clean?" I asked. "Granted I haven't seen him in a long time, but his deals were always on the edge."

"Simon has made his share of mistakes," she answered, "but down deep he is a man with a conscience and sincere regret for his past indiscretions. I simply had to help him see a way to make amends."

"It sounds like you've been very busy. How long has this been going on?"

"About a year."

"And how is Simon making amends?"

"We've researched hundreds of foundations over the past few months and Simon is getting ready to transfer all his wealth to charity."

I was stunned. I could not imagine Simon giving anything away. Well, that wasn't exactly true. The Simon I knew in college was altruistic to a fault. But by the time we parted company, that idealist was already a memory. The Simon that had always been in my peripheral vision had only one goal in mind: to dominate the world one dollar at a time.

"So Simon wants to give away all his money?"

"Well, not exactly all of it," Angel said. "He can't let the bitch-wife die in poverty can he? And we'll need a little to live on. But you can't imagine how much there is to give away. We can make a real difference."

Angel had a genuine fervor. I softened my judgment of her and began to think that perhaps there was more to Simon than I had given him credit for. Maybe that was why he'd left the message for me. But

I'd found nothing yet that indicated the kind of wealth that Angel was referring to. Wealth, yes, but not the kind that would allow you to endow several charities and still have enough to keep Brenda from living in poverty. From the look of it, I had to guess that Angel wasn't exactly low-maintenance either.

"Is there any reason that you can think of that Simon would disappear?" I asked.

"Well, yeah," she sang at me with that unique tonality that reminds you of a teenager. "His partner, his wife, the mob, and God knows who else. Jeremy, please find Simon for me." A tear collected in her eye and she dabbed it away before it could run her mascara.

"I'll do my best, Angel," I said. I gave her one of the cards I'd had printed up with Jeremy's name on it and my newly purchased cell number. "Just give me a call if you hear anything will you?"

"If Simon Says it's okay, then I'll call," she answered. "And if I hear anything from my clients, I'll let you know, too." We got up and left the coffee shop to walk back to the condo. It was nearly 11:00— my pre-arranged time to meet Riley. Angel slipped her hand through my arm and I wasn't sure if she was just being companionly or if she was actually thinking I could support her as we headed back down the hill.

"You mentioned clients. Do you have another job besides being a party hostess?" I asked.

"I'm a travel agent," she laughed. She pulled up closer to me and whispered in my ear. "I could take you around the world—for a price." I was stunned to silence by the implied offer. We'd no more than hit the curb when a late model sports car pulled up and Davy the security guard jumped out.

"We're not doing this again," he yelled at Angel.

"Davy, it's okay," she started.

"It's not okay. Get in the damn car."

"Hey!" I said stepping up to Davy. Angel was obediently getting into the car. "Just back off and leave the lady alone." He turned on me with a snarl.

"The lady is my business," he yelled in my face. "And you better keep away from her if you know what's good for you."

"Don't make threats at me, champ," I answered pulling up to my full and most intimidating height. He didn't answer. He just hauled off and slugged me. Hard. In the face.

I heard the car squeal away from the curb as I hit the pavement.

Riley to the Rescue

AFTER MY HEART ATTACK in Las Vegas last March, I woke up in a hospital bed. Riley was sitting in a chair beside the bed playing on my computer. That's no small task.

"How'd you get into my computer," I asked. She looked up at me.

"I turned it on and dragged your finger across the biometric scanner and I was in," she answered brightly.

"How did you know which finger?" I asked. It is only set to read one fingerprint.

"I had to try them one at a time until I got the right one," she answered, as if that were the most logical solution. "You've only got ten and I only had to try three."

Memo to self: secure your hands if you are going to be unconscious.

She caught me up on what had happened after my heart attack. She had gone to my room and taken care of Maizie. She guarded my belongings for me and extended my stay at the hotel. And she had waited by my bed for two days.

Resourceful. Intelligent. Likes my dog. What more could I ask.

"So you want a job," I said thoughtfully.

"I do," she answered looking me straight in the eye.

"Do you have a license?"

"You have to work three years before you can get an agency license. I've served two under Lars," she answered.

"I meant a driver's license," I said. You needn't have been around

46

the block a few times for me to be interested, but you do need a license.

"Oh, of course."

"Good. As soon as I can get out of here, your first job is to drive Maizie and me back to Seattle. I'm not leaving my Mustang in Las Vegas. It's like a bad joke." She laughed, but nodded her head.

"I can do that."

"We'll see," I answered. "I will pay you a decent wage—I'll ask Lars what that is these days—teach you what I know, sponsor you for your license, and help you defend your thesis before Lars. I won't do your work for you, give you advances on your salary, or listen to stories about your broken heart when some guy dumps you."

"What makes you think I'm the one who gets dumped," she asked repositioning herself provocatively in the chair. I pretended not to notice.

"There's a catch," I said. Her features straightened and she became serious and if anything a little guarded. I smiled. "I'm not planning to have another of these episodes, but I could use someone around who knows enough to shove an aspirin in my mouth if I'm having a heart attack. I'm not planning to drive much either, so I'll need someone who can chauffeur Maizie and me to the office and appointments. I may even need to have my laundry picked up and groceries delivered. If you can live with the crap side of working for me, I'll see that you get all the benefits, including work time to write your thesis. Deal?"

Now she jumped up out of her chair, leaned across the bed and kissed me on the forehead. "What more could a girl ask for?" she said. "Deal!"

And what do I get out of it? I asked myself. I get a beautiful woman sitting in the next room. I get to smell her scent in the office. I get to see her smile and appreciate the way she looks. I get to hear her voice on the phone. And it was all strictly business.

It turned out that she was also good at picking me up off the pavement when a heavyweight ex-Marine decked me. She took me home when I protested the idea of going to the emergency room and half-carried me up to my apartment. She patched up my cut eye, watered the dog, and left me asleep in my recliner.

Showdown with Billie the Kid

I CAN'T THINK OF A WORSE PLACE to die than a hospital. So I tend to avoid them. I finally got myself out of bed Monday morning and looked in a mirror at the damage Davy the doorkeeper had done to my face Saturday night. I wasn't much surprised when Riley drove me straight through the pelting rain to the hospital instead of to the office.

"I don't need to see a doctor. I just got punched in the face. It's not like I had a heart incident or anything," I complained.

"Dag," Riley said patiently, "if you want to play punching bag for guys who are half your age and twice your size, that's your business. I'm not going to interfere. But you've got an appointment with Dr. Roberts this morning."

"Newel? Why?" I asked.

"This is the first Monday of the month. It's your regular monthly appointment."

"Damn, Riley. How could I forget that?" I'd been seeing Newel Roberts, one of Seattle's finest heart surgeons at least once a month since my heart attack last March. I must be getting pretty pre-occupied with this case. I didn't even realize it was Monday. "Well, I'm glad you remembered. Thanks, Riley." I looked at her. She was still a little ticked off at me for the whole Saturday night affair.

Scratch that word. It was not an affair.

Anyway, she seemed to believe that if she'd gotten there sooner

48

I wouldn't have gotten hurt. I needed to debrief on what she learned Saturday night, but it would have to wait until after I'd seen the doc. She dropped me off at the hospital and I went in for my appointment.

"Dag," my cardiologist said to me. "This just isn't looking good to me. The wall of the left ventrical is so thin you can practically see through it. We've got to accelerate you on the program. If we don't get you a new heart soon, I can't guarantee that you'll be around for Christmas."

It was bleaker than I'd anticipated. Different symptoms told me that things weren't exactly right, but I'd been telling myself I was getting stronger. I'd followed all the routines he'd given me. Eat right, stay trim, get as much light exercise as I could, lots of liquids, don't get stressed. Well, that last one was a little harder to live by. I suppose getting clocked on Saturday night isn't exactly avoiding stress. Remind me to apologize to Riley.

I supposed my cup of espresso each morning wasn't exactly on the program either.

"What do I need to do?" I asked.

"There's not a lot you can do that you haven't been doing, though I'd try to quit running into things if I were you." He looked at the cut and bandage job Riley did on me Saturday night. "I'm moving you onto the active list. We've got to try to find a match for you and get you a new heart."

"When do you think?"

"You know the donor situation. There's probably a heart in a morgue someplace in Seattle right now that would be a perfect fit," he said, "if the corpse had been a donor. But we've got to watch a couple of other things with you as well. Your blood type is not the easiest to match and we've got to get you on the right anti-immune drugs before we put someone else's heart in your chest. That means you are going to be more susceptible to illness, which means you'll have to be even more careful about your health."

"Well, it's not like I'm planning any big illnesses this month," I joked. "I'll be sure to wash my hands."

"Okay, smart aleck. I'm prescribing the drugs and I want to see

49

you once a week now. And if I call, be here in 30 minutes or the heart will go somewhere else." Newel Roberts scrawled out the prescription and I took it a little shakily.

"Don't worry, Dag," he said. "Our success rate with this is pretty remarkable now. In all likelihood you'll live to be eighty if we get this taken care of."

"Thanks, Newel," I answered. "I'm looking forward to getting old."

"You will," he said. He put a hand gently on my shoulder before he left and I got dressed.

Damn.

I've known it was coming. According to the reports, I'd been going through a gradual deterioration of my heart muscle most of my life, caused by a childhood disease. It had been so gradual that no one noticed until my jackpot heart attack in Las Vegas last spring. Since then, the assessment was that the deterioration was accelerating. This old ticker was headed for the grave with or without me. It scared the crap out of me, but I was frankly willing to let it go first. The meds were making me feeble minded, too. I couldn't believe I'd forgotten it was time for my monthly appointment.

Out in the waiting room I stopped at the reception desk to make an appointment for the following Monday. When I'd finished I turned and almost stepped on a small person with a high voice.

"You got a bad ticker, mister?" she asked. Maybe nine years old, my little assailant was dressed in jeans, cowboy boots, and a red bandana. "Dr. Roberts says mine's gonna kill me if I don't get a new one soon."

"Billie!" An exasperated mother rushed to her side from the other receptionist. "I'm sorry, sir," she said. "Sometimes she is so blunt."

"That's okay," I answered. "Do you mind?" I gestured toward Billie and squatted down until I was about her height. "It's a tough life, isn't it Billie?" I asked the little girl.

"Not so bad once you learn to live with it," she answered. "It's really hard getting anybody else to understand though, don't you think?" This was a precocious youngster, I thought.

"Yes," I said, "unless you've got it there's really no way to understand

50

it. What happened to yours?"

"Dr. Roberts says its con…" she looked quickly at her mother, closed her eyes and concentrated, then spit out the word, "congenital. I was born with a bad heart and it's been going downhill ever since. How about you?"

"Uphill all the way," I answered. "I got sick when I was a bit smaller than you and it damaged my heart somehow. Now I've got to get a new one."

"Or you'll be sorry," she chimed like the ad on the radio. "You know what, though?" she asked innocently. "Somebody else has to die in order to get a new heart. That's not fair is it? I want to grow up to be president of the United States, but it's not fair for someone else to have to die so I can grow up."

"That's true, Billie," I said, "but people die every day. People have accidents or get sick. We don't have to kill someone to get a new heart. We're not going to take anything that they need."

"I know," Billie looked straight in my eyes. "I just want them to be proud in heaven when they see who got their heart."

I was near tears when the nurse called, "Billie Martin."

"Oops, gotta go."

"Come on, Billie," her mother said, reaching for a hand. I could see that our conversation had affected her as well.

"I need a few minutes alone with Dr. Roberts, Mom." She turned to me. "What's your name?"

"Dag Hamar," I said.

"Mr. Hamar, would you keep my mother company for a few minutes so I can ask the doctor some personal questions? Thank you." She marched over to the nurse and called back over her shoulder, "I'll call for you in a few minutes, Mom." Then she left with the nurse.

I stood and looked at Billie's mother and decided to introduce myself.

"I'm Dag Hamar," I said holding out my hand. She took it hesitantly.

"Wanda Martin," she responded. "I'm really sorry if my daughter bothered you Mr. Hamar."

"Not at all. She seems very mature for her age."

"She had to grow up fast," Wanda said. "Even faster than I did. I never wanted my baby to go through this." Her lip was quivering so I led her to a chair and sat with her.

"No parent should ever have to watch her child suffer," I said. "You should be very proud of her."

"She's adjusted to it much better than I have."

"Well, I'm sure there will be a heart donor soon," I said, thinking in part about my own position in the waiting line for donors. I'd have to do a little research to find out how low on the list I was.

"It won't make a difference," Wanda said. "She won't get it. We don't have insurance. I'm trying to raise the money, but I might not be able to make it in time." That was a gut-punch.

"There are assistance programs available, aren't there?"

"Oh yes. On the condition that I give up custody of my child and make her a ward of the State. And that is no guarantee that she'd get a heart. They'd evaluate her case and determine the urgency. Then in a couple of months when they decide, they'll put her on a list with all the other children who are sick and give her a number. Then maybe she'll still be alive when her number comes up. And maybe if she is, I'll still be allowed to visit her once in a while, if the State deems me fit to be near her. I won't let them take her away from me. Not now."

The impassioned plea set all kinds of ideas in motion for me. Heart transplants cost in the neighborhood of a hundred grand, but care and medication after surgery can cost double that.

"Can't Billie's father help?" I asked.

"I don't even know who Billie's father is," Wanda said bitterly. "I wasn't exactly a model teen. Billie's all I've got. I'm not even employed right now because I have to take care of her."

This looked bleak, but I was sure there must be a way to help her. I didn't have dough to give her. My own transplant was going to cost me my life savings after the insurance ran out. Healthcare is the privilege of the rich. I didn't know what to say to Wanda, and thankfully was spared the necessity when the nurse came back out and called for her to join her daughter.

"Good luck to you, Mr. Hamar," she said as she rose to leave.

"And to you and Billie, too," I answered.

I called Riley and told her with a little more force than was necessary not to bother coming up to pick me up, I'd take a cab to the office. She told me that she was already waiting at the front door.

Damn.

I needed to walk. I needed to run and fill my lungs with air. I needed to go to a gym and pump iron, play basketball, and work up a sweat. None of that is going to happen. It's all I can manage to walk the mile downhill from home to office with one or two rest stops on the way. I couldn't bear to think of a nine-year-old who couldn't run and play and was willing to tell a perfect stranger that her heart was going to kill her if she didn't get a new one. Not fair didn't even begin to describe it.

I ducked through the rain and got in the car next to Riley and sat in silence. She pulled away from the curb. She looked at me in a way that nearly melted what was left of my heart and asked, "Do you want me to take you home instead of to the office?"

"Don't patronize me, Riley," I said more sharply than I intended. "I have work to do."

"Yessir," she responded sharply and drove the rest of the way to the office in silence.

I closed the door to my office and sat staring out my window at the rain-swept Sound. Once before I die, I'd like to see Mount Rainier again.

Damn!

I heard Riley come into the office after she'd parked her car. I flicked on my laptop and connected to the network, and called her into my office to hear her report on what happened Saturday night. She entered a little hesitantly, not sure if I'd bite her head off again.

The reports that I'd set to run and compile on Saturday were ready and waiting. I scanned through them, not expecting much, as Riley told me about the girls who came to party at the condo. I figured now that Simon had set up the laptop to get me involved, but it wasn't going to lead me to him. I was much closer when I talked to Angel. Maybe Riley had found out something, too.

"Well, they all have jobs outside the condo," Riley began. "I met a couple and acted like I was interested in maybe joining them." I raised an eyebrow. I didn't want Riley to get herself into a bad position. "Don't worry," she assured me. "It was just research. Anyway, they are there for anonymous company to very powerful men. Officially, they don't know any of them. Of course, they aren't blind. They know who's there. But these guys, for all their money and power, are pretty pathetic. A lot of them have the typical wife and family that don't understand them, are out of town, or supposedly don't care. But mostly they want to be with women who make them feel young and attractive. They slip the girls "tips" to hang around them while they are talking sports or to play drinking games with them. There are private rooms, but usually those are where the men go to talk privately with each other and not with the girls, unless she's a professional."

"Come on," I said. "These guys are taking a huge risk even being in the same room with each other, let alone with anonymous women offering them sex."

"Not sex," Riley was quick to point out. "Some of the girls are professional escorts and are available for sex, but most are employed by the very companies that the men run."

"That's even worse. *Quid pro quo*," I recited. "An exec is open to a huge lawsuit if a woman's employment is dependent on a sexual relationship with her boss."

"Never with their bosses," Riley pointed out, "or with anyone who works for the same company. There is a strict rule forbidding contact between anyone in the same company at the condo. It's like an incest taboo. There is some kind of separate initiation that goes on. Cinnamon wouldn't talk about it. I'm going to try to talk to some of them outside the condo tomorrow."

"Did you tip her?" I asked, remembering the two hundred dollars

I gave her Saturday night.

"Uh…" Riley was blushing. "I didn't have to."

"Riley." She looked at me and pulled the money out of her purse that I gave her.

"Do you want the two hundred I earned, too?"

"You what?" I exclaimed.

"A couple of guys asked Cinnamon and me to join them for a game of cribbage. Cinnamon egged me on and I figured I'd better not blow the cover, so I joined. We played for about an hour and they slipped us each two hundred dollars when I said I had to go pick you up. It was really easy."

"They paid you two hundred dollars to play cribbage for an hour?" I asked in disbelief.

"We gave them shoulder rubs and flirted a lot," Riley said sheepishly. "Did I do wrong?"

I didn't know what to say. I knew that Riley—in spite of being an incredible flirt—avoided close contact with most men. I stared at the screen on my laptop as I shook my head, unable to say anything. The search for "Angel" in the files came up with a few dozen instances of Los Angeles, but nothing specific to the tall blonde I'd met at the condo. Something else in the report caught my eye. There were forty-two fuzzed documents on the drive. I chuckled. Then I laughed out loud.

"Dag?" Riley asked softly. "Is it okay?"

"Riley, what is the answer?" I asked, still laughing.

"The answer to what, Dag?" she wasn't sure yet that I wouldn't bite her head off.

"The answer to the ultimate question of life, the universe, and everything," I said. I watched Riley puzzle it out as I continued to laugh.

Just the Facts, Ma'am

RILEY PICKED UP MAIZIE AND ME in the morning and we went to vote before we got to the office, which meant that I missed my morning espresso again. Riley dropped us off at the office and said she had a couple of new leads that she was following up today. If I needed her I could reach her on her cell phone. She'd prefer if I text messaged her as she'd probably be in the library.

Well, that was okay. As soon as she left, Maizie and I went up to the Market and got a cup of coffee at the Eye of Dawn coffee shop. It was closer than trying to walk all the way back to Tovoni's, and there was an elevator that goes from Waterfront level up to the Market. After I'd read the paper we went back to the office. My old friend, Jordan Grant, was standing outside my office door. It wasn't too much of a surprise; I tore down a computer for him a couple of weeks prior and the case was scheduled for court on Thursday. We went into the office to chat and Maizie headed for her bed in the corner.

When Jordan and I were learning to be good detectives under Lars—a class we called Gumshoe U—we were always teamed up on the exercises that Lars gave the group. We worked well together, and when Jordan joined the FBI's cybercrimes unit, he became a great source of business for me. Now he works for the Financial Crimes Enforcement Network, or FinCEN. That's a division of the U.S. Department of the Treasury that is primarily interested in financial crimes like embezzlement, money laundering, and identity theft. The case we were to go to trial with on Thursday was a botched embezzlement that yielded evidence of kiddie-porn. It was going to be tough to prove that we were authorized to search for porn on the guy's computer instead of only evidence of embezzlement. I was interested in how Jordan was going to manage the case.

"We're going to drive a bargain," Jordan said. "The stuff on that guy's computer is disgusting, and I'd like to nail him. But if we attempt to introduce it as evidence, his lawyer will be all over unlawful seizure of property. At the very least, it could drag out for months before we even get a ruling on the porn stuff. But the guy has heard what happens in jail to those who take advantage of children. He'd be lucky to survive the first year of his sentence. So he's motivated to keep that information out of court. He can do that by pleading guilty to the embezzlement charges. He'll do the same jail time, but won't have the kiddie-rap in prison."

"I think someone should leak the information into the prison once he goes up," I said. "He deserves the added benefits."

Jordan laughed and we relaxed in the comfy chairs looking out at Puget Sound.

"Well, I tell you, I'm glad I'm chasing money launderers and not child pornographers," Jordan said. "It would be hard to deal with that crap every day. It's bad enough with the money games. I've got one I'm working on now that I'd like to put paid to, but it looks like it could go on for months."

"What's that?" I asked.

"I'm investigating a big Seattle holding company. It looks like they could be laundering a lot of money. All the signs are there, but I can't put my finger on where the money is coming from. I know they are on the take from some small time Midwestern hoods, but they simply aren't big enough operations to handle the volume of cash these guys carry."

"Sounds like big game," I said noncommittally.

"Yeah. If you hear anything about big money moving around Seattle—say maybe while you are attending private parties in a particular penthouse suite—you'll let me know, won't you?"

Damn.

Jordan and I are friends, but I don't want him mixing in my investigations. I daresay he would feel the same way.

"I've been trying to get someone in there for months," Jordan continued. "If there's no conflict of interest with your client, I'd like to piggyback on your assignment."

"As far as the condo goes, I think I've finished there. My quarry isn't attending at the moment. All I've got is a ghost-trail of where he's been, but not where he is."

"Well, if there is any way we can help each other, Dag, you know I've always been fair."

"I'll keep it in mind, Jordan. If I pick up anything I'll let you know," I answered.

Jordan left and I started going over my notes on Simon's forty-two fuzzed files. It wasn't impossible that I'd find something that would help Jordan, and I'd surely have to let him know. But I was solving a missing person case, not financial misdeeds.

It was a bit before noon that I had another visitor. This guy was a block of a man carrying a ten-year-old laptop—one from the era when you needed a really big lap, and he had one. I met him in the front office and he set the laptop on Riley's desk.

"Can I help you?" I asked.

"Broken," he answered shortly. I couldn't quite identify the slurred accent on so few words, and he wasn't volunteering to talk more.

"I don't repair computers," I answered. "I can give you the names of a couple of repair shops if you'd like."

"No," he said. He seemed to be struggling for words. This hulking man was not used to communicating with people in words, that much I could tell. "Stuff inside. I want it on a record."

"A record?" I realized that I was dealing with a man who wasn't stupid, but didn't speak English all that well. "You mean a CD?" I reached into Riley's top drawer and pulled out a CD to show him an example. He nodded his head vigorously. "You want me to get the data off the hard drive and burn it on a CD?" Again he nodded and then shook his head.

"Not burn. Give me." I nodded this time.

"It's just an expression," I answered. "What sort of data am I looking for?" He didn't seem to understand. "E-mail? Word processing? Spreadsheets?" He nodded at all of them then held up a finger and after struggling for a few minutes shot out another word.

"Favorites." He grinned as though he had just solved the New York Times Crossword.

"And Favorites," I affirmed. "Okay. Just fill out this form. I'll need your name, address, and phone number. Then sign here. This is a release form that says you permit me to copy all the information in your computer for you. My estimate is that it will be about $300 if the computer isn't too badly damaged. If it looks like it will go over $500, I'll call you before I proceed. If I can't recover the data, it will be a $50 service fee for checking it out. I'll call when the CDs are ready, probably Friday." While I was talking he busily filled out the form with a meticulous care that I found inconsistent with the slow-talking hulk that could barely hold the pen in his ham-sized fist. He pushed the form toward me and I read off his name.

"Okay, Mr. Oksamma. I'll need a deposit of $150. Would you like to write a check or credit card?" He reached in his wallet and pulled out two crisp hundred dollar bills and laid them on the desk. Money talks. I reached in my wallet and dug out two twenties and a ten and handed them to him. I signed the receipt and gave that to him. "Thank you for stopping by, Mr. Oksamma," I repeated. "I'll call on Friday."

I picked the computer up, walked into my office, and put it on my desk. My own laptop was the only other thing on my desk as I'd been trying to sort out Simon's files when he came in. I turned and found that he'd followed me into my office.

"Not until Friday, Mr. Oksamma," I repeated and pointed to the door. He showed a sign of being slightly startled as he looked carefully around my office, then retreated and headed out through the front door. I breathed a sigh of relief realizing that had he been aggressive I was in no condition to fight back. Always escort the client to the door, I reminded myself. I was too used to having Riley in the front office.

After I assured myself that the Refrigerator, as I started thinking of him, had really gone, I closed my door and opened the vault. I took the huge old laptop into the vault and set it on a shelf, hooked up the usual safeguards and set the system to make a copy of the hard drive. I'd tend to that later. I closed the vault and went back to my original task: finding Simon.

Of the fuzzed files, half a dozen looked like they'd accidentally had the name changed and lost their original extension in the process. There was nothing of significance on them as far as I could tell. But some of the other files were definitely worth a look. These were image files, text that was converted to a pattern of dots and then variously saved with either word processing or spreadsheet file extensions. They don't open as valid files in the program that matches the extension, and you can't search for text strings inside the file because the text is just a picture. It was a textbook example; in fact, now that I thought about it, one that I'd written an article about years ago. How long, I wondered, had Simon been planning this?

Well, I had something to start with. For the most part, the pictures were what seemed to be random number strings. Things like 76182060023046787. Each number string was followed by a name: Charles Hammond, George Brown, David Everest. Twenty-one numbers and twenty-one names in twenty-one fuzzed files. The file names themselves looked like they had been generated from the temp files on a computer: ptf4D.doc, _is1D5.xls. There was simply no shape or pattern to them. I tried following the directory trees. The files were located in a dozen different directories. Simply nothing was forthcoming. Yet the files all contained similar information—a number and a name.

I had to take a break and get Maizie out for a walk, and then I decided I'd try another tack in the investigation. Something Angel had said Saturday night reminded me of what else was missing in my investigation of Simon's computer. There were no travel arrangements. I checked through the browser history that I'd carefully copied and frozen from the day I'd gotten it so it wouldn't expire after twenty-one days. No travel Web sites.

I went back through the credit card billings. There were nowhere near as many airline tickets purchased as there were locations that charges came from. This time, I was going to short-cut the process. I dialed Brenda's number.

She answered on the first ring and called me by name before I'd said anything.

Damn caller ID.

"So have you finally decided to take me out to dinner?" she purred. "A girl could starve waiting for you to call." I had to remind myself that things that purr also have claws.

"Brenda, I can't find Simon's travel plans for Singapore. What airline was he flying on?" I snapped. I was not engaging on any personal level with her. It was strictly business.

"Airline? Silly boy, he took the plane." She sounded so smug.

"The plane?" I asked. "You mean he has a private plane?"

"Of course," she said. "Simon handles a variety of import and export for some of his clients. Since they are usually fairly small quantities of very pricey goods, he uses the jet to transport them. It's faster in customs than going through commercial channels. I thought you were going to own every bit of information about us once you had that laptop." I ignored the dig. Why hadn't I found anything about the private plane? I wondered.

"Does Simon fly himself?" I asked.

"Sometimes. Usually for long distance trips he has a private pilot and staff who fly with him. I assume that would be the case on a trip to Singapore."

After a few more not-too-subtle digs, at my computer competence and a few insertions about the urgency of finding Simon and getting my ass in gear, I managed to get the contact information out of her for the private jet. I hung up a little abruptly when she started in again about taking her out to dinner. That woman is flat-out trouble.

I swore there was nothing on Simon's computer about owning a plane. I called the leasing company Brenda said managed Simon's airplane and put together a new list of questions and places to investigate.

According to the manager, Simon flew the plane himself Thursday with no crew. He had filed a flight plan to Oakland. The management company for Simon's jet said that he picked up a crew in Oakland and a different pilot had filed a flight plan from there to Singapore with six passengers and crew. They had not received word that the plane was back in the U.S. again yet, but that they would certainly let me know when customs contacted them that the flight had returned. I had one more question for the manager.

"Did Simon make his own arrangements with you for his flight?" I asked.

"No sir," the manager answered. "Miss Angel always makes his travel arrangements. She makes the arrangements for several local execs." He gave me her number. Something was suddenly out of place. If Angel was concerned about Simon, why hadn't she told me she made his flight arrangements?

If Simon was still in Singapore, or had flown to other locations from there, I could spend the rest of my life looking for him. There had been no charges made to his personal credit cards, nor any ATM withdrawals as far as I could tell in the two weeks he had been missing. Either he was dead, or he was doing a good job of covering his tracks, and not spending any money.

My head was hurting by the time I locked the doors and Maizie and I walked down to catch a cab home to watch election results on TV. I knew I was missing something, but frankly I was too tired to think what it was.

Personal travel agent who makes his flight arrangements. Twenty-one names and numbers. Private jet. No evidence that Simon was on the flight to Singapore.

Maybe he wasn't.

A Partner Calls

MAIZIE AND I WERE A BIT LATE getting started this morning and rolled into the office about 9:00. It was good to get out and walk again, though I found that I needed to take it a bit slower in the light rain this morning, but the cup of coffee at Tovoni's left me with a pleasant buzz. Riley grabbed a towel and rubbed Maizie down quickly as I put my hat and coat in the closet. She cooed over the dog, rubbing her and talking about how she shouldn't have to walk in this nasty weather. By the time she was done, I was getting a little bit jealous. It was going to be a long dreary day. Maizie settled down on her bed after she'd dragged it halfway across the room to put it behind the sofa next to the heat vent. Smart dog. I almost joined her.

"Riley," I started, "what are the results from the file recovery on Simon's computer?"

"Not good," she answered. "The computer was definitely altered the day before we got it. But whoever did it used a blanking program. The disc was optimized and all unoccupied sectors were written over with zeros. I've been poking around, but it was a professional job."

"That puts it out of Brenda's league," I muttered. "She must have taken it somewhere after she deleted the files she didn't want me to see. There was nothing on the computer about Simon owning a private jet."

I gave Riley the hard drive from Mr. Oksamma and told her to have a go at it while I tried to make sense of the twenty-one names and numbers from Simon's computer.

Riley came in about 11:00 and plopped herself down on the edge of my desk. I looked up at her and she leaned back on one elbow like a lounge singer on a piano bar—her favorite vamp pose.

"I know who hit you Saturday night." I looked up at her. What was she playing at?

"I already knew who hit me," I said cautiously.

"Not the kind of guy who takes kindly to older men messing around with his girlfriend, is he?" Riley asked. I nodded. "I wonder what he'd do if he found out his girlfriend was planning to run away with one of those older men—say an older man who set her up with her own business."

I leaned back in my chair appreciating the view of Riley sprawled out across the edge of my desk.

"Okay," I said, "spill it. What were you investigating yesterday?"

"Angel Woodward," she answered. That was progress. I didn't know what her last name was. "Dag, there's more going on up there than meets the eye. When you go up there you just see girls catering to men who can pay them well."

"Ah, I see," I smiled. "You've become an expert on the 'hostess' industry, eh? So, how's tricks?"

"You want to know what's going on?" she scowled at me.

"What did you find out, Riley? You know I'm all ears."

"All except the part that's eyes." She grinned, but she didn't shift her provocative pose. "These girls are smart cookies. I've learned about several of them over the past few days talking to Cinnamon and then with Angel. Did you know that Cinnamon is a marketing director at a local pharmaceutical corporation? Sierra is a field sales rep for a medical products firm. Allison is an insurance claims adjuster. Portia owns a string of independent coffee stands and employs over twenty people. Diva is a software developer. The girls Cinnamon named who work up at the condo are all are college-educated, several have master's degrees, and one is a PhD doing cancer research. And you know what? They all got jobs or businesses through men who are clients at the condo."

"Nice work," I said. "But you missed Angel, who is a travel agent and makes all Simon's travel arrangements for him."

"Hey! You didn't even know her last name yesterday," she said.

"I didn't know her last name until you just mentioned it," I fessed up. "So are you suggesting that the condo is a front for a secret society of college educated women who are using their contacts there to take over the economic structure of Seattle?" I asked. "That's very Hollywood."

"No," Riley said, "I'm not suggesting that. I'm just saying that there are an awful lot of really smart women who are using more than their brains to break through the glass ceiling. Whether they ever use last names in the condo or not, they know who their clients are. They could do a lot of damage if they got upset. For insurance against ladies being upset, their clients are very nice to them."

"What about Angel?"

"Yes, then there is Angel," Riley continued. "Based on mathematic extrapolation of a limited sample-set, I believe that we could safely assume that Angel does a business of about $15 million a year and pulls down about $1.5 million in commissions and fees."

"As a hooker?" I exclaimed.

"No, as a travel agent," Riley said. "She's not a hooker, at least not in the way that she defines it. She books travel, escorts businessmen on their business dates, and sells ATM travel cash cards. It is a very, very lucrative business."

"Why on earth would she be working up at the condo in addition to that kind of a business?" I could not put this together.

"Well, it's probably not for the extra thousand or so a week in unreported cash that it brings in," Riley quipped. "That might motivate some of them, but most figure they could make six figures on their day-jobs. They figure that the condo puts them in the presence of very powerful men being very powerful. And if a powerful man likes you, he makes the way easier for you outside the condo, in the real world. He puts in a good word for you with a friend who knows someone who happens to be looking for a marketing executive."

"So Angel goes there to make contacts for her executive travel agency."

"No, I don't think so. The contacts get made for her. Simon Barnett set up her business and makes sure she has an unending supply of clients. She's there for Simon."

"The ladies sure didn't impress me like that when I was up there," I said shaking my head. If Riley was right, most of the women I met in the condo pull down more money each year than I do.

"Oh, they impressed you all right," Riley said sweeping her hair back off one side of her face as she turned to look at me with a sleepy-eyed grin that reminded me of Claudette Colbert in *It Happened One Night*. But it was Riley, and she was continuing.

"You never notice us for what we are. Here we are in all our beauty and brilliance, and you say 'Here, recover the data off this laptop,' or 'Pick up dogfood on your way to chauffeur me tonight.' We practically throw ourselves at you and you never realize the treasure you have right here in your hands."

Did I mention Riley can be a regular drama queen? Well, she wasn't exactly in my hands. More like lounging on my desk. But I have to admit, she gave me an idea, and even if it was an evil one, I couldn't help myself. I'd just found out yesterday that I was going to die before Christmas if I didn't get a heart transplant. And frankly, on a day to day basis, the chances of a transplant seemed slim.

"All right Riley," I said standing up from my desk. "I've wondered what you were really made of ever since I met you. It's time to put your money where your mouth is." She looked shocked, but then she recovered and went back on the attack.

"Whatever do you mean?" she asked.

I said, "Maizie, guard the office while Riley and I go out for lunch." Then I turned to Riley again as I slipped into my own coat, "I know just the place. It's not far from here." As we left the pier, I put up my umbrella and used one arm to pull Riley close to me so she wouldn't get wet. I could feel her tense a little. Oh, I do know a little about women... at least this one.

We walked down the Waterfront past the Aquarium in silence. Riley was tense, and she was surprised when we turned in at Pier 57—The Bay Pavilion. I unfurled the umbrella and led her to the end of the pier where there's a huge game arcade and a merry-go-round.

I bought two $10 rolls of quarters and handed one to her.

"All right, Riley. Let's see how hot you really are. Most tickets at the end of his roll of quarters gets lunch from the loser. And I'd like fish & chips if you please." I could see her visibly relax at last as a smile broke out across her face.

"Well, plan on buying your own when you pick up my calamari," she laughed. Then we hit the games. It was a riot. We did a side-by-side Skee-ball challenge, but soon discovered that even though I beat her by 10,000 points, the machines paid the same number of tickets. It was on to various coin drops, car racing, gator-beating, and even a dance contest. I about dropped on that one and conceded the tickets to her. When we were done, I had only 175 tickets to her 310. Well, she'd be just insufferable now. We bought various candy lollipops with the won tickets and headed toward the exit.

"Wait, Dag," Riley said. "I want a picture. Let's take it in the picture booth."

"Go ahead," I laughed. "I think I can dig up another dollar."

"No, together. I want a picture of the two of us together." I was surprised.

"I don't think the two of us will fit in that little booth."

"Oh, come on. People do it all the time."

"Aren't they little people?" Nonetheless she shoehorned me into the photo booth and climbed in with me. I think it is the closest I've ever held Riley. There was a fresh clean scent about her. She knew I was sensitive to perfumes, so was always careful not to use any floral scents. I was lost in thought, experiencing the sheer joy of being with her when the camera flashed four times and took me by surprise. Well, so much for that picture.

Riley collected the film strip and we left the building. We hit Ivar's Acres of Clams for fish & chips and calamari and sat laughing about the contest in the Bay Pavilion. I confessed that she played a good game and had fairly beaten me. I told her that I was probably going to have to bring her into full partnership in the firm now. The weather had broken briefly as we went back to the office, so I didn't need to put the umbrella up. Riley wrapped her arm around my waist anyway as we walked, and I placed mine carefully around her shoulders.

Damn the doctors. Life was too good to give up now.

We unlocked the outer door to the office and discovered my door open. That was unusual. I always close that door. I stepped through and caught the surprise of my life. A guy was stretched out on his stomach on the floor with Maizie perched in the middle of his back growling just loud enough that I'm sure he could hear. His arms and hands covered his ears and neck. I could see he was breathing, but he wasn't desperate enough to challenge the little pit bull perched in the middle of his back. Her pink bow lay in the middle of her bed and she looked every bit the vicious guard dog.

"Good girl, Maizie," I said. "Kennel up." I tossed her a ginger snap from the jar on my desk and Maizie leaped into the air off the stranger's back to catch it, then trotted off to her bed behind the sofa to munch it down. I stepped behind my desk and ordered the visitor up as I picked up the phone to call the police. I noticed that Riley had dropped her coat in the doorway and had stepped out of her shoes.

"Suppose you tell me why you'd be inside a locked office with a guard dog on your back," I said. "I need to tell the police something."

He yelled "No!" and lunged for the telephone. For all his efforts, he ended up sprawled back on the floor, this time with Riley standing over him. I hadn't even seen how she'd moved to intercept him, but he looked dazed as he got to his knees.

"Bitch!" he spat. She looked like she was ready to drop him again, but I held up a hand and she backed off a step. "I came for what's mine," he yelled. "That bitch had no right to give you his laptop."

"You'd better have a seat and talk before you try any more heroics, friend," I said calmly. Frankly my confidence picked up a lot when I saw Riley lay him out. I was impressed and winked at her. She smiled, but didn't take her eyes off the guy until he was firmly seated in the chair facing me. Then she moved quietly to stand behind him. "What laptop is it that you think I have?"

"Simon Barnett's. It's company property. His wife had no right to bring it to you. I came to get it back." He nodded toward the laptop lying on the floor next to where Maizie had first taken him down—my laptop.

"Can you describe this laptop to me," I said picking up my device and returning to my desk.

"You're holding it in your hand. What do you mean describe it?" he asked.

"Surely if you are with BKL you must be able to tell me where the asset tag is. You wouldn't leave company property lying around without an asset tag; your insurance company would insist," I said turning the laptop over in my hands. "Who are you?"

"Bradley Keane," he said automatically.

Simon Barnett's junior partner. According to Angel, the partner was doing work for some branch of organized crime. He must be afraid of what was on Simon's computer, but I can't imagine why. Apparently Bradley Keane didn't even know what Simon's computer looked like. He must be really spooked to dare a mission like this.

"Mr. Keane, there are a few things that you need to know," I said. "First off, this isn't Simon's computer; I don't leave valuable client property lying around where it can be walked off with. Secondly, Simon's laptop has no company asset tag, so I doubt very much that it is company property. If you can bring a police officer in with a subpoena, I'll be happy to take the laptop in question to court and testify, but unless you want what's on his laptop brought in as evidence, I'd suggest that you think that option over carefully."

"Look, Hamar, I know that Simon kept records of our business on his personal laptop. He has been laundering money for a syndicate and is planning to cut and run and leave me holding the bag. The only hope I've got is to go state's evidence with that computer beside me. I've got to have that computer." He was still eyeing my laptop, evidently unpersuaded that it wasn't Simon's.

"Breaking and entering won't look very good on your record when we go to the authorities," I said calmly. Was he the villain or the victim? He'd come up with good answers, but I certainly didn't trust him. "Why don't we leave it this way, Mr. Keane? I'll let you know if I find any incriminating evidence on the computer—which, by the way, I haven't yet. I'll even let you know before I let FinCEN know." He glared at me. "I'll assume that is an agreement on your part and I don't really need to call the police in right now. Fair enough?"

Simon's partner took my offered card, gave one last look at my computer, glared at Riley, and left. He carefully stepped directly on her coat in the doorway.

"That bastard!" Riley declared as she picked up her coat and brushed it off. She turned to me. "Why did you let him go without calling the police?"

"A couple of reasons Riley. First, I have a pit bull in my office."

"She's half dachshund and loveable as can be."

"She took down a six foot, 200-pound man and made him wet his pants," I said. "I don't know how she did it, but I don't want any kind of claim brought against us that would endanger Maizie."

"I understand that, but why else," Riley asked.

"A hunch," I answered. "Let's see if I'm right." I reached for the remote control. I'd never done this in front of Riley but I'd told her at lunch I was going to make her a partner. It was time she knew how this operation really ran. "Close the door for me, would you Riley?"

"You want me to leave?" she pouted.

"No," I answered. "If you are going to be my partner, you're going to have to learn a little more about the business." I'd never seen Riley quite so at a loss for words. She opened her mouth a couple of times, then quietly closed the door and turned toward me. I turned on the TV.

"We're going to watch TV?" she asked, then went silent as I keyed in the password and the wall behind my desk slid aside to reveal the vault. I heard her gasp a little as I turned and entered it. She was behind me like a magnet on steel. "How many servers do we have in here?" she asked in a hushed tone. I noticed that it didn't take her long to adopt the "we" pronoun.

"We have ten servers that run our little operation. As you know, we use cellular modems to open our virtual private network. That is more secure than WiFi, even though the connection is a little slower. There is an eight terabyte disk array that keeps our files backed up and an environmental system that keeps the room cooled to sixty-two degrees. This is where I hook the disks we recover into the system, then give you a copy of the drives to work on. It's also where I keep valuable things locked up. Like Simon's computer," I pointed it out. But that wasn't what I was in here for right now. I reached up and took the monster laptop that Mr. Oksamma brought in the day before off the shelf.

"Any luck on that disk I gave you this morning?" I asked.

"Not much to it," Riley answered. It's got an ancient operating system on it—Win97, I think, probably hasn't been upgraded since it was new ten years ago. Data's all intact. No problem restoring the whole drive even to boot capability. The file formats are all pretty old, too."

"Have you checked dates on any of the information?"

"Not really."

"I have a feeling this computer hasn't been used in years," I said turning it over. "I didn't pay much attention to it when Mr. Oksamma brought it in." I hadn't really bothered to examine it when I backed up the disk. Sure enough, an asset tag had been ripped off the device. Thing is, asset tags leave a tag in the residue as well and I grabbed an ultraviolet light and scanned the back. "BKL Ltd. Asset #7124" popped out clearly. I remembered Mr. Oksamma following me into my office when I thought he was leaving. The Refrigerator had actually been casing the place for Bradley Keane.

"Okay, lady. You showed me how good you are at arcade games this morning. Now I want you to show me how well you can break security on an old computer. It shouldn't really be that hard. Security wasn't as tight when this baby was in use. I'm betting that passwords for BKL's network are on here someplace. Find them."

A Day in Court

IT WAS SUPPOSED TO BE a preliminary hearing, but Jordan was hoping to push the defendant to an early confession, thereby getting an automatic conviction on the embezzlement in exchange for not bringing up the kiddie porn that I'd discovered.

I dropped Maizie off with Mrs. Prior. Maizie apparently speaks the same language as my landlady. I was listening to a pretty intense lecture on how worried Maizie was about how I was taking care of myself when Jordan drove up. I scratched Maizie's ears and joined Jordan.

We headed for the U.S. District Court on Stewart. It's the kind of building that you'd think would be corporate headquarters for a next generation dotcom company. It sits on close to three acres and rises 23 stories of glass and concrete into the sky, with a naturalistic monolith in its central courtyard, and a roof that looks like something off *The Flying Nun*.

It was just nine o'clock when we entered the building and I was already getting antsy—not for the opening arguments, but for what I'd put Riley up to while I was sitting here listening and waiting. We'd set up a new laptop, with the data from the old one that Mr. Oksamma had brought in, and some sophisticated hacking tools. The old computer had an early wireless card in it and must have been used to test the system when they were installing it. I was betting that of the dozen or so passwords we'd found on the device at least one was still valid on the network. One was all we needed.

I'd warned Riley about not being seen or recognized at BKL. Keane got a good look at her in the office, and I didn't think he'd hesitate to call in reinforcements if he spotted her in his territory. With Keane's current edginess around the idea of police, I had the image of the hulking Oksamma in the back of my mind.

I sat in the back of the courtroom and waited for Riley's message as the hearing opened. It wasn't long before a flash on my screen indicated I had an incoming message from her. She said she was in position and ready to start scanning for the network. She had managed to get into a bathroom right outside the doors of the top floor offices of BKL. We were ready to start hacking. This first part was going to be all up to her.

We'd set the laptop to mimic the old device that Oksamma had brought us, borrowing user names from Simon's laptop and passwords from the old computer. They were old, but I was betting that the small firm never thought about old equipment as a liability, especially an abandoned laptop back in a storage closet. The passwords collected on the device had shown a pattern. If the current password we had was expired (as was likely) my extrapolating software was likely to be able to suggest the right password for this month. Very careless.

As expected, the password was rejected, but the third try was a hit.

Now it was my turn. I linked into Riley's laptop through our VPN and began rifling through BKL's network searching for vulnerabilities and backdoors. There were plenty there. We set up our own user account, backed up all BKL's accounting data for the past three years, and closed up shop. If I needed back in later, I could now get in through remote access. Before I closed down my computer in the back of the courtroom, however, I gave Riley an encryption key and had her download all Simon Barnett's and Bradley Keane's e-mail, transfer it to our servers, and then set up a blind cc of everything that came into their inboxes forwarded to our account. We were going to have a fun afternoon.

By 2:00, having been called into the judge's chamber and given him my testimony, it was obvious that the case was not going to trial.

The attorneys had agreed to a plea bargain when presented with the evidence of child pornography on the defendant's computer. Technically, the computer belonged to the enterprise and not the defendant. They would gladly give me a new directive to look for anything that violated corporate policy. Faced with the overwhelming evidence, the defendant pled guilty to the embezzlement charges and was remanded over to custody to await maximum sentencing. Even though part of the plea bargain was to make restitution, he'd still be facing five to ten.

Personally, I'd have preferred to nail him on the child porn, but some days you take what you can get.

Jordan dropped me back at my office at about 3:30 and I found Riley at her desk looking smug as she scanned through e-mail messages. I called her into the office to talk about what she'd found. We sat in the comfy chairs facing the window where the rain had resumed pelting down with a fury.

"So how did you manage to get in without being seen?" I asked.

"Oh, it wasn't a matter of not being seen," she said. "It was just being seen in the right place. I went up to the office, started to say I had an appointment, but before I said with whom, I suddenly remembered that I'd forgotten my organizer and would have to run back down to my car. 'By the way,' I asked, 'is there a men's room near?' The receptionist was happy to point down the hall, out of sight of both the elevators and the reception desk. Once I was in, I went into a stall and camped out. It was very convenient."

"Wait a minute. You asked for a men's room?" I asked.

"Of course. James Whitcomb wouldn't ask for a ladies' room." She was enjoying this entirely too much. I had to admit that it was creasing my own face with a smile. She showed me a picture she'd snapped on her cell phone of herself in disguise. Without knowing for a fact that it was a woman dressed like a man, I would never have been able to tell.

"So you spent the whole day in the men's room," I said. "Educational?"

"Disgusting is more like it," she said. "I hung an out of order sign on the door of the stall and kept my feet out of sight whenever anyone

74

came in. You can learn a lot in a men's room, you know? Bradley Keane even walked in once with some other guy. I couldn't see who, but I could hear everything they said. They really should not continue business conversations in the men's room. You don't know who else might be there."

I was interested. I knew for a fact that men in restrooms and locker rooms tend to forget that they aren't in their own secure board rooms. I'd heard a number of explicit conversations under those circumstances myself.

"What did you learn?"

"Keane is trying to track down a shipment that was supposed to arrive on a container ship sometime last week. Apparently it was a last minute change of plans when Simon disappeared with the private jet. They seem to have lost track of exactly where the ship was supposed to dock. Bradley thought it was supposed to come into Seattle, but the other guy said he was sure it was coming into San Francisco because of the problems they had last time," Riley said. "There was considerable concern that the cargo not be investigated. I don't know what the cargo is, exactly, but apparently it is not what is printed on the manifest."

"Do you think it is being shipped to BKL?" I asked.

"No. They mentioned a fee warehouse, whatever that is. I'm betting that if we start digging into their finances, we'll find some reference to it."

We sat there looking at the rain for a few minutes. I was sure we had something to work with now. Somewhere Bradley and/or Simon were smuggling something. That in itself could account for a lot of their revenues and growth.

"Got any plans for tonight?" I asked.

"Hmmm… I'm hungry. Nothing particular on Thursday nights on TV. I'm single and don't drink. So I guess I'm yours. What do you want to do with me?"

I had to bite my tongue before answering. "Feed you first. Then, I think we should plan on a late night digging through the records of BKL. We'll set up a search routine on the e-mail first and look for key words. I've started a list already, but I think we should add to it based on your bathroom liaison. We can start tearing apart the company financials. If we divvy up the work, we should be able to find some of these shell companies that we know exist. Maybe we'll even find out what a fee warehouse is."

"Food first?" She looked pleadingly at me as I moved behind my desk. I paused, then returned and held out my hand to help her out of her chair. She took it and I pulled her to her feet.

"Food first, and then we dig into this."

We started out the front of the office and toward the entrance to the pier.

"Dag?" Riley asked as if she were puzzled about something. "Are they always like that?"

"Who like what?"

"Men in bathrooms."

"You mean talking business?" I asked.

"No, I mean talking all the other stuff. They were so disgusting." She shuddered.

"There's a reason it's called toilet talk, Riley. It's only good for flushing." She took my arm as we walked down toward Elliott's and gave it a little squeeze.

"Thanks."

Partners in Crime

I FELL ASLEEP on the sofa in the office around midnight and Riley mercifully threw a blanket over me and left. I don't know when.

I used to be able to pull all-nighters without even blinking an eye. A few cups of coffee and I'd be stoked for the night. That's probably the problem. I'm not drinking coffee beyond my morning espresso and if Doc Roberts knew I was doing that he'd have a hissy-fit. I'm going to have to quit.

I know it.

But at 6:00 this morning when I woke up in the office, all I wanted was a cup of coffee.

Riley left me a note and said she'd stop by my house to pick up clean clothes and Maizie this morning.

Damn.

I let her help me patch up my head, and now she thinks she can just go pick things up for me and make my life pleasant. She's a sweetheart. I figured I had a good couple of hours before she would grace my presence, though, so I slowly made my way up through the Market to the Eye of Dawn. I went in and ordered a strong Americano and a sweet roll. I sat to enjoy the cup and greet the daybreak.

Eye of Dawn doesn't make quite as perfect a cup of coffee as Tavoni's, but I wasn't about to walk all the way up to Belltown to get perfection. Eye of Dawn looks into the market on one side and out onto the Sound on the other. I could see the ferries all lit up, making their first journeys across the Sound. Out in the middle, there was a huge container ship wallowing deeply, surrounded by four tugs pulling her into the terminal. I was reminded that BKL was expecting a container or some number of them, either in Seattle or in San Francisco. What was the fee warehouse and what was Bradley expecting? Something had gone wrong on a previous shipment.

We don't hear that much about what comes in and out of the Port of Seattle. Container ships arrive every day, many from China and Japan. This one said Hoisan on the side clearly. It's funny how I can read the letters on a ship a mile away, but I need reading glasses to see my computer screen clearly.

This ship was probably headed for Terminal 18 where they installed the new heavy duty cranes a couple of years ago. What was it that had happened?

When it hit me I spit coffee out through my nose and nearly choked to death. Two police officers who were eating donuts and coffee nearby jumped to my assistance.

"You okay, old fella?" one of them said to me.

"I'm fine," I said shortly, still coughing a bit. So much for that shirt.

"Maybe we should get you a cab home. It looks like you had a rough night." One of them shone a flashlight in my eyes. Damn! It was broad daylight. Then I realized what they were thinking.

"Officers," I said as politely as I could. "May I reach for my wallet?" One of them moved behind me as the other faced me and nodded. I could feel that a hand was near a sidearm. I pulled out my wallet and handed my PI card to the officer. "It was a long night," I said, "but I'm not drunk, I don't need a cab, and my office is just a couple of blocks from here. I just inhaled my coffee." The officer smiled and relaxed.

"You look pretty rough, pal," he said. "Can't be too careful these days. You okay?"

"Yeah," I answered. It doesn't pay to escalate these things. I work well with the cops and I intend to keep it that way. "I understand. Say, do you guys know anything about ships?" I asked.

"Not much," said the officer on my right. "They come in full, they leave full. Somewhere in between a bunch of guys down on the docks and a bunch of drivers of big rigs have a lot of work to do."

"That's about what I know," I said. "I was just wondering where that big container ship was coming from and what it had on it."

"The Hoisan?" commented the barista, who had been watching our interchange with interest. "That comes in out of Hong Kong. We see her about every three months. Brings in all sorts of Asian mish mash and takes out mostly grain, beef, and agricultural products. I used to work down at the docks till I killed my back," he finished.

"Thanks," I said. "And thanks for coming to my rescue," I told the officers. "I need to get back to the office. I'm not done with my night yet, I'm afraid."

They wished me good luck and to take care 'old man' and I left. I hustled as fast as I could through the market and got back to the office while the ship was still hanging out in the harbor waiting for docking clearance. I dialed Jordan's phone number. He was still asleep but came awake fast when he heard my voice.

"You wanted a possible connection of a major Seattle holding company to some kind of illegal traffic that would bring them a lot of money," I said. "I think I've got something."

"Knew I could depend on you Dag. What's up?"

"There's a ship docking this morning that has something on it. I think we might have a lead on who it's registered to."

"What are the contents?" he asked.

"You remember a couple years ago when a bunch of illegal immigrants were stowed in a container—some of them were dead?" I could hear Jordan suck air into his lungs.

"You can't mean someone's trying it again," he said. "Who's the container addressed to?"

"I think I've got the information here. Riley was compiling a list of names last night. Let me see if she found it." I went to her desk and searched through the papers she'd left on top. Bad form. I was going to have to talk to her about that. But fortunately for me, the paper I wanted was right on top. She must have found it after I fell asleep. A name was circled in red with the initials FEE written beside it. "Far East Exchange."

"It's a fake," Jordan said, decisively.

"My guess is, an empty warehouse that was leased and may not even exist anymore. These guys don't need an office."

"When's this ship coming in?"

"It hasn't reached the docks yet," I said. "I can see it out in the Sound."

"I'm on it. Thanks for the tip, Dag," he said. "It could be our break." He was off the phone and I could picture him rallying troops and tying down the terminal. There would be some unhappy people out there this morning, but in the long-run, it was probably not enough to bring down a huge conglomerate like BKL. I'd bet that they were pretty well insulated from everything but the cash.

I'd just hung up the phone when Riley walked into the office and Maizie came bolting to jump up on my lap.

"What kind of dog is this?" I asked looking her over. She had blue and yellow ribbons tied to her collar and she proudly waved a pink bow from the tip of her tail.

"That's a champion dog," Riley said laughing. "Mrs. Prior said Maizie wanted to wear her ribbons to the office to show Dag. She won the costume contest at the doggie day camp yesterday."

"Do I want to know what she wore?"

"She was a ballerina," Riley giggled as she watched me scowl at Maizie.

"Who is ever going to take you seriously as a guard dog, sissy girl," I said rubbing her ears. "And what did they do to your toes?" Each of Maizie's toes was painted bright pink.

"Mrs. Prior says that Maizie likes to have her nails done," Riley said. "She went for a manicure and polish after the day camp as a reward." Mrs. Prior says. Mrs. Prior talks to dogs. Dogs talk to Mrs. Prior. Don't ask any more questions.

"Well, we've got some leads," I said as I took the clean clothes from Riley. "By the way, how did you get into my apartment?"

"I took the key off your key ring," she said handing it back to me proudly. "Here you go."

"I suppose you made yourself a copy," I said with one eyebrow raised. She looked at me so innocently and startled that I had to laugh. But she didn't deny that she'd made a key.

"I brought you a bran muffin and a cup of decaffeinated green tea. If you'd like we can go out for breakfast when you are dressed," she called after me in the bathroom.

"Not now," I answered. "I want to start triangulating the businesses that you've managed to track down so far. We may have a start, but we still don't have Simon. He may be hiding in one of the business locations."

"Do you think he's hiding, or being held?"

"That's what I really don't know."

Two phone calls changed the shape of our day.

The first was from the management company that staffed Simon's plane. It had landed in New York. According to the manager, the crew had been around the world at Simon's behest with stops in Tokyo, Singapore, New Delhi, Cairo, Paris, and London. He did not have specifics on the manifest other than it included the pilot, six passengers and crew, and cargo listed as "Asian antiques." I asked if Simon was on the list and was given a startling bit of information. The flight manifest only requires the number of people, not who they are. Customs and Immigration check the documentation of all arriving passengers. So all we really knew were the name of the pilot and the number of people on the plane.

"Riley, we need to know the most likely destinations for a plane-load of Asian antiques. What can you find from the list of BKL subsidiaries and shells that might be a place where they are headed?"

"I'm on it," she chimed in. "I'll let you know as soon as I get them all researched."

"You are a treasure, Riley," I said. "Don't ever let me forget it, partner."

"I plan to be a constant reminder to you, partner," she said.

I went to work on my list of numbers. Something about the accounting records for BKL rang a bell with me. They had bank accounts in different places around the world, which is not unusual for a multi-national company.

International Bank Account Numbers. Every bank in the world has an IBAN routing number. That is how money gets transferred from one location to another. You need a bank, a routing number, and an account. There is a specific formula for determining what country and what bank, followed by the account number. I was seeing similar patterns, though different numbers, between the records of BKL and the bitmap numbers in Simon's fuzzed files: 76182060023046787 Charles Hammond, said one of Simon's numbers, and indeed I matched CH76 1820 6000 1030 5696 7 from BKL accounts.

A quick check with the IBAN validator on the Internet and I had the name and address of a Swiss bank. Access to a bank account would require more than an account number, though. I would still need a password and User ID to poke into them.

The phone jangled me out of my excitement and I realized it was already mid-afternoon. During my intent focus, a plate of Thai noodles had somehow appeared on my desk with a cup of tea and, by all indications, I'd actually eaten most of it.

Riley called sweetly from the outer office, "It's our client, Dag," in the kind of sing-song voice that told me instantly that Brenda had already been obnoxious on the phone. I put her on speakerphone and waved Riley into the office.

"Have you got anything yet, Dag?" she demanded as soon as I'd answered. I was getting pretty sick and tired of her condescension and decided on the spur of the moment to unload.

"Yeah, I've got a boatload of illegal Chinese immigrants and a plane full of Asian antiques. Which would you like to bid on?"

"You are supposed to be finding Simon."

"I'm a lot closer today than I was yesterday, thank you," I said. "His partner paid me a little visit and it moved the investigation forward quite a ways. You should have cleared giving me the computer with him."

"You didn't give it to him, did you?"

"No. Should I?"

"It isn't company property. That is Simon's personal computer from home."

"Well," I said, "it seems as though Simon might have had some trouble telling the difference between what was personal and what was company property. Where was he planning to go after Singapore?"

"He usually clears customs in California," she said. "He claims they know him there and he doesn't get as much hassle as he does in Seattle. He's got a warehouse in San Diego that he uses as a base for shipping goods around the country."

"Anything in the East?" I asked.

"No further than the Midwest," she answered. "He does a lot business in St. Louis, Chicago, and Minneapolis."

"That will do," I answered. "Thank you for your help, Mrs. Barnett." I was already starting to hang up the phone when she practically screamed at me.

"Dag, wait! I made this call to tell you something else. Don't be rude."

"Wouldn't dream of it. What did you want?"

"I'm leaving town for a few days. Just a little vacation that I had planned for some time. So I'll call in a few days. If you absolutely must reach me, here is my cell phone number. I can't guarantee that it will be on, though." She rattled off the number and I jotted it down. Height of concern, if you ask me. Missing husband so she is taking a vacation. I was pleased. I'd have a little peace at least.

"Have a nice vacation, Brenda," I said. "May I hang up now?" The receiver clicked and I assumed that was permission enough.

"Riley!"

"I've got it," she said, rushing back to her desk and returning with a yellow legal pad. "Six companies all told. One in St. Louis, three in Chicago, and two in Minneapolis."

"So which one is it? Where are they headed?" I mumbled.

"Chicago," Riley said. I looked up at her. "That's where Far East Exchange is located."

"Riley, I love you," I said enthusiastically.

"Oh, Dag," she swooned against the doorway in a dramatic pose borrowed from the cover of a bodice-ripping romance novel. "How long I've waited."

"Well, wait a little longer, Sugar. I've got another task for you."

"Damn!" she exclaimed. I looked up at her. That's my line.

How to Become
a Private Investigator
On Two Weeks' Notice or Less

I WAS SO EXHAUSTED after my near-all-nighter and another late night on Friday that I spent most of Saturday in bed. I couldn't leave it alone even then; my mind kept flitting back to how I got started in this business. Embezzlement, fraud, and computer files were the constant of my career.

It started on a Monday in September fifteen years ago. It happened to be the day after my forty-second birthday—unmarked and uncelebrated.

Don't feel sorry. I just don't do birthdays. I'd spent the weekend like any other weekend, hiking, socializing, and trying to get laid. A birthday could only be significant in that it helped me achieve one of the other three. This time it hadn't been helpful.

Cynical.

Yes. I suppose so. I was grouchy as a spring bear when I got to my office at Anderson Elliott Consulting, and found the entire network in collapse.

Discovering why would change my life.

I'd managed the tech department since we had one, starting on a mini-computer which, by today's standards, was a giant. An entire room was dedicated to the computer and three workstations. Over time, we became part of the desktop revolution, consolidating and then distributing the network so that everyone in the company had a computer on his or her desk. We were way ahead of our time in many ways.

On this particular Monday morning, my Sunday night tech was standing in a corner of the server room, sweating and shifting from foot to foot while a police officer stood barring the door and two dark-suited guys with gravy stains on their ties systematically dismantled our servers. Amy, our receptionist came rushing up behind me.

"I'm sorry, Dag," she started. "There was nothing I could do. They just flashed badges and came in."

Neal was nodding his head from his corner of the room. I addressed the uniform.

"You are standing in the door of my office," I said. "Want to show me your warrant?"

One of the suits stopped what he was doing and the officer stepped aside. The suit flashed what looked like a valid search and seizure warrant and started to put it back in his pocket. I reached out and took it from him so I could read what was written there.

"We are seizing these computers as evidence in an embezzlement and fraud case," the suit intoned. I looked quickly through the warrant and found nothing that authorized the dismantling of my network.

"There is nothing in here that says you are authorized to shut down this business," I remarked. "If I can be of help to get you the actual data you need, I'd be happy to oblige. I'm the Director of Technical Services here." Two or three others from the office had approached, though thankfully none of the officers seemed to be here yet.

"Dag, my computer won't connect to the network," one started in while walking up and then stopping short when he saw the activity.

"It will have to wait, Stanley," I answered. I turned back to the suit. "You see, you unplug the cables and no one can do any work."

"If we don't unplug and take them, we can't prevent data from being changed and erased," he answered. He was definitely a little

86

nervous. He obviously knew how to unplug cables, but I had a feeling that he didn't really know much about computers.

"I see," I said. "But taking the servers isn't going to get you what you want."

"How do you know what we want?" he asked.

"The search warrant says to search for paper or electronic files that evidence embezzlement or fraud on the part of senior executives," I said. "I don't know exactly what evidence you expect to find, but it's more likely to be on someone's desktop computer than on the servers."

"All right smart guy, why don't you just tell us where it is. You in on this? You concealing the evidence?"

"No," I said. "I had no knowledge of any wrongdoing. But as a basic security provision, we run a full back-up of everything that is on the system and on each desktop computer every night. We maintain the backups for two months, then recycle all but the end of week ones. Now unless you were so careless as to alert the suspects of your intentions a long time ago, the evidence you are looking for will be on those tapes. Current through midnight Sunday. You ran the backups last night didn't you Neal?" I asked my tech. He nodded vigorously. "So," I said, "If you have the backup tapes, you have the evidence. It's not on the servers and you can reconnect them so all the normal honest people here can go back to work."

The suit went to confer with the officer and the other suit. He came back a short time later, but work had stopped on disconnecting the network. "I demand the backup tapes for this system and all desktop computers on the network," he intoned. I smiled.

"According to this warrant," I said, "as far as I can see you are entitled to it, without being so demanding. Neal, open the safe." I'd had a fireproof cabinet that we referred to as "the safe" installed a year earlier. I asked Amy to get us some packing boxes and she disappeared and was back in a flash. Neal started unloading the safe into the boxes and labeling them. In the meantime I sat at my desk and scratched out a receipt longhand since my computer was down.

"Why so cooperative?" the suit asked me.

"According to this warrant, you have reason to suspect one or more of our execs of embezzling funds. That means that he's stealing from the company. All these people standing around you are share-holders in this company. The data on these tapes will either exonerate your suspect or nail his ass to a cross. If he's been stealing my money, I vote for the latter. Now, before you take those boxes, I'll need your signature here," I said. I produced the receipt for him to sign. He started to sign and then read the short document and looked up at me.

"You a lawyer?" he asked.

"No," I answered. "I'm just someone who wants to make sure that his own ass is covered if any of those tapes come up missing. You've got them; it's your responsibility." He signed. "Of course, there is one other thing," I said. "You'll probably want the encryption keys." He looked at me blankly. "Without the keys the data on the tapes is a useless hash. Maybe you need someone to decode the information, too," I said low enough so that only he could hear.

"You could save us a lot of time if we had your full cooperation," he said equally low. There was no question that he understood my suggestion.

That was the moment when the CEO and CFO chose to get to work and come charging toward the server room.

"Do me a favor," I said. "Cuff me and get me out of here. Also, take my desktop computer." The suit nodded and went to work. "Neal," I called. "Reconnect the servers and get people up and operating again. Make a fresh set of backups."

"What the bloody hell is going on here?" bellowed our beloved president. My new friend shoved the warrant at him and snapped at the officer to cuff me and bring me along. He grabbed my tower under one arm and his buddy rolled the boxes of tapes out on a cart. We were out of the office and in the parking garage before the boss had reached the phone to call his lawyer.

"Thanks," I said as he took the cuffs off. We shook hands. "I'm Dag Hamar, formerly the Director of Tech Services at Anderson Elliott and Associates."

"Detective Jordan Grant, King County Sheriff's Department," he answered.

"How did you get into taking down computers instead of speeders?" I asked good-humoredly. Now that he was out of the situation inside, Jordan was relaxing and becoming quite friendly. I thought that I might end up liking him.

"I took a class," he said. "Frankly, I'm in way over my head on this one. I'm glad you decided to cooperate."

"With those tapes and my computer we have access to everything of significance that has happened on that computer system in the past year. The system I put together would go back further than that if I'd thought of it sooner. But I've only been doing this kind of backup for a year. If you tell me what you are looking for, we can pop it out in no time."

"So why did you suddenly jump ship?" Jordan asked. "Maybe I should be suspicious of you."

"What I told you is true," I said. "There are a lot of good people who work in that company and if I can save them their jobs I will. But I've been working at Anderson Elliott since I graduated from college almost twenty years ago, and this is the first thing of interest that has happened in all that time. And I happen to have a thing about people who steal and people who break their trust. You hit three for three in there."

"Well, I'm happy to have you aboard," Jordan grinned. "What else will you need?"

"I'll need a tape drive, monitor and keyboard. Other than that we're good." We pulled into a computer superstore and I bought the drive I would need on my own credit card. I figured I could use it eventually.

Damn.

It was suddenly crystal clear that my life had changed. Inside of two hours when I was forty-two years old, I had left the corporate world and become a private investigator.

I soon discovered that I needed more than a business license to do all the things I wanted to do. Jordan offered to introduce me to his instructor and I went with him to a class titled simply "Undercover." I don't know why I was surprised to see a face from the past loom in front of me when I entered the classroom.

"I've been expecting you, Hamar," he said as he motioned me to a chair. "I've been expecting you for twenty years." Jordan looked at me in question and I smiled and shrugged. Lars Andersen, the venerable professor of this class was my commander in the U.S. Navy in Viet Nam in 1969. I had lucked out when I showed an affinity for electronics and computers and he requisitioned me for his Countermeasures and Deceit (CM&D) unit. It was a branch of Navy Intelligence and he kept me busy for two years while I amassed enough veteran's credit to go to college. He also introduced me to the fundamentals of sneaking around. It seemed that none of the equipment that we needed to do our job was ever delivered to our department. So, we arranged to have it requisitioned from other departments.

Now he was in command again, and I was establishing the two relationships that would carry through all my years as a private investigator—Jordan Grant and Lars Anderson.

One thing Lars emphasized to us repeatedly: There is no substitute for personal observation. If you were investigating a crime, you needed a witness. You wouldn't find the witness by randomly selecting phone numbers from the telephone directory, nor would you find one on a computer disk. If you wanted to find out the truth, you had to go where the truth was.

"If you are going to open the floodgates," he intoned, "you have to be ready to wade in the water."

I'd been living in a virtual world for too long. It was time to go to the truth. I got my lazy ass out of bed and packed a bag.

Redeye to Hell
(with Connections)

I CAUGHT THE FIRST FLIGHT to Chicago that I could get a business class seat on. It was a red-eye at 12:20 in the morning. I swung by the office on the way to the airport to grab a few last minute things and write a note for Riley. The brief respite from the rain this morning had ended and I was pelted as I left the cab and moved as quickly as I could into the office.

Riley had found the information that I needed to follow up on, though even she didn't know yet what I was looking for. Far East Exchange was located, not in Seattle, but in Chicago. It had an address of Wacker Drive near the river. I grabbed a GPS transmitter and programmed the server to broadcast and record my position. Of course, I couldn't legally broadcast from a commercial flight, but I figured that I would entertain Riley by showing her where I was at any given time.

I didn't want to just disappear and never be heard of again like Simon. This way, Riley would know where I was at all times. She knew how to "call in the cavalry," as she liked to say, if there was an emergency. That possibility nagged at me; I could be headed into Mob HQ for all I knew.

She would be pissed that I took this trip without her. Hell, she'd be pissed that I took the trip at all. But I'm not going to play sick just because I'm a little sick.

The flight was comfortable and not too full. I stretched out my legs and considered sleeping. My head was splitting and I detected the change of air pressure as we taxied to the runway. I was getting a little woozy. The vibration of the engines, the movement of take-off, and my general exhaustion, and I was out like a light.

The next thing I knew, the flight attendant was standing over me shaking me by the shoulder and calling my name.

"Mr. Hamar? Mr. Hamar?" I pried my eyes open to look at her. "Sir, we've landed. You need to deplane now."

Damn. It must be an unexpected side-effect of the heart medication. I needed to remember that the change of air pressure was going to affect me more radically than it used to. I gathered up my bag and realized that the plane was empty except for the flight crew, who were preparing to leave the craft, and the service crew who had moved on to clean it. I shook my head to clear it and left for the terminal. I had to pee so badly I was about to wet myself.

As I was leaving the plane the lead flight attendant smiled pleasantly at me and said, "Welcome to Houston, Mr. Hamar."

I was on the jetway when that hit me. Houston? What the hell was I doing in Houston? There was no sense getting back on the plane. It obviously wasn't going anyplace. It was 6:30 in the morning. First things first. I had to get to a bathroom or I'd burst right there.

It took longer than I expected.

When I dragged myself out of the restroom, I'd washed my face and brushed my teeth and run a comb through my hair. I looked almost human. Time to locate a service counter and find out why I was in Houston.

"Oh, Mr. Hamar," the nice woman said. "You were supposed to connect here to a flight on to Chicago. I'm afraid you've missed that connection." I looked at the ticket that I'd bought on-line as the first available flight to Chicago. Seattle to Chicago, connecting in Houston. Too bad I wasn't collecting frequent flyer miles for this.

"When is the next flight you can get me on?" I asked. She consulted her timetable, tapped on her keys, and said "Hmmm" a lot.

"The first flight that I can get you on in business class is at 2:25 this afternoon," she said. "If you want to change to coach I could get you out at 11:45." She smiled at me waiting for an answer. I calculated the stress of waiting versus the stress of flying in a sardine can.

"I'll take the 2:30 flight, please," I said. I looked around at the terminal trying to figure out where I was going to hang out for six hours.

"Here you are," she said handing me a boarding pass. "Gate C33 boarding at 1:45. If you'd like to relax, feel free to use our President's Club lounge. It's between gates C22 and C23. Just show your boarding pass."

"Thank you," I said.

I headed off down the concourse toward the distant lounge and discovered I had already passed it. I had to turn around and by the time I got there, I'd had to stop twice to rest. When I entered, however, I found a pleasant place with soft furniture and a continental breakfast spread out. It included a self-serve espresso machine. I looked around as if someone might stop me if I had a shot and then pulled it and went to sit down.

The last cup of coffee I had I'd spit out my nose. What a waste. This cup was not near the quality of either Eye of Dawn or Tovoni's. But the aroma brought me further awake before I determined that the flavor wasn't worth suffering for. I had breakfast and then went back to the reception desk. A young man greeted me as if he'd had to get up at 4:00 a.m. after a hard drunk the night before to open the lounge. Nonetheless, he promised to wake me in adequate time to make my flight if I fell asleep. I found a carousel desk, plugged my laptop in to recharge the battery, and logged into my virtual network.

I'd figured out the names and numbers had to be bank accounts, but I was still missing passwords. My first inclination was to search all Simon's files for the account numbers, but that turned up a blank. Then I tried searching for the names whose initials spelled out the country in which the account was located.

I hit my desktop search button and entered Charles Hammond. Instantly an e-mail popped up, sent to Simon by himself. Subject: Flight conditions. Text: Charles Hammond 4178311. A phone number? Or could this possible be the password for the Swiss account.

I kept searching, this time for George Brown. GB was the country code for Great Britain. I had to wade through a lot of different files as Simon had not conveniently sent an e-mail message for George. It was buried in a business report followed by a string of numbers. When I reached Aldus Dominic, I found no match at all. I searched another name and got a hit, but the following name was missing. Continuing down the list, only two more of the names yielded results. It looked like I hit another dead end.

I checked my own e-mail for messages while I thought about what to do next. Half a dozen messages had been routed to junk mail and the rest should have been. I scanned through the titles in the junk mail and noted one advertising a popular male dysfunction drug. My junk filter had caught it, but the way it was written caught my eye: v i g o r m a l e. There were spaces between the characters. Of course the routines in the junk mail catch variations on keywords as well. I switched to my search program and entered A l d u s D o m i n i c. There he was, complete with code number. Finding the rest of the files if Simon had decided to mask the names was going to be a pain. But, if junk mail could find them, so could I.

I spent the next two hours adapting a hacking tool with a search algorithm that would include common variants, substituting numbers for letters, inserting asterisks and spaces, and generally looking for patterns instead of words. When I looked up, the male receptionist was looking down the row of carousels at me.

"Your flight is boarding, Mr. Hamar," he said calmly.

"Boarding?" I said. "How much time do I have?"

"Oh if you hurry, you shouldn't have any trouble."

Damn.

I don't do hurry all that well.

I shoved my computer in my bag and headed out the door. It was already almost 2:00. There was no way I was going to make this. I reached Gate C27 on my way to C33 with plenty of time. But that gate proved to be a dead end. Gate C33 was the opposite direction.

But that was where I got my first big break of the day. An electric cart was just leaving C27 and I flagged it down. It took me only a minute to explain to a competent man, who was apparently used to dealing with everyone else's emergencies, that I was about to miss my plane because I couldn't walk fast enough because of a heart condition, etc. etc. He looked at me, took my flight number and gate information and told me to hang on tight.

I'm sure there are speed limits for electric carts in airports, but when they heard the constant beep, beep, beep of the oncoming cart, people scattered and we reached the gate as the attendant was announcing my name and asking for immediate boarding. I slid into my seat and fastened my seatbelt as the door closed. I flagged the flight attendant.

"This plane is going to Chicago, isn't it?" I asked.

"That's right, sir. We'll have you there in three hours." I relaxed and when the plane taxied out onto the runway, I fell immediately asleep.

Wet Welcome in the Windy City

I WOKE UP IN A STRANGE BED in a strange city. The sounds were not my sounds, the smells were not my smells.

Chicago.

I lay staring straight up at the ceiling trying to put the pieces of the story together that got me in this place. A shipment of antiques. Far East Exchange. Chicago. A harebrained notion to take a midnight flight and check it out personally. I'd gotten to my hotel in Chicago at about six o'clock. It was a decent hotel right in the center of the Loop.

Blessed sleep.

I looked at my watch. I'd slept late. It was nine o'clock. Riley would be in the office and getting my note. I'd better get up and prepare for the indignation. Then I realized that it was only 7:00 in Seattle. I had an hour to get ready at least.

I dragged myself to the window and looked out. Rain pelted the window for about 30 seconds, and then dissipated to a fine mist that clung to the building and cut visibility. I could just see the building across the alley and a pinch of the street below. It looked pretty much the same as Seattle. The rumble of the El a dozen stories below me confirmed that I wasn't in Washington any more. This was a city that believed in mass transit.

I showered and shaved the two-day stubble off my face, trimmed my mustache, and dressed. I hadn't brought many clothes in the roll-aboard bag that I packed, but one spare suit and two shirts was likely to be all that I would need since I spent all the previous two days and a night in the same clothes. Once I was dressed and had a tie on, I felt almost human. Coffee would take me the rest of the way.

There is nothing harder than ordering coffee in a foreign city, and when you are from Seattle, all cities are foreign. I stepped up to the coffee stand in the hotel lobby and asked for an Americano. The barista reached for a coffee pot that looked like it had been on the burner for a week.

"No, no," I said quickly. "Espresso fixed with a shot of hot water."

"Mister," she answered, "all espresso is made with hot water."

She pressed a button on her machine and handed me a cup of something that made me wish I'd taken what was in the pot. Well, Doc Roberts would be happy I was going without coffee again. This was my second day without, and I had the withdrawal headache to prove it.

I ate breakfast in the hotel café and logged into the network on my laptop. I had results for my searches waiting for me. Eating my oatmeal before it got cold, I started scanning the new names and numbers. Every name from the account numbers was coupled with a number of five to ten digits.

An idea crossed my mind and I looked up one of the banks on-line. Indeed it had a log-in screen. I entered the corresponding name under "UserID" and the number under "Password." There was a momentary pause and the screen refreshed with "my account" highlighted and the current balance: $12,557,827.80, €9,829,098.30, 6,906,933.90, displayed in three different currencies. In this bank alone, Simon had access to over twelve and a half million dollars. I had a list of his user names and passwords for twenty-one such banks.

Before I checked the next one, I looked at the transaction history. The account had been largely idle for the past two years, but in the last ten days, over half the current balance had been deposited in multiple small chunks.

Simon, or someone who had the same information I did, was very much alive and financially active. Since the activity I saw were deposits, I was betting it was Simon.

A waitress came up to my booth at that moment.

"You gonna order lunch now, Pops?" she asked. "If not, you better get outa here. The rush is about to start."

I glanced at my watch. It was 11:45. Not only was I not ordering lunch, I needed to make the contact that I wanted or the trip to Chicago was a waste. I paid the check and gave the waitress a $20 tip.

"Come back tomorrow," she called after me. "You can sit here all morning." I waved and headed out to get a taxi, dialing the office number as I went. There was no answer and I left a message telling Riley I was about to visit Far East Exchange.

I gave the driver the address on Wacker Drive and he wagged his eyebrows; it was only four blocks away. It wasn't a bad looking building. Small by comparison to the towering behemoths around it, but in good condition. The front entrance was a door beside an oversized garage door. I assumed they must get shipments in here of some sort, though I couldn't imagine a sixteen wheeler negotiating the angles with Chicago traffic.

I walked in.

I was surrounded by walls of drygoods, furniture, and artwork. An old man in shirtsleeves and old-fashioned arm-garters poked his head up over a handcart of bolts of fabric to look at me. "Are you from the theatre?" he asked. "You weren't supposed to be here until two o'clock. I'm not ready."

"I'm not from the theatre," I answered. "I just stopped in to see if you could answer a couple of questions for me. Are you the owner?"

"Owner, shmoner. I'm the only one here."

"Do you have a minute that I could ask you some questions."

"I got no time," he said. "I got work to do. Theatre crew is coming and they want forty-seven different bolts of Japanese Silk for 'Madame Butterfly.' Not the forty-seven that are up here in front. No, they want one each from forty-seven different lots around the warehouse. For theatre! Damn actors will be better dressed than half of Chinatown."

I didn't bother to mention that the people in Chinatown probably didn't dress in Japanese silk. I weighed my options and then made a rash offer.

"Maybe we could talk while I help you get those bolts down," I said. I couldn't be in any worse shape than this old guy, I thought. If he can do it, so can I.

"I won't turn down your offer, but I don't know that I'll answer your questions. You from the IRS?" I shook my head. "Police? Homeland security?" Each time I indicated no.

"I'm interested in Asian antiquities and I've heard that you are an expert."

"Eh," he was noncommittal as he motioned me toward a ladder. "Bolt 1247. It should be red and in that bin right next to the fourth step." I climbed the ladder, paused to rest and reached for the bolt. I hauled it out and handed it down to him. He motioned me to stay on the ladder as he heaved the fabric onto the hand cart. He moved the ladder to the next bin and rattled off another number. "What kind of antiquities do you want to know about and what do you want to do with them?"

I thought fast. I should really have prepared my story better, but I wasn't expecting an old man with a silk emporium. "I'm buying a franchise restaurant. Thai place. Thai is really big right now. Everything's Thai, you know?"

"You're telling me," he laughed. "Tom Yum. Phad Thai. It's all you can get now."

"Exactly. Well, I heard you could buy Thai antique furnishings for less than you can get repros from the restaurant supply. I thought before I put the money down on the franchise I'd check with a pro who could give me some advice." I'd handed him six bolts by now and I was panting. Most of the time he just pushed me on the ladder to the right place so at least I didn't have to climb up and down.

"It's true you can get a bargain. Of course, it's cheaper to buy Chinese than Thai. The good thing is that most people can't tell the difference. If it has an elephant on it they assume it's Thai."

"Too many people have watched 'The King and I' and figure that everything with elephants comes from there," I agreed. "I wouldn't turn down a good deal if it looked reasonable."

"So who pointed you in my direction," the old man asked.

"An old friend of mine from college," I answered casually. "Guy named Simon Barnett." I handed him the last bolt and he motioned me to get down off the ladder. He walked away from me and I followed. He motioned me to a chair beside his desk and fell heavily into his own.

"I didn't catch your name," he said.

"Hamar," I answered. "Dag Hamar." All right, I admit. It's not quite as dramatic as "Bond, James Bond."

"Yes, Mr. Hamar, and Swedes don't open Thai restaurants," he said bluntly. "Why don't you just come out and tell me why you are here?" Okay. Either he was an especially sharp cookie, or he already knew a lot about the case.

"Simon Barnett is missing," I said.

"I heard that already," he answered. "You work for that lousy two-bit partner of his?"

"No," I answered. His assessment of Bradley Keane matched my own. "Simon's wife hired me to find him."

"I'm not sure I like her any better," the old man said.

"Nor I," I agreed. "I took it on because Simon left me a note asking me to."

"If you are a friend of Simon's, then I'll help you anyway I can. I'm Earl Schwartz." We shook hands again.

"Like I said, we went to college together. We used to be a lot closer than we are now. Apparently, though, he thought I could find him." The old guy just nodded wisely. "Are you expecting a shipment of Asian antiques soon?"

"Yes. It landed in New York Saturday. It was being unloaded and trucked here."

"Trucked? Why aren't they flying it on into Chicago?" I asked.

"Well now, that's a good question," Earl responded. "Apparently the plane is needed elsewhere."

"Do you know if Simon was on the plane?"

"I do not, but I don't think so. When Simon brings in a load of antiques, he sees me directly. It's a good business if we deal with each other."

100

"I take it you don't get along well with his partner, though," I ventured. He swore vehemently.

"That sonabitch isn't worth the paper he wipes his ass with. And what's more, he's had a goon sniffing around here this week, too. Guy hardly speaks English, but he's hard as nails."

"Big guy, looks like a refrigerator?" I asked.

"That's him. You know him?"

"He paid me a visit last week."

"Well, watch out for him. If he doesn't get what he wants, he takes what he can get." The old man was angry to say the least. He was going to be even more upset when I told him about the shipment coming into Seattle. I was willing to bet he didn't know about that shipment from Asia. Before I could say anything, though, a young man came in the door, slapped a button beside it and the garage door began to open. A panel van backed in and Earl said that the theatre was here for their silk. I helped load up the van and they pulled out. Before I could return to my conversation, my cell phone chimed. I flipped it open.

"Where the hell are you?" I expected Riley to be mad at me, but it was Jordan on the phone.

"I'm in Chicago," I answered, "interviewing the manager of Far East Exchange. What did you find?"

"Nothing, damn it!" he swore. "I've had a full crew down here— ambulance rescue standing by, drug sniffing dogs—since the ship docked Saturday night. We scanned and inspected every container that was unloaded which succeeded in slowing down the job even more than the Longshoremen's slowdown that they pulled this weekend. We got to the container addressed to Far East Exchange and opened it. It was full of furniture. We sent dogs in, nothing. I called to get you down here this morning and Riley was the only one in the office. Normally I like seeing her, but it was your ass I wanted to chew today."

"You knew it was a hunch, Jordan," I defended myself.

"Well, we played it and it didn't work." I suddenly thought of something else.

101

"Hang on, Jordan," I said. I turned to Earl. "You said you were expecting a shipment from New York. Is one coming in from Seattle as well?"

"No," Earl said. "Simon only told me about the one from New York."

"Jordan," I said into the phone again. "Where is that container headed? I don't think it's coming here to Chicago."

"No," he said. "It's slated for a warehouse in Spokane."

"I know it's still a long-shot," I said, "but if I were you, I'd follow it. It isn't going to Far East Exchange."

"All right, Dag. I trust your instincts, but I've already sent some men to interview this Schwarz guy you are with. You know the routine."

"Oh Christ!" I swore. "Jordan, this guy doesn't know anything about it. And I'd bet Simon didn't either unless he recently discovered it."

"Well, we're going to have to question him anyway."

"I know. How soon?"

"Probably ten to twenty minutes," Jordan said. "If he's not there when we get there, I'm holding you responsible."

"Don't worry, Jordan," I said and hung up. He didn't need to worry; I was doing the worrying right now. I turned back to the old man.

"Look," I said, "I'm not going to hide this from you, Mr. Schwarz. You're about to get a visit from Internal Revenue's Financial Crimes Unit. There's a shipment addressed to Far East Exchange that arrived in Seattle this weekend. I'm not telling you anything else about the shipment because if you don't already know, then you shouldn't."

"Simon warned me," he said. "Two weeks ago. He said something wasn't right and he was warning all the businesses that he had acquired himself to keep everything clean and to expect police. We take the good with the bad, you know? Do you think that bastard Keane cooked enough evidence to hold me?"

"I doubt it. The whole thing smacks of a bad spy story. I don't think they'll be able to touch you if you've run the business cleanly." I felt sorry for the old man. Even innocent, this wasn't going to go easily on him just because of how old he was. He was eighty if a day. He sank down in his chair and opened a drawer, and then he pulled out a bottle of Scotch and a couple of glasses. He poured a finger in each and handed me one. I don't drink much and would have refused, but it seemed like an insult to not take at least a sip.

"You like jazz?" he asked out of the blue.

"Yes," I answered. "Very much."

"Most detectives do, don't they? There's a nice club just across the river. I know the manager. They've got a trio playing tonight with one of the best bass players you'll ever hear. I'll make sure they save you a table." He dialed the number and raised his glass. We touched them together and drank off the last of it as two men entered from the street. The Feds had arrived.

There was no small amount of confusion regarding who was whom when they started, but when I showed them my ID they waved me aside and said Jordan told them I was here. They were kind enough not to cuff the old man as they led us out into the street, and they let him lock the door behind him and set his alarm. I was left standing on Wacker Drive as they drove away.

I spent the rest of the afternoon back in my hotel room making phone calls. I patched things up as best as I could with Riley. She'd been watching my movements on the channel I left her and was poised to call the police at any sign of trouble, but Jordan had called her down to the docks early this morning. She'd taken the brunt of his frustration over my tip. I didn't blame her for being ticked at me now and assured her that I'd make it up to her. I told her what I'd found regarding the names. She was suitably impressed.

After she'd returned from the freight terminal with Jordan, she continued sifting through Bradley's email. She was detecting a number of people to whom Bradley sent messages that sounded like veiled threats. In my eyes, there was little that Bradley wouldn't do. I warned Riley to be extra careful. She repeated the same warning back at me.

Then, I made the inevitable call to Mrs. Prior to see how Maizie was doing.

"Maizie is very worried, Dagget Hamar," Mrs. Prior announced, "and a little upset that you would go on this trip without her. She is your partner, after all." This was sounding like the same conversation that I'd had with Riley.

"I couldn't bring her on the airplane with me," I said. "They aren't kind to dogs on airplanes. She would have had to ride in a box in the luggage compartment. She wouldn't have liked it at all."

"Maizie is hiding her eyes and is sending me pictures of her howling in a kennel," Mrs. Prior said. "Did you leave her in a kennel and go away?"

"No, she's remembering the last time we tried to travel by plane together," I said. I was talking to my dog through a pet psychic.

Damn.

After dinner, I decided to take Earl up on his offer to have a table saved for me at Alex's Jazz Alley. Located just off State Street on the north side of the river, it was a flat walk. And it was a great club. The trio was indeed everything that Earl had led me to expect. The crowd (yes a crowd on a Monday night!) was enjoying the beat to the extent of getting up to dance, whenever they felt like it, whether they had partners or not. It was a young crowd. The energy was incredible and before I knew it I'd passed several hours drinking tonic and bobbing my head to the music. They took a break, promising to be back for another set and a woman danced over to my table and plopped herself down in the other chair.

"Whee, that was fun, wasn't it?" she asked as she turned to me. "You weren't out there dancing," she continued. "Your feet wanted to dance. Even your head wanted to dance. What was holding you back?"

"My heart," I said matter-of-factly. "Besides, I didn't have a dance partner." She was about five foot three with dark hair that had been streaked with blonde so she reminded me of a tiger. As I looked at her she mussed it up with her fingers and flung it back and forth. A little older than the average in the club, I guessed she must be in her mid-thirties.

"Who needs a partner?" she asked. "I didn't have one and I'd still be out there if my feet weren't hurting. I've got new boots on." She lifted a foot to the table and pulled her pants leg up to show me the high-heeled leather she wore under them. When I was in the Navy we'd have called them "Follow me home" boots. "What do you think of them?" she asked.

"Very sexy," I said honestly.

"Right answer," she said. "I'm Peg."

"Nice to meet you Peg," I said, "I'm Dag." I decided against a repeat of the James Bond line. If you're not James Bond, you shouldn't really try it.

When the next set started, she got me up to dance a little. I'm afraid I wasn't much of a partner. She led me back to the table and ordered another tonic. Hmmm... She knew what I was drinking? Well, there was no question of the fact that even with sparkling water, I was nearing my limit. I wanted to walk home, but I was also a bit loathe to leave the company of my charming companion.

We'd pretty much talked about miscellany from the music to the weather, and had even skirted a few political issues. It was nothing particularly significant, but it was pleasant. And there is something about being with an attractive woman. You just want to stay in her orbit. I regretfully rose to make my excuses and leave.

"Do you want me to call a cab?" she asked as she stood with me.

"No, I think I'll walk. It's just a few blocks south on State Street."

"That's great!" she said. "Will you walk me home? I live on your way and I hate to make the walk alone."

Why not? I agreed. Lucky for me. It was misting again, a wet heavy fog and Peg had an umbrella that we huddled under while we walked toward the river.

"I live in the circular tower over there," she pointed. "It's a great location."

"It looks terrific. View of the river?"

"No. That's expensive. I mean even more expensive. I try to stay within my means."

By the looks of it, her means must paint a pretty big circle within which to live. We walked along the river, a few feet above the water in front of the building.

"It has been a very pleasant evening, Peg," I said. "I should really get going, though."

"Care to come up for a nightcap?" she asked. "or a cup of coffee." She could scarcely have tempted me more. I shook my head.

"I'm flattered that you'd ask," I said, "but I'm really bushed and need to get back to my hotel."

"How about dinner tomorrow night?" she suggested. Hmm… Would I be in Chicago tomorrow, or would I just catch a plane back home and return to the computer? This trip hadn't exactly yielded the results I'd fantasized about. I had to admit, I'd dreamed of walking into Far East Exchange and just finding Simon there waiting for me.

I was about to answer when a hulking man passed and made a grab for my computer case, still slung around my neck and over my shoulder. That slowed him down and I swung at him. It didn't help. He jerked the bag hard enough to break either the strap or my neck, and I was thankful that it was the strap. I looked up and realized the hulk was none other than Oksamma, the refrigerator.

Peg had come to my aid as well, but he brushed her off like a fly, knocking her to the ground. I yelled something unintelligible grappling with him again. This time he wasted no more time with me than he had with Peg. He belted me in the jaw and I fell backward and over the railing into the Chicago River.

Everything slowed to a standstill. I heard Peg scream. I knew without a doubt that I was going into the water. It would be very cold. I would have a heart attack and die.

I hit the water and it felt like concrete.

Oh fuck the heart attack, I thought. I can't swim.

Dead or Dying

TWO YEARS IN THE NAVY and the best I could guarantee was that I could survive in a swimming pool if I had a life jacket. I was floating up through the murk and mud. I couldn't figure out why it wasn't cold. My lungs weren't hurting particularly. I knew what had happened. I was dead. The murk was just the mess I'd made of my life. Maybe I would have eternity to clear it up. For some reason I remembered just when I'd lost Hope.

My mid-life crisis hit the day I realized thirty-three was half-way through my life expectancy. Of course technically, having already survived Viet Nam, I should have had a much longer life expectancy than the sixty-six that was estimated in 1982, but apparently I had seriously over-estimated.

At thirty-three, I'd just been promoted to full partner and celebrated by buying a brand new bright yellow Mustang convertible. I moved to a new apartment in a trendy part of town where I could hold huge parties for young, equally trendy people. There was just one thing missing in my life, and I went hunting for a beautiful, young, and trendy girlfriend. Hope springs eternal.

Hope was her name.

We met at the top of Mt. Si on a Saturday afternoon, looking across the lowlands toward Puget Sound. We hiked back down the mountain together and shared a drink at a cozy North Bend watering hole. Much to my surprise and delight, we spent the night in my trendy, downtown apartment. Smart, funny, and beautiful, Hope was twelve years my junior; but we made each other happy and, clearly, that is what mattered. Within two months, Hope had moved in with me and I couldn't have been more pleased.

Having eye-candy on my arm at company gatherings added to my status among my male coworkers. For her part, Hope liked the gatherings because she was drawn to power like a magnet. Power that comes from money, position, and oh, yes, did I mention money? Hope liked people who were powerful, they got her into doors and then she left them behind. She loved power. Did I mention that? Power that you get from wealth and position.

Power like my boss's.

Damn.

It was a big hairy falling out. She said I never understood her. I'd always held her back. I was just plain mean.

Don't turn me into a martyr. For my part I told her she was an incompetent gold-digger and a slut. Besides which, I'd been sleeping with a college girl who was in a class I taught and didn't really care what she did.

Except that she backed a truck up to the apartment while I was working one day, emptied it of everything but my one painting and my recliner, and drove away.

And you know what? I was perfectly fine with that. She'd taken everything; she couldn't possibly ask me for any more.

I bought a mattress and put it on the floor of my once cool apartment. I didn't mind so much that she'd taken all my LPs. After a few weeks I began to slowly acquire the new CD format. I had a girl over occasionally, but no more big parties. I didn't look at women the same way anymore. It wasn't that I didn't like them, but it didn't seem they wanted the same things in life that I did.

The more I thought about my life, the more I hated it. When the lease expired, I moved out and found a small furnished apartment on Capitol Hill. I took my picture, my mattress, my clothes, and my chair and moved. I stuck my Mustang in a garage, and ignored it.

I painted the apartment black, grew a straggly beard at a time when most of the men in the office were shaving, and became an organic vegetarian. I even started wearing jeans to work. I didn't see any clients anymore. I just lived with the machines. We were changing over from the big dedicated systems by '86 to personal computers and networking. The job was changing and I was suddenly feeling very old.

That's when I discovered what men want from young women.

They want to feel young.

They want to feel that they've cheated the clock and that they've retained their youth in the face of years. I wasn't avoiding women, and I wasn't doing without women in my life. I just discovered that I wasn't expecting anything from them. It made life easier.

I discovered that there were women in the office that I made it a point to pass each day, just so I could feel my heart speed up a little—that feeling where it is beating up in your throat a little higher than it should. I would pass where a woman had just walked by and stop to inhale the fragrance she left behind. And when I did, I walked a little straighter.

I shaved (mostly—all but the mustache) and went back to wearing suits. I wasn't mean. I was certainly not going to complicate women's lives with mine any more. We'd deal with each other the way we were. Someday, someplace, I'd find the right one for me—maybe somebody my own age who knew who the Beatles were and what it was like to face the choice of being drafted or enlisting. I instituted the fifty percent rule. I wouldn't go out with anyone who was less than half my age.

Of course, when I made the rule, it included everyone that it was legal to date.

I quit thinking about it. Hope was as gone then as it was now in my watery grave.

If This Be a Dream, Sleep On and Wake Me Not

I WOKE UP IN A STRANGE BED in a strange city. The sounds were not my sounds, the smells were not my smells. The warm soft body lying next to me was not my body.

Damn!

I sat up straight pulling the covers off the waking, naked form of Peg beside me. She opened her eyes and pulled me back down onto the pillow.

"How did I get here?" I asked.

"That's an improvement," she answered. "Last time it was 'who are you?' Remember anything?"

"Last time? How long have I been here?"

"No, you have to answer one to get one."

"I remember…" Drowning. That's what I remembered. Being knocked into the river and drowning, knowing I'd never see the light of day again. "…being pushed into the river." I finished lamely.

"More like being catapulted," she said. "There was no mistaking that the incredible hulk intended to kill you."

"Intended to," I repeated. "I'm not dead then?"

I don't know what I expected, but the kiss she planted on me was not it. In fact it was like nothing I'd experienced in a long time. I didn't make a move to break it and neither did she. After while she pulled away and asked softly, "Do you feel dead?" I most certainly did not.

"Have we been... I mean did we...?" I felt like an idiot.

"No. You haven't been up to it so far. I haven't given up hope, though." She threw that off as if it was just a saying.

"How long have I been here?" I asked. She looked at her clock. It was nearly ten. I wasn't sure if it was morning or night.

"About 34 hours," she said calculating. "It's Wednesday morning."

"My God," I said. "I need to check in. Riley will be panicked."

"Don't tell me Riley is your wife," Peg moaned.

"No, my partner," I answered.

"Thank goodness," she said and rolled on top of me with another kiss. "I did not haul your ass out of that river and thaw your freezing body with my own for someone else."

I blame it on the pollution in the Chicago River affecting my brain. I couldn't for the life of me sort out my priorities just then. In fact, it was about half an hour before I could think at all.

Eventually the reality of my situation dawned on me and I struggled to separate myself from the warm and willing woman still nestled in my arms.

"I really need to make that call," I said. "Where are my clothes?"

"You need clothes to make a phone call?" she handed me a bed-side phone.

"I was going to use my cell phone and not call on your home line."

"Only if it's waterproof," she answered. She slid out of bed and padded naked to the dressing table and picked up my cell phone. She brought it back and noted that I hadn't begun to dial. I was simply staring. She smiled and pirouetted in place so I could see her from all sides. "I hope you like," she said as she handed me my waterlogged device and slid back in under the covers. It didn't take long to realize that the phone was ruined. I got up and dialed the office on Peg's landline.

When she answered, I could tell she had been crying by the catch in her voice. "Riley, it's me," I said.

"Dag?" she sounded stunned. "Really? Is it you?"

"It's me, Riley," I repeated. "I'm fine. I wanted to let you know." I wasn't prepared for the stifled sobs I heard at the other end of the line.

"Your GPS blanked out in the Chicago River. I didn't know until I came in yesterday. I thought you were dead," she said through the choked voice that meant she was crying. "I called Jordan and he's on his way to Chicago." The calm control of her words belied the emotion I could hear in her voice. I don't remember anyone caring about me like that.

"I wasn't conscious," I said. "I came to my senses enough to call you just now. Really, I'm okay now, but apparently I've been out of it for a day."

"Thirty-five hours," Riley whispered softly. "Dag, I thought I'd lost you."

"Not this time," I said. "But it was a close call. The big guy who brought the laptop to our office decided he wanted my computer in trade. He grabbed my laptop and dumped me in the river. Kiddo, I thought I was done for, too."

"Where are you now?"

"I'm with a friend who hauled me out of the river and nursed me through the fever," I said looking at Peg. It was not necessary to get into the details with Riley.

"Jordan is going to land this afternoon. He'll want to see you."

"As soon as he calls you, tell him that I've been found. I'll see him tonight."

Peg whispered to me. "Not unless you want to see him naked. Your clothes are at the cleaners."

"Uhhh. Make that tomorrow morning, Riley. I'll call him with directions. My cell is dead after being dunked. I suppose the GPS transmitter is too."

"Yes. The signal went dark at 12:21 Central time yesterday morning. Dag, I thought…"

"I know Riley. I thought so too. You know Lars's old saying about opening the floodgates?"

"You have to be ready to wade in the water?"

"Well, it seems we should take it literally."

"I'm so glad you are okay, Dag. I'm just so glad."

"Do me a favor, would you Riley? Get me on a flight back home tomorrow, okay?" I said. "This was really more adventure than I'd planned."

Somehow we managed to get through a good-bye.

I looked around for the first time rather than just looking at Peg. It was a nice apartment. I went into the bath off the bedroom and I could see through the open door that it was a nicely furnished modern apartment. I'm not too self-conscious, but I wasn't used to parading around naked in front of a woman. I grabbed a towel from the bathroom and wrapped it around me before I returned to the bedroom.

"Formal attire?" Peg asked. "Does that mean you want me to get dressed, too?" She threw off the covers and stood up. It could be that she was really that good looking, or it could be that I simply had not seen anything like her up close for a long time. I wasn't finding any fault with her body or reason to want her to cover it.

"Don't dress on my account," I answered. "I just thought perhaps I should make myself useful. Kitchen through there?"

She crossed toward me and wrapped her arms around me for another kiss. "I found you useful," she cooed.

"If you are thinking that I can do that again now," I said, "don't get your expectations up too high. I've got a heart condition and speaking of that, I should take a pill."

"Not until noon," she answered. I looked at her. "I found your pill bottles in your pockets when I emptied them to send your suit to the cleaners. I've been shoving one down your throat on a regular schedule."

"Are you a nurse?" I asked.

"Not anymore. Now I'm a bartender," she said. "I manage Alex's. You remember?"

"You are the manager? I thought you were a customer."

"No, but I work there because it's fun," she smiled. "Grandpa said to take care of you when you came in. When I saw you weren't dancing, I decided to take matters into my own hands, so to speak. I didn't intend to have to fish you out of the river in order to get you up to my place, though."

"Grandpa? Earl Schwarz is your grandfather? He told you to seduce me?"

"Pretty accusatory," she snapped. "No, I wasn't ordered to seduce you. I just found you to be a nice, attractive man, and frankly it's been a long dry spell. It was all spur of the moment. I wish we hadn't gone down by the river, though. I'm really sorry about that."

"Did you report it?" I asked.

"No," she answered bluntly. "Grandpa told me that he was in the police station when he called and that you had warned him that they were coming. I was afraid that if Grandpa was in trouble and you were discovered in or near the river, it would be assumed that he set you up. I've stayed clear of the import company ever since the big holding company bought it a few years ago."

"Seems like an awfully big place for one old guy to run," I speculated.

"Grandpa got a call almost three weeks ago now. Apparently, some guy from the holding company told him there was trouble with shipments that were being sent to him without ever getting there. He told him to exercise his own discretion regarding keeping the business open any longer. Grandpa's discretion said to fire everyone who worked for him and sit there by himself until they dragged him away. He doesn't own it anymore, but I don't think that message ever reached his brain."

All the time she was telling me this, she was setting things up to brew an espresso in a countertop machine. I leaned on the countertop and thought about nude baristas. For some reason, that made it really hard to concentrate. She handed me a freshly pulled shot in a demitasse. The aroma broke my train of distraction.

"There's cream and sugar if you want them," she said motioning toward the refrigerator. I shook my head silently and raised the tiny cup to my lips. A long slow, tongue-scalding sip. Where had this woman been all my life? She watched me as I focused on the coffee. Sex and coffee in one day.

Damn.

I finished and set the espresso cup down to see her still watching me and smiling. I was a little embarrassed about being watched so closely.

"Nice place you have here, for a bartender," I commented.

"Compliments of my ex-husband," she said frankly. I decided it was best not to pursue that line. I went to the window and looked northward toward the John Hancock building. I felt her presence before I felt her touch.

"You really shouldn't be up for too long," she said. Her arms slipped around my waist and she rested her cheek against my back. "Come on," she said, pulling me back toward the bedroom. "Let's get you back into bed so you can rest."

Somewhere along the way, I lost the towel again.

Bone-Chilling Cold

I WOKE UP ALONE in a cold bed. Peg had been gone for some time. My clothes, fresh from the cleaners were hung on the back of the door. The shoes were going to be a pain. She'd filled them with crinkled newspaper and sat them next to a register to dry, but they were stiff and tight. As I put them on, I noticed her sexy boots sitting beside them. They were ruined. She dove into the river to save me, and somehow I had emerged intact. I examined the brand and size.

A note was sitting next to the things she had taken from my pockets on the dressing table. It was simple and to the point.

"Dag, it was a lovely time (except for the bath). Help yourself to coffee and anything in the fridge before you go. The door will lock behind you automatically. Kisses, Peg"

She was not expecting me to be here when she got back.

She was not expecting anything.

I sneezed. A cold, acquired, no doubt, from my dip in the river and subsequent fever, was settling into my head and chest. Just the thing the doctor warned me against. It would be a great flight back to Seattle.

I gathered my things and checked them off. Dead cell phone. Dead GPS transmitter. Keys. Wallet, dried beside my shoes. Credit cards and cash all there. In the kitchen, I cleaned up the remains of last night's delivered food and washed the dishes. I looked around and found the pad of paper she had used for my note. I wrote simply.

"Peg, thanks for reviving me. I have to fly back to Seattle, but I'll be thinking of you. Hugs, Dag"

Some things you simply don't put in writing. I called Jordan and he was waiting at the front door of the apartment building when I left. He lectured me soundly on going out without backup and said he was glad I had survived. Riley would have held him personally responsible if anything had happened to me. We went by my hotel and picked up the remainder of my clothes and roll-aboard. I got him to stop at an electronics superstore, and bought a new laptop, a GPS transmitter, and a cell phone. On the way to the airport, I put the things I needed from the computer box in my bag and activated the GPS transmitter. I called Riley from the phone and realized that everything I had would need to be charged before I used them for long, but it wasn't like the bad old days when you couldn't turn a new device on without charging the battery first.

"What are the arrangements?" I asked Riley on the phone.

"I've got you booked back to Seattle with a plane change in Minneapolis," she answered.

"Weren't there any direct flights?" I asked.

"Travel agent's discretion," she answered. "This may prove to be nothing, but I got a call last night from the airplane leasing company. Simon's plane has been routed to Minneapolis." She left unspoken the assumption that I would want to be there.

"That's interesting," I answered, "but I can't imagine how I'd go about finding Simon's plane in Minneapolis. There must be more than one airport there." It was intriguing, but, damn it, I was tired. I'd nearly drowned, I was sick, and I wanted to go home.

"Angel's flying to Minneapolis late this morning." She dropped that bomb on me and waited for my reaction. I was too numb to react.

"Good work, Riley. Watch my new GPS."

This time I checked my flights carefully. There was a new hollowness inside me, along with the cold and a feeling of getting old all too quickly. In Minneapolis, I found a place near the gate where I could plug in the phone and computer. I logged onto the Internet and looked up the brand of the sexy boots Peg had been wearing when I met her. I ordered a new pair in her size and had them shipped to her.

I'd been sitting in the gate area for nearly an hour, having heard the announcement that the incoming flight from Seattle was late and we would depart about half an hour later than scheduled. The gate agent picked up a mic and announced that the flight had just arrived from Seattle and passengers would deplane shortly.

I began packing up my equipment and just looked up as the passengers were coming off the flight. The double-take I did was mimicked by nearly every man in the gate area. Leading the line of people getting off the plane was Angel Woodward. Riley had done her work well. I snatched up my roll-aboard and fell in with the line of people headed toward baggage claim. Just the glow on Angel's face told me everything I needed to know. She had to be in Minneapolis to meet Simon. I stayed well back from her in the crowd, but she was hard to miss as she strode along in high heels that put her height at well above mine.

She wasn't carrying anything but her handbag and small roll-aboard like my own, but she skirted the baggage claim carousels and headed for the metro train stop in the lower concourse. I stopped long enough at a machine to buy a ticket and stepped onto the train at the back of the car she entered. I was going to have to be careful here. I was sure that she could recognize me if she had paid any attention at all that night we faced each other in an all-night diner. I looked around uneasily, thinking that she might have a bodyguard with her even here. I didn't spot Davy.

Angel rode the southbound train to its last stop—The Mall of America—and headed for Bloomingdale's. I followed more closely because the crowds in the Mall were insane. Huge displays for the holidays were already up and the stores were playing Christmas music over their loudspeakers. Santa Claus and The Polar Express had already arrived and were doing a booming business.

I watched as Angel selected at least two dozen outfits from several areas, mostly in sports and casual clothing. Then with a saleswoman in tow, she headed for the dressing rooms. Conveniently, the men's shoe department was located in the line of sight from the dressing rooms and I walked over to get a new pair of shoes so I could ditch the stiff pair that was still not completely dry from the river dowsing. I was being fitted when I saw the sales woman come out with a load of the clothes that Angel had taken in. She draped them over a counter and ran out to pick out at least a dozen more outfits to take back in to Angel.

My cell phone rang and I quickly silenced it and ducked down in case Angel glanced toward the sound. It was Riley. She wanted to know why I was at the Mall of America.

"I followed Angel," I answered. "This could be a waste of time. It looks like she's just on a shopping trip."

"Dag, I'm worried about you."

"Riley, I've already decided not to die on this trip. That last brush was close enough. I'll be careful, and you keep watching me on TV."

I paid for the shoes and chose a hat from the nearby men's department and picked up a heavy overcoat as well. It was cold in Minneapolis and my hat, at least, hadn't made it out of the river with me. If I'd been wearing an overcoat in Chicago, chances are that Peg never would have pulled me out of the River. Of course, adding the coat and hat to my outfit would throw Angel if she caught a glimpse of me on the train. I hardly looked like the same man now.

When she finally emerged from the dressing room, she looked like a new woman herself. She was wearing one new outfit and had half a dozen more in her arms. She paid and the clerk wrapped the purchases up in parcels that Angel could carry. Some she packed in her carry-on bag. She made a stop at the ladies shoe department and bought three new pair of shoes, one that matched the new outfit she was wearing. In the space of two and a half hours, a casual observer would not have been able to tell it was the same woman except for the height. That has always amazed me about women. They can change so rapidly. Perhaps she, too, was worried about being followed.

She went from the department store to a wine bar in the food court and took a seat. The waiter brought wine and took her order for dinner, so I decided to take advantage of the opportunity to eat as well.

119

I stopped at a walk-up sushi bar located just outside the doors to the restaurant and ordered several pieces. I could see Angel through the window as she ate and was interrupted by a phone call. She chatted for a few minutes while she arranged her packages, stood and slipped a bill onto the table next to her unfinished plate of food. She was on the move again. I followed suit and dropped a twenty to pay for the sushi and followed her out of the Mall and back to the train.

Well, it looked like we were headed back to the airport, and I settled into my seat near the back of the car. The doors were about to close at the third stop when I saw her on the platform walking away. I dove out as they closed and took a look around to see where I was.

I was cold. It was well below freezing on the desolate platform and the wind was picking up. No doubt the weather broadcasters were describing it in terms of wind-chill. I was thankful for the overcoat but wished I'd bought gloves.

The stop was for the charter terminal and Angel had just turned into a long covered walkway that looked like a construction shelter. I passed the end and realized it went all the way to the parking garage, straight as an arrow for a couple hundred yards. If she turned around or glanced back she would see me clearly since we were the only two people in the area. I stepped around the outside of the walkway to see where it went. The parking garage was straight ahead; off to the right was the terminal. This seemed to be the route you took to get from the train platform to the terminal.

On the diagonal, between the platform and the terminal was a wide, cold, windswept parking lot—all but deserted.

I didn't have a choice. My only option was to cut across the parking lot and hope I didn't freeze or have a heart attack before I reached the warmth of the terminal. It was touch and go. I had to stop to breathe, but I couldn't stop or I'd freeze. I had to carry my roll-aboard and watch for ice that was scattered in huge black patches across the parking lot. Even though it was only a couple hundred yards, I had visions of freezing in the wilderness before I finally made it to the entrance.

I crossed the threshold at the near end of the terminal. I had no idea how this concourse was laid out. I scanned the length of it as I moved forward and saw that the entry from the parking ramp was on the second level. A long escalator led from it to the main concourse. There at the top of the escalator was Angel, stepping on and waving as if she'd recognized me. I started forward slowly. I was hurting bad from the forced march across the open parking lot. My ears were cold, and I could hardly feel my right hand carrying my roll-aboard. My eyes were watering from the chill, and my nose dripped profusely as I attempted to get a handkerchief to it.

Angel was faster and she reached the bottom of the escalator long before I got there. She ran forward and straight into the arms of Simon Barnett, waiting for her a few feet ahead of me. There was no need to hurry as the public display of affection that was underway showed no sign of a quick end. By the time they broke the clinch I was right behind Simon.

"Hello, Simon," I said as casually as I could. He spun around to face me.

"Dag Hamar!" he exclaimed. "Well I'll be go-to-hell. You finally found me. I was beginning to think I'd have to call you and give you directions." He had aged some since the last time I saw him, but that was to be expected after thirty years. His tightly trimmed black beard was heavily streaked with gray. He might have put on a few pounds from good living, but he looked fit.

"What are you doing here, Jeremy?" Angel asked confusedly.

"Jeremy?" Simon asked. "He told you his name was Jeremy?"

"Yes," Angel replied. "We met at the condo." Simon turned to me.

"Jeremy Brett?" he asked. I nodded. "I will so be damned," Simon laughed.

"What's so funny?" Angel was turning indignant.

"Detective mysteries," Simon wailed. "Jeremy Brett played Sherlock Holmes on television years and years ago. It's a fake name, honey. This is Dag Hamar, probably the only man in the world who could have found me. I'll bet you've uncovered the entire rotten kettle of fish that is known as Barnett, Keane, and Lamb Ltd."

"It's pretty smelly, Simon," I said. I gripped his shoulder. I needed his shoulder. Simon was once my best friend and my head was absolutely spinning. I tried to speak again.

"Dag! Dag, old friend. Are you okay?"

"I don't think I'll make it, Simon," I said. I could hear a ringing in my ears that was drowning out the noise of the terminal around me and Simon's voice. I sat heavily on my roll-aboard and Simon caught me and propped me up. He kneeled in front of me and looked me straight in the eye. I could barely make out the words he was saying.

"Dag, I can call you an ambulance and send you to a hospital, or you can trust Angel and me to take care of you. But we've got to leave here tonight. It will all have been a waste if you don't come with us." I shook my head to clear it and struggled back to my feet.

Breathe, damn it. Inhale deeper. It will pass. I just told Riley I wouldn't die on this trip. Focus.

I took a long shuddering breath, fumbled in my pocket for a bottle of pills and popped one in my mouth. I focused all my energy on breathing—which was no small task considering that my nose had plugged up as soon as I got in out of the cold.

Simon and Angel were both still looking intently at me. I nodded.

"What's the plan?" I asked.

"Simon Says, board the plane," Simon answered. We headed for security.

Charter Flight

BEFORE I KNEW IT, I was on Simon's private jet and we were airborne. Regulations or not, I opened the cell phone and called Riley. She was still at the office.

"I thought you'd be headed home with Simon," Riley said immediately. "Why is the plane going south."

"Let's hope not," I answered. "I'm not sure where I'm headed but Simon is in the cockpit."

"You found him?"

"Angel led me right to him. I can't arrest him and he was getting ready to take off. If I wanted to talk to him, I'd have to get on board. I got on board."

"So you are calling from the plane, but you don't know where you are going?" In spite of having given me the information I needed to find Simon, Riley was getting a little exasperated with this wild goose chase. I can't blame her. I'd have been in the nuthouse if she had pulled this kind of stunt.

"I haven't been able to ask yet," I said. "Simon and Angel are both in the cockpit."

"Puts a whole new meaning on that term," Riley snorted. It felt good to laugh.

"Well, keep track of me, and if I call and say 'where am I?' just tell me, okay?"

"Okay, Dag. Get some sleep."

"Hey, Riley," I said before she hung up. "Go home. *Battlestar Galactica* is on tonight."

"Thanks, Dag," she said. "Love you too." And then she disconnected.

Damn.

Shortly thereafter, Angel emerged and came to sit beside me. She brought a welcome bottle of sparkling water with her.

"Simon Says you don't drink," she said handing it to me. I wasn't sure if that was just a statement or an instruction.

"I usually avoid it," I said noncommittally.

"Simon Says you are the best there is." Simon Says. What was Simon playing?

"Simon hasn't seen me in a long time," I answered. "I'm not sure I'm the best at what he wants."

"Simon Says there is no one he trusts more than you." Third time. I was going to have to break this cycle.

"So where are we going?" I asked.

"Simon Says, don't ask," she replied. This time I knew a command when I heard it. Simon was warming me up. "Get some sleep," she continued.

"Does Simon Say?" I asked.

"No, you just look like you need it." She smiled at me and went back to the cockpit. Whether Simon said or not, I decided to take her advice.

I don't know how long we were in the air, or how long I napped. The seats in Simon's plane made up into full beds, and somewhere along the line Angel had come back and made one up for me. I was so exhausted that I didn't wake up again until Angel came in and shook me awake. There had been rough weather during the night, but frankly it just served to put me further under.

I sat up, strapped in, and called Riley. She answered on first ring.

"Where am I?" I asked immediately.

"Where have you been?" she responded. "It looked like you were headed into a hurricane off the Texas coast, then you skirted it out into the Caribbean, and ended up coming up the Eastern Seaboard. It looks like you are landing in Atlanta, but you've easily flown three times that distance. Are you okay?"

"I'm fine, Riley. I wasn't flying the plane. I was sleeping." I gathered my wits. "Does Simon have anything in Atlanta?" I couldn't remember anything.

"Nothing I've found yet, but that's not where you were headed. At first I thought it was Mexico. He could easily have swung further out into the Caribbean and gone to Jamaica, the Virgin Islands, even as far east as the Bahamas before he swung back north. How big is that plane?"

"Big. It's a luxury jet. I haven't even explored the whole thing. I'm surprised Simon could fly it without a crew. He must not have been planning to come back."

"Just in case, Dag, do you have your passport?" Riley was making a joke but I gave her a little dig anyway.

"Yes, I've got two or three with me. You never can tell when I might need to get across a border undetected." I chuckled.

"Very funny," Riley said. She was sounding a little more relaxed than in our recent conversations. "Have you been taking your pills?"

"Like clockwork," I said glancing at my watch. Damn. I was an hour late for this one. Well, I didn't have any water, so it would have to wait till we were on the ground. I had another thought, though. "Riley, check around with some of your new friends from the condo and see if I should be expecting Angel's boyfriend to show up. Can you do that?"

"Can I? Come on Dag. Of course I can. But I don't know. Why should I?" The old teasing Riley was back. I grinned to myself.

"Well, let's see. Assuming that having a job and a salary isn't enough motivation, why would you do this? Surely not for the cause of social and criminal justice. Certainly not because you would do anything for poor old Dag if he asked. Maybe you'd do it for dinner at the Ninety-nine when I get back to town?"

"Consider it done," she laughed. "The things a girl has to do to get a date these days. Geez! I better get started. See you soon." She was about to disconnect but I caught her before she could.

125

"Riley," I said. "Thank you."

"Dag, you don't have to thank me for just doing my job, no matter how much I tease," she answered.

"Improving my mood and brightening my day wasn't part of the job description," I said. "That's what I'm thanking you for." There was a little pause. "Bye," I said.

"Bye, Dag. Be careful."

I had no more than hung up before I felt the wheels bounce on the ground. I relaxed until Simon had taxied to a hangar and the engines died. Then I stood up and stretched. Simon and Angel came out of the cockpit. He looked tired, but I assumed that was just the strain of having flown all night.

"Well, you look better than last night," Simon said brightening. "It would have complicated things if you'd croaked on me before we could talk."

"I like to keep your life simple, Simon," I cracked. "So why are we in Atlanta instead of Cuba?" I asked directly. Simon was surprised, but grinned and turned to Angel.

"Didn't I tell you he was the best?" he asked her. Then he turned back to me. "Let's just say the weather there turned suddenly cold and leave it at that. Atlanta was the nearest airport I could get clearance to land at that I wanted to trust. Miami is way too complicated."

"I see," I said. "You know people here and they smooth the path for you, right?"

"In a manner of speaking," Simon agreed. "Actually, this was the best place Angel could get us a reservation on such short notice." He opened the hatch and let down the stairs. We disembarked, each carrying our light luggage. A limousine was stopped about fifty yards away with a uniformed driver approaching us to take our bags.

"It looks like you were expected, Simon," I commented.

"It helps to have a travel agent in the family," he answered giving Angel a squeeze around the waist. "She made all the arrangements while we were in the air." We got into the spacious car. I had plenty of room, but Angel and Simon looked a little crowded where they were sitting practically in the same seat. I had to chuckle. Even in the car, Angel towered over Simon's 5'7" frame. When they were standing, Simon faced her chest rather than her face.

Well, maybe that was the way they liked it.

"Did you bring it?" Simon was asking me. I pulled myself back into the moment.

"Bring what?"

"The laptop, of course."

"Of course not. You can't imagine that I'd bring a client's property with me when I'm out in the field, can you?"

"Damn it, Dag. Everything we need is on that laptop. That's why I had our mutual friend deliver it to you." I noted that he didn't call Brenda his wife. Perhaps that was just sparing Angel the insult.

"If I had brought the laptop, Bradley would have it now." I related the story of my laptop being grabbed and how I was thrown in the river. I omitted my rescuer and resuscitation afterward. But I did sneeze into my handkerchief. I'd woken up this morning with a stuffy head and runny nose.

"Christ Almighty! Angel did you hear that? We're lucky to have Dag with us at all. You're tough as nails, old buddy. But that was brilliant, carrying a decoy. So how long will it take to get the laptop here? Do you have someone who can ship it reliably? Maybe hand-carry it. I know. We can get one of the girls to pick it up from your office and fly out here with it. Angel says you were up at the condo and all chummy with Cinnamon. It'll be nice for you to have some company while we're working, don't you think?"

"Simon," I said. "I'm not having the laptop delivered out here. Suppose you tell me what this is all about. You take off and leave clues for your wife to bring me a laptop. You ask me, after thirty years of staying away from you, to find you. I find you and discover you are playing a game to get me out here to join you for something, but you haven't told me what. Your company is being investigated for money laundering, fraud, and possibly smuggling. This is the end. Unless you start getting into some details that explain your actions, I'm calling a friend at FinCEN who will be very interested in your activities and current whereabouts. That's it, Simon. Give."

Simon settled back into Angel's arms and looked at the roof of the car.

"Simon Says wait till we are at the hotel."

Damn and blast!

The hotel was the Ritz Carlton and the suite occupied the top two floors, with a grand staircase leading from the lower level to the master suite. It seemed silly to arrive with our cumulative luggage, all of which fit beneath the arms of a skinny bellhop. I'm not sure what Simon tipped the guy, but he actually bowed on his way out.

I tossed my bag in the room I was told to occupy and returned to the sitting room. I heard giggles from the upstairs suite and decided enough was enough.

"Simon!" I yelled. "Time to get serious. I want some answers."

He appeared at the top of the stairs without his jacket and tie and with his shirt half unbuttoned.

"Answers," he said, leaning over the rail. "You were always one to have to get to the bottom of things. That's what I was counting on. Angel, honey, Dag wants a meeting. I think I'll have to delay this a while. Why don't you order us up some breakfast. I'm starving."

"Spoil sport!" she yelled from the bedroom, but Simon was on his way downstairs. He sat on the sofa opposite me and squared off.

"Dag," he said, "I'm a successful businessman. I made a company out of nothing through being smart and putting money where it counted. You were supposed to be my partner, remember?"

"We don't have to go through that part, Simon. From what I've seen, I'm glad I'm not."

"Well, don't be too happy about it. I'm bringing you in late. Not to that business, but partnership with me. Christ! I wouldn't saddle anyone with that cesspool. I made a bad choice with that Bradley Keane. I needed someone who could manage operations and finances while I put together deals. Then I find out he's made a few deals himself, and they aren't kosher. He's got his finger into everything—drugs, prostitution, gambling—you name it and he's got a piece of the action or could get one. Worst thing is he used my company to build his credibility with the shysters that he deals with, and laundered the money through BKL." Simon sat back on the sofa, the very image of an injured partner. Yeah. Everything was Bradley's fault. I could believe that—if I was ten. But Simon wasn't done.

"The truth of the matter is that Bradley is a coward. He's got bullies that do his dirty-work for him, but fundamentally, he's scared shitless that his external partners will come down on him if he balks at anything. That's what got us into this current mess. It was inevitable. They want in. They want part of the legitimate action because we've done such a good job of building a rich, privately held company. And Bradley can't keep them out. Hell, by the time I figured it out, I can't keep them out. That's why I disappeared."

"Did he make threats against you, Simon?" I asked.

"Didn't have to. He's got a goon who was assigned to him. Recently, I spotted the guy following me. Every time I looked up, there was this big lummox in the shadows."

"Big guy, doesn't speak much English, and looks like a refrigerator?" I asked.

"Ah, you've met him."

"He helped me into the Chicago River," I said. "FBI has an all-points bulletin out on him now."

"That's not likely to help, but maybe the next guy will be smaller, or meaner, or speak English. They're not going to stop with one dowsing. I've been moving from place to place on the QT all around the country for the last few weeks. I set it up to look like I was headed for Singapore and sent the jet on without me. Otherwise they'd have figured out when I was back in the country through Passport Control."

"What have you been doing for money?" I asked. "There's been no bank activity, credit card charges, or ATM withdrawals."

Simon reached in his pocket.

"These," he said, pulling a fistful of credit cards from his wallet. "They look like an ordinary credit card, but you deposit cash for them.

They contain no identifying personal info—just a balance and a PIN." Riley had told me part of Angel's business was selling ATM cash cards. "I've been buying a couple a day for almost a year now," Simon finished.

"I've found enough in the books and in actual actions to put your partner away if you want to testify," I offered. "You gave me a lot of clues, and Bradley provided a lot more without knowing it."

"What? And go to jail, too? I've talked to them. I don't trust them. I'm good for ten to fifteen if I cooperate. I'm the majority partner in BKL. Do you think they'll take Bradley down without taking me out? Why go for the little coward when you can get the big entrepreneur." Simon had a point. If BKL was in it, he was culpable.

"What brings me into this?" I asked

"I've been following your career for thirty years," Simon said. "I don't know what color underwear you're wearing, but if there's a public record of it, I know it. Who do you think tipped the County Sherriff about embezzlement at Anderson Elliott?"

"You're saying you manipulated me into becoming a private investigator?" I asked, incredulously.

"No. That was a surprise to me, but at least it dislodged you from that cesspit you were stuck in. And your life got a whole lot more interesting after that. I knew that when the time came you'd be the person I'd call to manage the whole liquidation of my estate," he said. "I'm liquidating now. I have to disappear. Permanently. And in the process, I'm gonna dismantle the entire company and expose the dirty parts that lead to the only one who is truly responsible for it. If I'm gone, there's only one recourse," he finished.

"What about Brenda?" I asked. The doorbell chimed and I saw Simon's eyes shift up to the staircase. I glanced back. Angel was coming down in a fetching robe. From the way the gown split apart as she swished down the stairs, I'd have to say she wasn't wearing much else. She went to the door to admit a steward with a huge breakfast table.

"What about who?" Simon asked looking back at me. "What do you think? I won't leave her penniless. She's got a pre-nup. It spells out exactly how much of the company is hers. I'll protect her, even if she doesn't deserve it. But geez, Dag, Brenda and me never should have been together in the first place. You know that better than anyone." I knew it. Maybe I had more reason to be thankful than anyone.

"So what's your plan?" I asked. The breakfast tray was set up and Angel called us to the table.

"I've been manipulating assets of the company remotely for the past three weeks. I've had to do it all by phone. I don't have my laptop and I'm not brilliant at computer systems like you anyway. What I have is everything positioned for rapid dismantling. With you and me working together, we could tear down the whole company so that the only thing that's left is the trail that leads to Bradley. We just need my laptop, and you to finesse the system."

"Doesn't exactly fit what Angel told me," I said noncommittally. "She said it was all about charity."

"Well she's right," Simon said, "and I'm not back-pedaling here. The businesses are going back to their original owners where appropriate, or to trusts set up in their behalf. I need money someplace where I can get hold of it so I can effectively disappear—more than I've got in cash cards. And then there is all the cash that Bradley is pushing through the company to underworld organizations, even terrorists. That's not even on the books. I figure we should do a little re-routing of the assets into a whole lot of charities. We could make anonymous donations of it to hundreds of charities and do a world of good. We could endow medical research, education—community theatre, for God's sake. Got a favorite charity? It's on the list."

"How much are you talking about moving?" I asked.

"Upwards of two billion dollars," Simon said without batting an eye. I stared at him. No wonder Jordan was after this guy. "Want to take two billion dollars from organized crime and terror and give it to the needy? All we need is you and that laptop. Simon Says, 'let's make a difference.' What do you say, Dag?"

Damn.

What could I say?

"We don't need your laptop," I answered.

131

Simon Says

COLLEGE IN THE 70s was a heady time for me. I was fresh out of the service and going to school on my GI benefits. I'd survived Viet Nam and the world was filled with possibilities. I was a couple of years older than my fellow freshmen at the University, but among those headed for business degrees, my age seemed to be a benefit rather than a detriment. I was more experienced. And when the draft lottery came about, I hung a sign on my door that said, "Been there, done that."

Into the chaos of my college life stepped two of the most remarkable people I'd ever met: Simon Barnett and Brenda Lamb. They swept me into a social life like I'd never had before. If there was a party happening on campus, we were there. We went to ballgames, lectures, concerts, and plays. If there weren't three tickets, either we didn't go, or Simon pulled strings and found three. It was all new and different to me, and I don't know how I got included. If anything, I was an accounting geek, Simon was an entrepreneur, and Brenda knew more than anyone about how to have a good time.

Among us, though, we were going to change the world. We were going to do great things so that Viet Nam couldn't happen again. We were going to find cures for cancer and end world hunger. We were going to do such great things.

I didn't drink and wouldn't touch drugs because of what I'd seen among my friends in Viet Nam. Brenda and Simon thought that was funny, but loved having me along as their chauffeur. And whenever

132

there was a dispute, we always yielded to what "Simon Says." With Simon so much the dominant personality among the three of us, maybe it wasn't surprising that Brenda and I connected in a different way. Despite the fact that I'd been in the service and was older than the other two, Brenda became my first lover. There was nothing that I wouldn't do for her, and very little that I didn't.

We were married a month out of college.

All three of us remained close. Simon was my best man. Our plan was that Brenda and I would work in the corporate world while Simon found the deal that would put us in business together. Brenda and I both got good jobs. I was recruited and started working for Anderson Elliott Consulting right out of college. Brenda got a great job with a local bank, but two years later, when Simon had acquired his first business, she went to work for him. We had our timetable down. I would join the new business the next year and it would be a three-way partnership. No one questioned that Simon would have the controlling share.

It was Simon who found the house. It was a big old house in Madison Park overlooking Lake Washington. I couldn't imagine how we'd pay for it, but Simon, as usual, had a plan. He would finance the house and we would pay the mortgage to him. And since he intended to live there with us, he would pay us rent. Brenda and I would have our dream home while we were young enough to enjoy it. Simon figured a way to manage the cash flow so we'd all benefit. He couldn't wait until we had kids so he could be an "uncle." The deal was closed.

We moved into the house and began furnishing it. We each had private spaces and we had public ones. My special space was where I had a reclining chair, a stereo, and a picture on the wall. I'd sit there in the evening while the TV was on in the next room and listen to Crosby, Stills, Nash, & Young, or Credence Clearwater Revival while I vacationed in that seascape picture.

About three months after we moved in, I got sick at the office and came home at noon, intent on going straight to bed.

The bed was occupied by Simon and Brenda. Apparently we weren't being fast enough about having kids for Simon.

Damn.

The confrontation was remarkably brief.

I threw up on them.

They were both all over me, getting things cleaned up, getting me to bed, tending my fever. I was so sick that for a while I thought I had hallucinated the whole affair. But I knew that wasn't true. On the morning I woke up and could stand up, I packed up.

As it turned out, I didn't have all that much to pack. My clothes, my car, my chair, and the one painting that I owned.

I signed a quit-claim deed on the property and filed for divorce. There was no contest and no partnership. I kept working at Anderson Elliott. Simon and Brenda got married. I got an invitation to the wedding, but declined to attend.

Now that I saw the size of the fortune we liquidated, I wondered selfishly whether I'd made the right decision. But looking at the way things turned out, I wouldn't trade my feeble life for either of theirs.

Banking

I'D BEEN TRANSFERRING FUNDS from account to account. I knew how to hide tracks when moving money, Simon knew where to put it. The twenty-one named accounts that I'd found were the shadow accounts that Simon had set up and into which he was gradually bleeding off the assets of the company.

I couldn't believe how quickly I had fallen back under Simon's charismatic spell. I didn't for a minute believe that he was doing anything out of his altruistic nature, though I came to suspect that it pleased Angel to see money going to various charities. And it pleased me to see title to Far East Exchange transferred back to Earl Schwarz.

It was going to take a couple of days for me to move all the funds that Simon had identified and not leave tracks until it was too late to follow them. Simon sat across from me with his sleeves rolled up and his collar unbuttoned. Gold chains hung loosely around his neck. I shook my head to myself and went back to work. Sometimes he was such a little bantam rooster. But to him it was all part of the role he'd chosen.

I looked back up at Simon. One of the gold chains had a state-of-the-art jump-drive hanging from it. He saw me looking and automatically reached a hand to his neck.

"What's that?" I asked pointing. I studiously tried to focus my attention back on my computer screen. I glanced back up. He had a pursed-lip smile that I recognized as Simon when he perceived he had been too, too clever.

"That is my life insurance policy," he said. "If anything ever happens to me, all you have to do is look on this and you will know exactly who the villain is. You cracked my laptop, long before I gave you my password, and found lots of interesting things, but what's on here, you can't imagine. It's my insurance policy. Anything happens to me, I release this. Instant calamity, earth-shaking disaster that would collapse the economies of half a dozen countries and even more businesses. Bradley and Brenda think I kept everything on my computer. The real goods are on here."

"Seems like an albatross around your neck," I quipped. "So if something happens to you, you release the disk?"

"Right."

"How? You're dead."

"They'll find it."

"Which they? And what if you aren't found?" I continued. It wasn't often in my life that I'd caught an outright fallacy in Simon's thinking, but when I did it was always incumbent upon me to make the most of it.

"I'll be go-to-hell," he said and left the room.

I worked late into the night. When I finally lay down, I'd transferred ten businesses on a time-clock so that they would all move at one time on the day before Thanksgiving next week. That would reduce the risk of discovery until all transactions had cleared in Europe and Asia.

I was back under Simon's spell. I asked myself a dozen times before I fell asleep if what I was doing was right. The answer always came back in the form of a question.

Does what I'm doing make a difference?

To Die or Not to Die;
That Is the Question

OH! GOD DAMN!

The sudden jab of pain startled me awake, but waking didn't lessen the pain. It radiated from the very center of my chest out into every limb of my body. I gasped once for air and felt my ears go numb and every sound disappear. My hair felt like it was standing on end with the electrical force that was frying my head.

Shit! Fuck! Stupid son of a bitch! Stop it. Stop the pain. Jesus Christ, don't do this now. I can't stand it.

I knew tears had puddled in my eyes because I could feel them dripping into my ears, but I couldn't get my eyes to open. I had them clenched tight like my fists were clenched at my sides. Even my toes were curled and I could feel cramps climbing my legs multiplying the pain with spasms in my lower back.

Stop it, you stupid mother-fucking cock sucker! I'm not going to die here! I'm not!

I had to get control. I couldn't move. I couldn't call for help. My voice wasn't working, and I wasn't breathing. I could feel sweat running off of me, dampening the sheets.

Breathe you worthless pile of shit! Breathe! Take in air and let it out, asshole!

I fearfully let a little of the air that was caught in my lungs escape

137

and rapidly sucked in enough to replace it. It wasn't enough. I'd have to do better. A little out, a little in.

You cowardly pussy. That won't do it. Breathe, goddamn you!

More air out. More air in. If I wasn't dead yet, I wasn't about to die now. With a shuddering gasp I released all the air in my lungs and sucked it back. The pain shot through my chest in waves. I sobbed the air in and out now.

Open your eyes, you cowardly bastard! I can't. You have to. Open them up!

I got my eyes open in slits that admitted enough dull glow to know that I could see light of some sort.

More!

My vision swam in and out of focus on nothing that I could recognize. I heaved a deep sigh, risking having my lungs explode, and blinked repeatedly. I still couldn't make out anything definite. What was happening? I couldn't see anything but a white blur with fine lines gathered at one corner of my sight. But I realized that I'd become distracted and the pain had lessened. I focused all my attention on the white blur and blinked again. The ceiling swam into focus. In one corner an industrious spider had stretched a net that was black with dust.

You are not going to die in a fucking hotel room where the maid forgot to clean the corners!

I focused on my toes and willed them to unclench, to relieve the cramp in my calves. With every breath I drew I focused on my limbs, demanding that they relax. I felt my hands unclench. I didn't try to move them. A low hum was coming to my ears now and, as I concentrated on breathing, it gradually overcame the pounding of my heartbeat. There was nothing much to hear, but I could hear the presence of the room in the low hum of the heating and an out-of-phase electrical circuit.

I knew what all these things were and I wasn't going to die. Not now. Not here.

Damn.

I was exhausted. I lay there on my back breathing and trying to come back to reality. I was so tired. I let my eyes drift closed again and was asleep.

I was awakened by a golden-haired vision leaning over me. The long curls were only partly caught up in a knot in back, and stray wisps floated around her face.

"Riley?" I thought. Apparently the words didn't make it out of my mouth. What would Riley be doing here?

"Dag! Wake up. Dag!" No, not Riley. Angel. Was I going to wake up every time I thought I was dying to a beautiful woman leaning over me? I could get used to it. She was certainly lovely.

My eyes were wide open now and I looked squarely into her face. I knew it was Angel, but it wasn't the face I was expecting. Had I ever actually looked at her face? Well, of course, I could recognize her. But I hadn't noticed that she had brown eyes with little dark streaks running through the irises. Why did I just assume she had blue eyes? I'd made disparaging comments to myself about her bottle blonde hair. Had I looked at it? Had I seen any more than I expected to see—a beautiful woman selling herself for money and power?

She had no mascara on. Apparently it was morning and she hadn't put on her makeup yet. I could see a faint tracery of lines around her eyes, silent witness to the fact that she was not quite as young as I originally thought, but not more than thirty even so. I could see how, in the future, they would deepen, and that the result would still be beautiful, but perhaps more dignified. In age she would be like Ingrid Bergman. It occurred to me to ask if she was Swedish.

But concern and worry tinged the beauty. Perhaps there was too much of a difficult life hidden beneath her usual makeup, which was exposed as she now looked at me without its mask. A hint of shadow beneath her eyes spoke of too little sleep and too frantic a life. I wondered how much of that care and worry she had brought to her relationship with Simon, and how much was a result of it.

"Dag, breakfast is here and Simon wants to get started right away," she said. I couldn't help myself. I lifted a hand toward her face.

139

She started away, but it wasn't from my touch. She took my hand in hers and opened it, then sought the other one and looked into my palms.

"What have you done?" she asked, then without waiting for an answer called out, "Simon! Come in here."

I realized that I still hadn't spoken and didn't know what she was referring to. I held my hands up where I could see them. They were covered in dried blood. On each of my palms were the perfect crescent cuts from my fingernails. I guessed I should get them trimmed.

As Simon came into the room I became suddenly aware that the sheets I on which I lay were soaked, and where I had started feeling warm, I was now feeling chilled.

Simon looked quickly at my hands and the damp sheets and was instantly concerned.

"Dag, are you okay?" he asked. At last I managed to pry my lips apart to answer.

"Pills," I croaked, waving feebly toward the bathroom. Angel was immediately in action getting water and returning with three bottles of medicine.

"Which one of these are you supposed to have?" she asked. I pointed to the right bottle and held up two fingers. She shook out the pills and popped them into my open mouth, then held the glass as I swallowed them down. I'll have to remember to keep those nearer to my bed from now on. It was a miracle that I had lived to take them.

"Dag, what's wrong with you, old buddy?" Simon said. "What can we do to help?" I managed to clear my head and tongue. I just hoped that I wasn't going to find that I was slurring my words when I spoke.

"I had an attack in the night. It obviously wasn't that bad since I'm awake this morning, but I guess it was pretty rough then." I looked at my hands. "Looks like I need a manicure."

"An attack of what?" Angel said.

"Heart," I answered briefly.

"I heard that you were sick recently," Simon said, "but I didn't know it was this serious."

"I'm on a waiting list for a transplant," I said, "if I survive long enough to get one."

"Let's get it moving," Simon said, "jumping to his feet. We'll call around to the area hospitals and see who can get you in." That was Simon, all right. If it needed doing, let's get the troops in line and do it. I'm sure he thought that all he had to do was call a local hospital and tell them I needed a new heart and I'd get one this afternoon. He had no concept of how long a recovery it was going to be and how hard it is to get a new heart.

"Right now, I need a shower," I said. "There's no sense in calling hospitals, Simon. Every one of them has a waiting list of patients for heart transplants. They take them in order when a heart that matches comes available. But there still aren't that many donors. Half of them will never get to the operation. My best bet is to get finished with our business and get back to Seattle where I'm at least on the list. But right now," I said again, "I stink and I really need that shower."

"I'll help you," Angel said immediately.

"No way," Simon said. "I'll do it. I'm not likely to give him another heart attack getting him into the shower. You are." We all laughed at that and Angel said to get a move on then, breakfast was ready.

I was pretty shaky getting into the shower and out, and I was glad that Simon was standing by. I felt a lot better when I came to the breakfast table. In the intervening time, Angel had made up her face and dressed in a casual, but sexy looking, shirt and jeans. I was still wearing suit pants and a dress shirt, though I hadn't put on a tie yet. I noticed that her makeup masked all the subtle beauties I'd seen in her earlier this morning. She had transformed herself from person to object in a few short minutes, though she still treated me warmly. She was comfortable in that role, and I feared that she might never be free of it.

Simon and I went back to work and spent the day setting up cash bleeds and transfers. When we were done, there would not be much left of Barnett, Keane, and Lamb. Riley called about noon.

"Dag, I hope this is okay," she started. I was instantly alert for what wasn't okay. "Brenda Barnett called this noon. She was back from

141

her vacation and said she was trying to track you down. She'd been dialing your number for days, she claims, but there's been no answer."

"It's my cell phone. She doesn't have the number for my new phone."

"I know that. I explained to her that you had found Simon and were with him in Atlanta," Riley said. "Then she really blew up. I have never taken so much verbal abuse in my life." I could tell she was still pretty steamed and was thankful she had restrained herself with Brenda. "The short of it is that she's planning to fly to Atlanta tomorrow herself to—and I quote—'drag the bastard home where he belongs and ditch the whore he's shacked up with.' I assumed that she was referring to Simon and not to you, right?"

"Presumably," I chuckled, "but with Brenda you never know for sure."

"Does that mean you are shacked up with a whore?" she asked.

"No one is, Riley. I've told you how Brenda thinks." At the first mention of Brenda, Simon had turned his attention fully on me and was listening to what was being said. I thanked Riley for the information, assured her that I was fine, and hung up."

"Brenda knows I'm here, Dag?" Simon asked with some concern.

"Yes," I answered. "And it sounds like she's out for blood."

"Or Money." Simon muttered. "Shit. That means Bradley knows."

"I don't follow. Bradley and Brenda didn't seem to be on great terms when I met with each of them," I said. I can't imagine that Brenda would tell him."

"He was probably listening when she made the call. He's been fucking her for years," Simon said bitterly. I was amused that someone so casual with whom he had sex, in fact who had slept with and later married my wife, was still bitter about who she slept with.

"This is serious," Simon continued. "How much do we have to go?"

"You tell me," I said. "We've transferred close to 1.5 billion in business assets in a mass divestiture and have given half a billion to charity. How much more is there?" Simon thought for a bit.

"There's still enough for one more donation," he said. "This account has one-and-a-half million in it." He pointed to the last of the named accounts that we hadn't dealt with. "It's yours." I was stunned. "You need to pay for an operation and get yourself healthy, Dag. You've done a good thing for me. It's the only way I can pay you back."

"Simon, I can't take your money. I'm not likely to even be around long enough to use it."

"That's a fine way to talk. Look, you've got the transfer numbers and I'm telling you the account belongs to you. Now if you want to give it away, that's up to you. Otherwise, leave it to your heirs. Just make sure they know it's theirs. One-and-a-half mil left in a Swiss bank account after you are dead is just going to stay in the bank." I tried to protest again, but Simon insisted that it was now my problem—he was quit of the whole thing. We had essentially liquidated a two billion dollar business in 48 hours, with all the transfers set up to execute on a timetable that would leave Bradley in the dark until Monday after Thanksgiving.

I thought about Simon's offer. Then I made a decision. I set up a holding account and wired $500,000 to it in the name of Billie and Wanda Martin. That much, at least, I could do. I sent an e-mail to my lawyer with the particulars and asked that he contact them on behalf of an anonymous donor. And that he do it fast.

Simon ordered dinner and champagne. He said it was time to celebrate, but I noticed that when they brought dinner to the room, he answered the doorbell himself, and spent a long time looking through the privacy glass before he opened the door to let the server in.

Simon was acting scared.

I had a salmon dinner with long grain brown rice and steamed broccoli. Angel had suddenly taken it upon herself to make sure I was eating a heart-healthy diet. She poured the champagne and poured me only half a glass. Just to toast with, she said. That was fine with me.

After dinner we sat in the sitting room, papers and my laptop still on the coffee table. Simon wanted to know if I'd look one more thing up for him and I agreed. But I was surprised when he said he wanted

143

me to check on flights from Seattle to Atlanta. Was there anything Brenda could have gotten on today?

"There's a red-eye at 10:30 tonight," I said. "It gets in tomorrow morning at 6:00. You aren't really worried about Brenda coming here, are you Simon?"

"I could turn my back and walk away from Brenda," Simon said. "It's Bradley's goon I'm worried about. He could be here by 6:00 a.m." He paused and brightened. "Well, she doesn't know where I'm staying, does she? We've got time to get to the airport tomorrow and get you back to Seattle and Angel and me to Croatia. It's going to be a lovely flight, Angel honey." It was a forced levity. Simon was worried.

His mention of the refrigerator-sized Oksamma worried me, too. I checked a couple more things on the computer. The last time I saw the big man, Oksamma was in Chicago where presumably he was still lying low.

There were half a dozen flights from Chicago that arrived this evening.

Vanishing Act

I RETIRED EARLY and lay restless in my bed. Too much contact with Simon could definitely warp your sense of reality. Someplace along the line I went to sleep.

For the second morning in a row, I was awakened by Angel. This time, however, she was not as gentle.

"Dag!" she yelled, bursting into my room. I sat up in bed fast enough to make my head swim and looked at her. It must have been something about my expression that alerted her to the fact that her robe was not tidily closed. For a moment it looked as if she didn't care, but then she pulled it closed and tightened the belt. I could tell this was done reflexively, though as she blurted out, "Simon's gone! I've looked everywhere. There is no note and he's not here. I called the front desk and they said he left this morning after ordering breakfast to be delivered."

"He must have gone out for a walk," I said. "It is getting a little stuffy in here after three days."

"You don't understand, Dag," she sobbed. "They said he checked out and paid the bill for a late departure so we didn't have to hurry."

"He checked out?" I was having a hard time processing this. "And left us here?"

"Yes," she sobbed as she sank down on the edge of my bed and buried her face in her hands. I patted her on the back, not knowing quite what the proper response should be. I was saved by the chime on the front door. "That's breakfast," she said. "How could he do this?"

"Well, look, you go out and let room service in while I get dressed. I'll be out in a minute and we'll start looking for him." She started to protest, but it's hard for me to get out of bed in the morning with a woman in the room. It's not like I'm a pajamas kind of guy. "Maybe he sent a note with breakfast," I said. Her eyes lit up and I was truly sorry I'd said that, but she left the room to rush to the door.

I slid out of bed and cranked the shower on full and hot. After I'd shaved, I selected my traveling suit and my one clean shirt and tie. Life in a luxury penthouse was obviously drawing to a close. I went out to join Angel at the breakfast table.

She was still in her robe and sat at the table solemnly spreading butter on whole wheat toast. She hadn't bothered with makeup yet and the creases around her eyes were deeper and sadder than I had observed yesterday. Her eyes were red and a little puffy. A tear still trickled down her cheek. I reached across with my napkin and gently dried her eye. She looked up at me directly then.

"He's gone," she said flatly.

"Did he leave a note?" I asked. She pointed at my plate. Under the dome covering my dish of oatmeal was a small envelope with my name on it. I somehow didn't think it was a get well card. I opened it and read it over.

"I don't know what I was thinking, Dag," I read. "They'll hunt me for as long as they think I can be found. I certainly can't drag Angel through that. My only hope is to get out of town and never come back. I've got plenty of cash in lots of places in the world. I can buy a new identity and disappear for good. But they'd spot me again in no time if I had Angel with me. I can see the contract now: look for an ugly little man with a tall golden goddess.

"When I bought the estate in Croatia, I put it in Angel's name, so I hope she takes that Marine of hers and settles down there. I know she's got plenty of money.

"I called the airport and there was a guy there last night asking about me and my plane. I asked for a description and was told that he didn't speak English too well and was the size of a pro-ball tackle. You can guess who that was. So now I'm out of here.

"Good luck on getting a new heart, buddy. If anything happens to me, you know what to do. Bury the fuckers."

I handed it to Angel, but she refused.

"I already read it," she said.

I made a quick call to the airport and discovered that Simon's plane had taken off 40 minutes ago. They could not patch a call through no matter what I said. I'd no more than hung up when my cell phone rang and my dear ex-wife started bending my ear about finding her husband.

"I'm at the airport getting ready to fly to Atlanta," Brenda said. "Make sure Simon is there and for her own safety, get rid of the bitch."

"It's too late, Brenda," I said, almost relieved. "Simon left this morning. Did you happen to tell Bradley where he was?"

"Well, I might have mentioned it."

"Well, there was a welcoming committee here already. Simon ran."

"Ridiculous," Brenda went on. "What would he have to run from? He's much more powerful than Bradley. Find him."

"I'm not going hunting for Simon again," I said. "I'm tired and I need to go home."

"Just track him on his tracking thing," Brenda said. She had come a long way. She wasn't always so technical.

"What tracking thing?" I asked.

"The one on his airplane," she said. "You have his computer, don't you? I can't imagine you didn't do this from the start. He has a tracking program on the computer that connects to the plane to keep track of it when he has sent it someplace. What kind of a computer hacker are you anyway?"

I had seen the application, but I didn't find a way to track anything on it. I'd tried entering the call numbers of the plane, Simon's social security number, any number of things, but it never connected to anything. I let Brenda know that it was a waste of time.

"It's fated to die," she said.

"What?" I asked.

"Simon's morbidity got to him a few years ago and he named the plane Fated to Die. He has it tattooed on his butt." Way too much information.

"Okay, I'll try it. But if I can't make contact with him I'm coming home. In fact, I'm getting a flight back regardless. I'm through." I told Angel that for what it was worth, I might be able to track where Simon was flying to.

"I'll take a look at the tracking system and see if I can locate the plane, but frankly, I don't know what good that will do. Unless we see that he's changed his mind and is coming back, I'd suggest we get a ticket back to Seattle. He checked us out of the hotel. Why don't you get dressed and we'll see what we can find. I'd rather not be here when Brenda lands."

Angel was subdued. Simon had left her and she was not certain that she wanted him to come back now, but she went up to their shared room nonetheless, and said that she would make flight arrangements for us. I doubted that she would be going. I sat at my computer and connected in through the VPN to Simon's computer. The flight tracker was there, but it remained unresponsive. I entered the name Simon had given the plane and tried several different capitalization combinations. If this was even the right name, it could take forever to find the right combination. And for all I knew he might have changed the name.

I became aware of Angel standing behind me. I looked up at her and she looked puzzled at the screen. She was dressed at her elegant best and had carefully applied her makeup and used eye drops. I explained to her what I was doing.

"Brenda said the name of the plane was Fated to Die. Simon had it tattooed on his butt," I said.

"That's not what his tattoo says," Angel said. "We were all pretty drunk one night up at the condo. There were only Simon and his partner and me left when Simon had an idea that we'd all go out and get tattoos. He assigned code words to each of us and we got them tattooed at about 2:00 a.m. that morning by a guy who was about as stoned as we were."

"So what is the tattoo?" I asked.

"F8ed2d1e," she answered and typed it in on the keyboard.

I pressed Enter and the screen changed to a world map with a comment box that said "Acquiring Data…" Inside a couple of minutes the map repositioned, and an icon of a plane appeared. It took a minute to realize that I was looking at the Eastern Seaboard map upside down and that the plane was flying generally southward. It was passing over the Florida Keys.

We watched fascinated for fifteen minutes. As the plane approached Cuba, it suddenly disappeared. The comment box returned with its message "Acquiring data…" The message was on the screen for nearly five minutes before it was replaced with "Unable to locate device." I entered the code again, with the same two messages.

"It appears that Simon does not wish to be tracked," I said.

We left the hotel. Angel had arranged a limousine back to the airport. I noticed she had a suitcase this time instead of her packages from Bloomingdale's.

"Simon didn't take any clothes with him. He dressed and took his wallet. His cell phone is even here." She was grieving. "He didn't really think that Davy was more important to me the he was, did he?"

"I thought that is what Davy was for," I answered. "To make sure your clients are a little afraid?" She looked at me sharply.

"That Debbie really is your girlfriend, isn't she," she said. It was a statement, not a question.

"You called her Debbie and lived?" I asked, avoiding the question. I still didn't want to reveal everything to Angel. Or maybe I just didn't want to answer her question.

We boarded the airplane in first class. Angel helped me into my seat and put my bag up overhead for me when I had a sudden feeling of wooziness creep over me again. The flight attendant was immediately by our seats asking if there was anything she could do or if we needed anything. We both assured her that we would be fine. She spoke to Angel as she returned to her duties and said, "If you or your dad need anything, just let me know."

Damn.

I suddenly felt very old. The "young woman effect" had abandoned me completely. As I turned to look at Angel now, I didn't feel immortal at all. I only felt old.

And suddenly a little curious.

She was wearing a blouse with a plunging neckline. I'd gotten used to Angel showing a lot of cleavage over the past few days. It even amused me to see Simon stop in mid-sentence when she walked by and pick up again where he'd left off after he recovered from her presence. But when my gaze fell to that valley between her breasts this time, I noticed something different.

She looked at me curiously, but unflinchingly as I reached toward her. I lifted the gold chain from her collar bone and gave a little tug. From out of the depths of that valley rose a small, state-of-the-art jump-drive. I held it in my hand and looked into her eyes.

"Simon gave it to me yesterday," she said. "I forgot. He said you would know what to do with it." She lifted her hair with both hands to expose the back of her neck and I reached around to unfasten the clasp. She smiled at me as she leaned her neck into my hand. Even when her lover left her, she automatically turned subtle charm and caresses toward a man who would pay attention to her. I realized that it really wouldn't make a difference how much money she had; she would still need to be worshipped by a man.

It wasn't going to be me. I congratulated myself on what little good judgment I had left, pocketed the jump-drive, and settled back into my seat to go to sleep. Five hours later, we were getting off the plane in Seattle.

SeaTac airport is one of those that have television monitors every few feet in the departure lounges, all playing the same version of news over and over again. You get used to ignoring it. I wouldn't have glanced at the monitors had Angel not suddenly gripped my arm and stopped me in my tracks. She was staring at a monitor that showed a screen not unlike the tracking screen we'd looked at in Atlanta.

"Authorities are still investigating the explosion of a private jet en route from Atlanta to Jamaica in Cuban airspace," the reporter said.

"Cuban authorities have denied firing on the craft, but security levels have been raised to orange. Flight records indicate that the craft carried only the pilot, who is presumed dead."

Angel fainted.

My Broken Heart

I KNEW I WAS IN TROUBLE. I'd missed my doctor's appointment last week. In fact, I missed two since yesterday was Monday.

I also knew Doc Roberts was not going to be happy about it, no matter what my excuse. The sniffling cold that I'd acquired after my dowsing in the Chicago River was still hanging on and I had no doubts that it had to do with the immunosuppressant I was taking.

I didn't count on the vehemence of Doc's reaction to me, though, or the other news he had.

"I told you to stay within half an hour of the hospital, Dag," he said. "I'm pretty sure I explained the importance of keeping your scheduled appointments. You have to be serious about this if you want to actually be in line for a heart. I don't have time or sympathy to waste on people who don't want to get well."

He wasn't exactly yelling at me. I was sure he meant it to be a severe warning. I couldn't help but feel he was treating me like a disobedient child. Maybe I was, but I still didn't like being treated that way.

"I'm sorry. It seemed very important. A man's life was at stake."

Not that anything I did mattered. What did I really accomplish while I was gone? I moved some money to places where it might do some good. Got it out of the hands of bad guys. Got laid. Almost drowned. Almost died in a hotel room. And lost an old friend in an airplane accident that had "suspicious circumstances" written all over

152

it. I couldn't even explain why I did it. It just seemed like the right thing to do at the time.

"I'm finished," I said. "No more running around. I'm on the program a hundred percent."

"You don't get it, Dag," he practically yelled at me. "You missed a donor. After an hour of trying to reach you, we had to ship it to Phoenix where they planted in an eighty-year-old geezer who wants to live to a hundred. The difference between you and him is that he wanted it enough to do what he was told."

I'd been punched recently—a couple of times. But neither of the thugs had hit me as hard as this news.

"How could that happen?" I asked. "You said it could be weeks before I came to the top of the list and there was a heart available."

"Could be," he answered. "It was a fluke. You were third and bottom on the list locally with that blood-type. A thirty-year-old male died in a traffic accident on I-5 late last Monday night. The first guy on the list has pneumonia and I don't dare cut him. The second passed on the night before. That brought me to you. It was a good match. It hurt to pack it in ice and send it to Arizona."

"Do I stand a chance of coming to the top of the list again?" I asked.

"I never give up hope for my patients, Dag," he responded. "Let's get you healthy again so you can survive a transplant if we get one." He paused and I had the feeling he wasn't telling everything. Hell, he'd just given me a sucker-punch to the brain. What could be holding him back now?"

"But...?" I prompted.

"Dag," he said quietly, "I don't know what is keeping your heart beating now. Make sure you use what time you've got wisely. Put your house in order."

I guess he could have been more blunt. I wasn't sure how.

I walked out of his office under my own power and waved off a nurse's offer of a wheel chair. As long as I could stand I wasn't going to be pushed around like an invalid. I felt that if I sat in it I would never get out again. I was at the door when it opened from the other side. There stood Billie the Kid and her mother, Wanda.

"Mr. Hamar!" the child exclaimed. "I was worried about you. Guess what!"

"Hello Billie," I greeted her. "Hello Ms. Martin." I nodded to Wanda who seemed to be positively beaming. "What's up?"

"I'm coming to live at the hospital so I can be ready when my new heart comes," the pint-sized patient exclaimed.

"That's good news," I said raising an eyebrow at her mother.

"It's a miracle," Wanda said. "I was meeting with a social worker to sign over custody and make Billie a ward of the State when a lawyer I'd never heard of called and said that an anonymous donor had set up a half-million dollar trust for Billie. He had to talk to the social worker and had her drive us to his office to verify the papers. Suddenly the State has become very helpful. Dr. Roberts said that the approach of the holiday season often results in an increase of donors and we should be here so there is no chance of her missing an opportunity."

Even though she could not have known about my delinquency, I couldn't help but hear a rebuke from Dr. Roberts over missing my opportunity.

"That's truly wonderful news," I said. I reached into my wallet for a business card and gave it to Wanda. "Please let me know when Billie gets her new heart," I said. "I'd like to come and visit."

"Can I have one, too?" Billie asked. I smiled and handed her a card over her mother's shush. Billie looked at it carefully. "What's a private investigator?" she asked.

"I solve mysteries," I answered. "Usually I investigate what is on computer systems. If you ever need anything investigated, you just call on D. H. Investigations. We'll get to the bottom of it." We parted, and in spite of the shocking news I'd had this morning, I felt a little better.

Some things, however, I was taking very seriously. I had Riley take me by my attorney's office and made some changes to my will. I would rest easier once that was signed. I thanked him for taking care of the business with Billie Martin and deflected his questions about where the money had come from.

After a very sensible, heart-healthy lunch, I convinced Riley to take me back to the office instead of straight home. I'd missed the one day during this month of record-breaking rainfall that I might have seen the mountain from my office window, but I once again wanted to stand there looking. There had been occasional sun breaks on this windy day and I didn't want to miss a chance of seeing it again.

I do want to live. I'm not ready to give up and die. I'm fifty-seven years old, and I want to live forever. Or at least until Christmas. I'd like to live long enough to retire. I'd like to live long enough to see the next version of Windows for my computer. I'd like to see Riley get her degree, and a PhD if she wants one. I want to see Billie get her new heart, and see her go to school like a normal kid. I want to go for hikes in the mountains with Maizie running along by my side. Or at least be able to walk to the office again. I'd like to know if there is such a thing as true love and whether anyone was really right for me.

Damn it! Why me?

I don't know how long I'd been standing there. It got dark earlier and earlier now. I could see the lights from the ferries crisscrossing the sound. I returned to my desk and opened my computer. I inserted the jump-drive and waited to see what would come up.

The dialog box was not what I expected. It asked for the encryption key. Encryption. The one place that Simon absolutely should not have used encryption. It required a key—an alphanumeric sequence that could be between eight and eighty characters. What was he thinking? Well, there was one chance, and that was that. Perhaps if I inserted it in Simon's computer it would get the key automatically.

"Riley!" I called. She'd been sitting quietly at her desk fiddling with a stack of CDs the entire time we'd been back at the office. Probably working on her thesis, I assumed. She was in my doorway in a flash.

"What is it Dag?" she asked. "Are you okay."

"Yeah, don't worry," I said. "I'd just like you to open the vault for me." She looked at me a little strangely.

"'I don't know how to open the vault, Dag," she said hesitantly. "You didn't give me the code."

"I thought you would have figured it out by now," I said with a smile. "Well that means I still have something I can teach you." I handed her the remote control. She took it with the kind of expression that showed she didn't really want to learn this. She turned that reluctance around on me.

"Are you sure you want to show me this, Dag?" she asked.

"Consider it an insurance policy, Riley. I don't want to worry about people having to tear down the walls if anything should happen to me. It would ruin the decorating." We laughed. I was reminded of the time, such a short time ago when I'd gotten the news that I needed a heart transplant and had discovered forty-two fuzzed files on Simon's computer. Forty-two—according to Douglas Adams, the answer to life, the universe, and everything. But we never found out the question. We'd laughed that night until tears ran down my cheeks and had chased away the specter of death in the shadows.

I was drifting off subject again.

Damn.

I showed her what channel to turn to and what sequence to key in. The panel that led to the vault slid open. Riley started humming "Secret Agent Man."

"That reminds me," I said, "Have you seen the new flick? We should go on Thanksgiving." Riley brightened considerably, apparently figuring that I wasn't planning to die that soon at least. I decided to go a step further. "You can come to Thanksgiving Dinner with me if you'd like to see how a bunch of Swedes celebrate. Of course, don't feel obligated if you have other plans."

"Sounds like fun," she said. "Let me check my busy social calendar. Yup all free." She shot it all out in one breath and we both had a chuckle. If I really thought she was as socially inept as she sometimes lets on, I'd worry.

I explained how the servers were arrayed and the security safeguards I'd put in place around them. There was an alert beacon and back-up power supply if either the main power or the cooling system failed. On various shelves were neatly arranged hard drives that were backups of all the systems I've investigated over the past ten years. The current investigations were whirring away on a shelf including Simon's computer and the computer Oksamma borrowed from BKL.

"The last thing you need to know is that you can't move or open one of these boxes," I said, "unless you enter its code on the panel inside the door. It's a tripwire that I learned in the Navy for wiring explosives. If you disconnect the computer case from the shelving, like opening the box where it sits, I've rigged an acid bath inside each hard drive that will physically pit the drive so it can't be read. It is much more effective than trying to erase the data quickly."

"And too bad if your hands happen to be in there," she said thoughtfully. "Dag, this all scares me. What if you had... if you hadn't... come back from this trip?"

"Well, a clever partner would have simply sucked all the data off the disks onto her own backup system and then would have erased the whole system remotely. If anyone ever managed to get into the vault, even the dataless disks would have been destroyed. But the clever partner would have everything that was running in the vault long before that could have happened."

"You've got a lot more confidence in me than I do," Riley said thoughtfully. "Unless you've got another partner you are thinking of."

"You deserve the confidence I place in you, Riley. Now let's plug this jump-drive into Simon's computer," I said handing it to her.

"Directly?" she asked.

"I wish I knew a better way," I said. "But the truth is, we've got all his data backed up onto separate hard drives, and I didn't find encrypted data on his laptop. Sometimes an encryption key is tied to the hardware ID number. If he just put the device in and had it encrypt automatically, that might be the case. That way, it's encrypted if it is separated from the computer and accessible if you log-in with Simon's password. He gave me the password before he... left."

Something about the latest disappearance of Simon gnawed at my mind, but I still couldn't place what it was. He'd been spooked by the news that Bradley probably knew where he was. He decided to run for it again and couldn't risk Angel or me knowing where he was headed. Then he filed a flight plan for Jamaica and blew up over Cuba, nearly creating an international incident. No. Something was wrong.

Was it a storm? The Cubans denied shooting him down. What happened to his plane? It was going to be hard for authorities to investigate since it occurred over Cuba. It bothered me.

I'd been running on automatic as I fired up Simon's laptop and entered the password that brought it to life. Before I plugged the jump-drive in, Riley snatched it form my hand and backed it up on the remote system from her laptop. Smart girl. I'm definitely losing it. She came back and inserted the drive in the port on Simon's laptop. I saw it identify the new device and tell me it was ready to use. I opened the file system. An alert box appeared stating that the file was encrypted and to enter the code. Riley and I both groaned at the same time.

"It looks as though Simon outsmarted himself this time," I said. I went wearily back to my desk and sat down. Riley came up quietly behind me and rubbed my neck. Then she came around to the front of my desk and perched on the edge in her most usual position.

"I have some news from my research," she said. I raised an eyebrow. "The muffin-top's little vacation was in Cabo San Lucas. She rented a condo there for a week."

"Well, she told us she was going," I said.

"Yes, but she didn't tell you that she was going with Bradley Keane."

Apparently Simon was right about Brenda and Bradley hooking up. I kept waiting for her to continue, but she seemed to be finished. "How did you get all this information?" I asked.

"I paid an unauthorized visit to the Barnett home yesterday. Bradley and Brenda both left at the same time."

"I'm not sure I want to know any more about your unauthorized visit," I said. Riley was slightly more free with the latitude that the law allows than I was. She was looking at the laptop.

Then she asked me the question that I knew had to be on her mind from the start.

"Dag, the company name is Barnett, Keane, and Lamb Ltd. All this time we've been dealing with Barnett and Keane. Who is Lamb?" she asked. I wouldn't have been surprised if she already knew but was waiting for me to come clean.

"Lamb is my ex-wife's maiden name. The company was supposed to be Barnett, Hamar, and Lamb. We had a falling out."

"Brenda Lamb?"

"Yes."

"You were married to that? I mean her?" Riley exclaimed.

"No. I was married to the most fiery, fun, and intelligent woman I'd ever known. She made instant friends with everyone she met. But people change. If anything, she was too gregarious. She was free with her love and she loved freely. That's not that out of character with my generation in the 70s. But the one that I couldn't stand sharing her with was Simon Barnett. So there you have it. But for one infidelity, I would be the multi-millionaire partner of Simon and Brenda and you'd be chasing me down instead of Bradley."

She looked at me intently for a moment and I held her eyes. I don't really want to get involved in telling about her eyes. Once you locked with her, it was really hard to look away.

"I don't believe it for a minute," she said.

"It's true," I said, somewhat taken aback.

"No," she answered. "The story may be true, but I don't believe you would ever be the person who would make deals with who-knows-what mobster and attempt to do away with your partner. For that, I would never be chasing you down."

The phone rang and mercifully cut our conversation short. It was Jordan.

"Dag, I thought you should know," he said. "We've confirmed that Oksamma was seen sneaking around Simon's plane late Sunday night. It seems he was interrupted and a night watchman was found stuffed in an oil drum in the hangar where the plane was kept. The

FBI has a warrant out for the arrest of Oksamma for the murder of the watchman, the suspected murder of Simon Barnett, and the attempted murder of Dag Hamar.

"He's still on the loose, friend. Be careful."

Investigating Angel

I WAS SLOW GETTING UP and would still be asleep if Riley had not been knocking on my door. I dragged myself upright and couldn't figure out what she was doing here in the middle of the night.

It was 9:00 in the morning.

Damn.

Well, what could I tell? As close as I could come to it, I hadn't had a cup of coffee since I was at Peg's apartment and I had the headache to prove it. That was when? A different life ago? At least a week. But I was dedicated to being on the program now.

No caffeine.

I could sure use a cup of coffee, though.

Riley took Maizie out for a walk while I showered and shaved. I was in my robe in the kitchen when Riley got back.

"Can I make your oatmeal for you?" she asked. "You can go ahead and get dressed." I suppose it was a nice offer and she didn't mean anything by it. I suppose I should have been happy to have the help. I suppose I'm an ass.

"Don't rush me, Riley," I snapped. "I can take care of myself."

"I just thought I could help," she said.

"I don't need a mother to look after me. I just need to sort out which pills I should take."

The instant crushed look on her face was more than I could bear. I turned my back on her. I could hear the stunned silence behind me. I

161

still couldn't bear to face her. I had to do something but I could scarcely trust myself to speak.

"Please put the oats in the water when it boils, would you," I spoke very softly, but I heard her say "Okay." I went into my bedroom and closed the door.

I sat on my bed and tried to get a grip on myself. What was happening to me? Riley didn't deserve to be treated like this. I didn't mean to hurt her, but it was evident that everything I said was wrong. I just needed to get a grip.

Then I started to panic. What if I hurt her and she left? What if she was already gone?

The anxiety I felt sent my heart racing and I was afraid I was going to have another attack. I almost called for her, but I was in my robe and nothing else. I moved quickly and pulled on underwear and socks. I went to my closet to choose a suit.

I froze.

There were too many of them. How could I have gotten so many suits. I could never make a choice among so many. What if I offended one?

Damn.

They are inanimate objects, I thought. I can't offend them.

I closed my eyes and grabbed one out of the closet. I did the same with my shirt and tie. It didn't make a difference. I got dressed and rushed into the kitchen.

Riley was still there. She smiled at me tentatively and I did my best to smile back. She placed a steaming bowl of oatmeal on the table and I sat down.

"Thank you," I muttered.

"You're welcome," she said. She turned back to the kitchen door.

"Riley, please don't leave me. I'm sorry," I said in a rush, half rising from the table.

"I won't leave you, Dag," she said, turning back to me. She came around the table and laid a hand on my shoulder. I looked up at her and took a bite of oatmeal. I didn't taste it, but it didn't make a difference.

Riley wasn't leaving. There was no need to panic. The world was slowing back to normal. I was okay. She reached around and straightened my tie, flooding my senses with her fresh clean scent.

"Can I ask you a question, Dag?" she said, sitting across from me.

"That's one," I said. "Do you have another?" She smiled.

"Why do you always wear gray suits and white shirts?" she asked. "You have different styles, but they are all gray. All your shirts look the same. You'd look good with a little color on." This time it was my turn to chuckle. The panic had subsided.

"It's a big secret," I said. "I manage to function just like a normal person most of the time, but the fact is I'm colorblind. Not quite completely. I can see a small range of colors, but they are muted and I don't see colors in the red range at all. I know what colors are there most of the time, but I don't really see them. I identify colors by what is missing rather than by what I see."

"Dag, I had no idea!" she exclaimed. "When you commented on my red leather peep-toed pumps with the stacked wooden heel a few weeks ago, do you mean you couldn't see the color?"

"Red leather peep-toed pumps with the stacked wooden heel," I repeated. "I'm sure that is not what I said. It was the wrong shade of gray. I knew I had to be missing some of the color information. I merely deduced that it was red. I do it automatically. It's embarrassing when I'm wrong."

Riley glanced toward the living room and my one piece of artwork.

"You spend so much time looking at that painting, but you can't see the colors?" she asked.

"I know they are there," I said. "Knowing is what's important."

We loaded Maizie into Riley's car and went to the office. I was feeling a lot better.

"I think we should change the passwords," I said when we got into the office and Maizie had settled into her bed. I looked at her a little enviously.

"Do you think it's a good idea to change passwords now?" Riley asked. "Maybe we should wait till the end of the month."

"Why? Because I'm acting irrationally?" I asked.

"No, Dag. I wasn't implying anything." I could see that this was going the same direction as our earlier conversation. It was time to nip it in the bud.

"You are right," I said. "I have been acting irrationally. For some reason, I'm having spells where nothing seems real and I can't control how I'm responding. It has to be the drugs. So what should we do today instead?"

It was the right thing to say. Riley had several ideas of what we should get started on. Top of the list was getting started on our investigation of Simon's murder. Riley was ready to press her investigation of the girls at the condo based on references to it that she found in "Simon's things." She held out a stack of discs from her file recovery work on Simon's computer. I didn't even think about the fact she'd told me the file recovery had failed. She must have gotten something for her effort.

Something else had finally dawned on me. It had bothered me from the start. There was no "accidental explosion" of Simon's plane. Oksamma had booby-trapped it and then had blown it up exactly where it would be the hardest to investigate. But he had been seen and had left one body behind at the airport. What else did we know?

Oksamma appeared to work for, or at least with Bradley Keane. Jordan was not moving on Bradley because he wanted to crack the smuggling and money laundering scheme and still didn't have enough hard evidence to link him to Oksamma.

We decided to do some more investigating. I started sifting through Bradley's personal finances to see if I could provide Jordan with the evidence he needed. If Simon could uncover Bradley's illegal activity, I could do it with the help of Simon's laptop. Riley wanted to see if there was any connection between Angel and what Simon had discovered. She was determined that there was a connection between the women of the condo and Bradley's activities. I couldn't see it, but it got us working.

As it turned out, it was Riley that uncovered the only clue of the day. It was nearly four and it was already dark outside.

"Remember how I told you there was a link between the condo and Simon and Bradley?" Riley said as she came into my office. She sprawled in her usual fashion on my sofa while I stood looking out the window.

"We haven't found any link, though," I said. "I've been through all Simon and Bradley's personal accounts as well as all the business accounts. The only record I ever found was Simon's cash machine transactions at the market. That and he obviously met Angel there."

"We were looking for the wrong thing," she said. "It isn't Simon and Bradley. The condo is owned by Brenda Lamb." That got my attention.

"She hasn't used her maiden name for years. I always assumed they'd put it on the business just so it wouldn't be Barnett, Barnett, and Keane. But even with that, what's the connection?"

"There is no sign that she has been active in the business for years," Riley continued. "I doubt that she even has an office there. But look at all the pictures that have been published over the past ten or fifteen years. She's on all the boards of all the important arts organizations, governor's task forces, community fund drives. She knows everyone."

"Everyone who is male," I said remembering the number of pictures Riley pulled up.

"And who is the clientele of the private party at the condo?" Riley asked. "Important men who exercise a code of silence. Why? Because someone has something they all want."

"Or because someone has something on them." Bingo. The condo was a perfect front for blackmail. I'd seen the security cameras. No doubt the image of Riley and me arriving with Cinnamon was somewhere in their files. Brenda may have looked at it and filed it away for future use.

"How much do you think Bradley and Brenda could make a year on private fees for "membership" in their little club?" Riley asked. "Business contracts? Deals? Acquisitions? Cash under the table?"

"Riley," I said, "Simon told me he's been converting cash into cash cards for nearly a year."

"Yes. It's actually a pretty popular new service. They work exactly the same way a bank ATM card works, except that the card is 'charged' with the amount you pay for and there is no other personal information on it. So if a thief got hold of your cash card, even if they got your PIN with it, your maximum liability would be what you put on the card. It has no links to any other bank accounts or personal data like a bank card would have."

"And how long has Angel been in business?"

"A year or more, raking in cash hand over fist. She said someone else owned the business before her and Simon helped her acquire it."

"Are there any more of these places?"

"Sure, it's a franchise."

My brain shifted into overdrive. Riley had seen Angel take in $25,000 in cash card orders in one day. It took five transactions. Cash transactions of less than $10,000 didn't have to have a bank form filed for FinCEN, but when Angel took $25,000 to the bank, she had no difficulty filing a form on legitimate cash sales. If there were even five of these franchises in a city, times, say, ten cities, they could process over six and a quarter million dollars a week. Jordan was going to love this. I picked up my phone.

"Riley, you are a genius," I said. "I love you."

"Last time you said that I at least got dinner out of it," she responded.

"I promised dinner at the Ninety-nine when I got back. We'll go."

"Let's try some place different," she suggested rapidly. "I'd rather not go back there just now. It's 25 for $25 month. Want to try something new? I've heard Andaluca is good."

"You make the reservation. We'll go after I talk to Jordan." She was off and happy, and so was I.

Thanksgiving

THANKSGIVING DAY DAWNED DREARY and gray like every other November day in Seattle. I woke up feeling pleasantly well. I did an assessment of all my vital signs to make sure I was alive. After dinner with Riley Wednesday night, I came home and went soundly to sleep in my bed instead of my chair. This morning my heart rate was normal, I had no headache, even my back didn't hurt, and I could take deep even breaths without gasping. As Methuselah said, "I feel like I'm ninety again."

I was relaxing with the morning newspaper and a bit of Sibelius on the stereo when the phone rang.

"Mr. Hamar," the woman on the other end said, "I hope I'm not bothering you too early in the morning, but you said you wanted to know. Oh. This is Wanda Martin. Billie had heart surgery early this morning. She is in intensive care now, but the doctors say it was successful."

"Wanda, that's wonderful," I exclaimed. I was so afraid that it was going to be bad news that my breath must have sounded like an explosion. "I'm so happy," I continued. "You must be exhausted. Is Billie awake yet?" I looked at the clock. It was after ten, but I had no idea what "early in the morning" meant.

"She's awake, but pretty groggy," Wanda said. "The first thing she said was tell Mr. Hamar. You've had a big impact on her, and she's been talking about becoming a private investigator when she grows up." When she grows up. I thought about it. The real victory was that she would grow up.

"Tell Billie that I will come see her soon," I said. "And congratulations! It's truly wonderful news."

I hung up and sat in my chair thinking. I'd had a long leisurely morning and was still in my robe. I got up, got dressed, and called a cab.

I arrived at the hospital a little before noon and went to the IC Unit to see if I could look in on Billie. Her mother came out to meet me and begged a nurse to let me in to see her daughter. After a quick phone consultation with Doc Roberts, she approved a five-minute visit.

Five minutes isn't much, even when you are visiting a ten-year-old. But I left that room filled with hope and confidence. "Don't worry, Mr. Hamar," she said as I was leaving. "Your heart is trying to find its way to you." How true, in so many ways.

I glanced at my watch. It was nearly 12:30.

I called Riley. She was just leaving to pick me up for Thanksgiving Dinner at the Swedish American Center in Ballard. I could hear her gasp when I said I was at the hospital and quickly explained that I was visiting a friend and to please swing by there and pick me up instead of at my apartment. She arrived about fifteen minutes later.

I must have been looking pretty fit because she relaxed visibly when I got in the car.

"You had me worried for a minute there," she said as we pulled away. "Is everything okay?"

"It is," I smiled. I told her about my original encounter with Billie and the issues surrounding her wait for a new heart. I omitted the part about setting up a trust fund for her, but Riley looked at me a little strangely when I said an anonymous donor had come to the rescue. I'm sure she was associating it with Simon's dispersal of funds. She was kind enough not to pursue the idea out loud.

"Well, I have a bit of news, too," she said. "I got a call last night from Cinnamon. She invited me to the girls' night holiday party at the condo Saturday night. Apparently they are closed to men for that night."

"Do you really think it's a good idea to go?" I asked. "You know they are recruiting."

"That's their problem," she answered confidently. "I just want to see inside again. Besides, I have a feeling there is a clue there that a man's eyes might not notice, being so filled with female beauty." I let that pass in silence. If she thought I hadn't noticed the security cameras she was wrong. But knowing Riley like I was beginning to know her, she was probably thinking about removing some evidence that I couldn't approve of. Better I kept my mouth shut.

We got to the cultural center and found parking. I was amazed that my euphoria was holding on and that I had no trouble making the block-long walk from our parking spot to the doors. Riley wanted to drop me off, but I told her I wasn't giving her the opportunity to escape. We would walk in together. She took my arm as we walked to the doors, but I couldn't tell if it was for her security or mine.

It made no difference when we walked in. Chaos reigned. Our coats and hats were hung on a rack and we were ushered into the milling throng. In one corner of the room a television had been set up and a fuzzy picture of the Thanksgiving Day Parade was being broadcast for a crowd of older men and children.

I introduced Riley to old friends. Several spoke to her in Swedish. I leaned over and whispered in her ear.

"Just smile and say 'thank you'," I said.

"What did he say?" she asked.

"I have no idea. I don't speak Swedish." We shared the laugh, but whenever anyone said anything to her in Swedish, she smiled and said "thank you."

"Dag!" said matronly Mrs. Seafeld. "Did you bring *knäckerbröd?*"

"I'm sorry, Mrs. Seafeld. I completely forgot it. I left it on my table," I said, picturing the neat package sitting next to the door as I left to catch a cab this morning.

"It's okay, Dag," she beamed. "You know we always have plenty. And I see you brought a feast for the eyes with you instead. No wonder you forgot the crackers!"

I glanced over at Riley and was surprised that she was actually blushing under Mrs. Seafeld's happy gaze.

"It's only fair." I said. "Mrs. Seafeld this is my partner Deb Riley. Deb, if you want to taste the best *risgrynsgrot* ever made, the one you want will be on the table today made by Mrs. Seafeld."

Mrs. Seafeld said something in Swedish, to which Riley bobbed and said "thank you". I'm not sure what she said, but she went away happy.

By the time the meal was served, we had circulated among many of the hundred or so gathered for the huge feast and had sampled appetizers from pickled herring and smoked salmon to *gravlox* and *bulla*. Riley had a cup of coffee and I leaned a little closer to her than strictly necessary in order to smell the delicious brew. I was on the program. No caffeine, easy on the fats and salt. For me it was going to be a thin Thanksgiving.

"Is everything made of fish?" Riley asked at one point.

"No," I said, "but I'd avoid that particular coffee cake if I were you."

"It's not…" she said looking at me.

"Oh, but it is," I smiled.

After Reverend Olson had said a blessing, we were shepherded into the food line and handed huge paper plates and plastic flatware. The first thing scooped onto our waiting dishes was pasta followed by a generous helping of meatballs in gravy. Onto the same plate went potato sausage, boiled potatoes, rutabagas, and lentil salad with radishes. French cut green beans with slivered almonds and bits of bacon were nudged into a corner, and last we were handed a small plate holding a jiggling green mass with orange flecks.

"What is that?" Riley asked, wiggling it on her plate.

"Lime Jello with shredded carrots," I answered. "No one can ever figure out if it's dessert, salad, or vegetable, so they put it on a plate by itself."

She looked at the multi-colored mass on her plate as we sat and started eating.

"Dag, I missed the turkey," she said.

"Didn't miss it," I said. "It's missing. It's not that we don't like turkey for Thanksgiving, but everyone has special dishes that they always bring and turkey just gets left out. We can get some at the deli tomorrow if you'd like." She looked at me with an expression of complete disbelief, but settled in to her meal with a hearty appetite and good humor.

I ate lightly, even though my plate was filled. I had to avoid the real fatty things, but I had my fill of salads, fish, and bread. After dishes were cleared, the *risgrynsgrot* was brought around in little dishes. It is a rice pudding in cream that is one of Sweden's most popular holiday dishes. I had been good up to this point, but I wasn't going to miss that. At a signal when everyone had been served, we lifted our spoons.

Riley sampled the dish and smiled broadly.

"It's good," she said. She took another big bite, looked curiously at me and said, "Oh, it's got almonds in it too." This time, I looked curiously at her and looked around the room to see if Mrs. Seafeld was watching me. She was. Cagey old woman. I began tapping my fork against my water glass. Soon everyone was joining me and I stood.

"Friends," I said in the ensuing silence. "For the past eight months I have had the privilege of working with a young woman of exceptional talent, brains, and beauty. She is the best partner that anyone in my business could possibly ask for, and she has extended her help to me while I've been battling this heart thing. She runs errands, drives me to work, and walks my dog. If she weren't my employee, you would think she was my wife." Everyone laughed, but Riley was blushing again. "And now, the fates have bestowed upon her the *risgrynsgrot* almond." Everyone applauded and cheered. Riley had no idea what was going on. I pulled her to her feet. "Deb Riley," I said, "there is only one almond in the *risgrynsgrot* and you got it. That means that you get your wish today. Any wish you want, all you have to do is think of it while you chew that almond and it is yours. Ladies and Gentlemen, the *risgrynsgrot* Queen!" I turned her to face everyone as they applauded. "Be careful what you wish for," I said quietly to Riley. "Sometimes they come true."

We sat back down and finished our pudding, then the tables were folded up and the chairs all moved to the sides of the room. Then Tore, Inga, and Sven set up with their fiddles and piano and started playing lively folk tunes. It didn't take long before people were up dancing, some traditional dances, and some just having fun with the music. I tried to show Riley one of the dances, but my breath, for all it was better today, was still not good enough to keep up with dancing. Fortunately, there were many other boys there who were all too happy to have her company. I watched and chatted with old friends while the music played and the dancing continued.

I was getting a little tired by the time we packed up and left, at nearly six.

"Do you mind if we put off the movie until tomorrow?" I asked. "I'm pretty tired right now."

Riley drove to my apartment and jumped out to help me. I'd made it to the sidewalk as quickly as she made it to me. "Do you need me to help you upstairs, Dag?" she asked.

"No. I'm fine," I said. "Just a little tired. Thank you for joining me for Thanksgiving, though."

"Oh Dag!" she said, flinging her arms around my neck. "Thank you for the best day ever." She kissed me. It was brief and accompanied by a hug that nearly broke my bones. As quickly as it was begun she was back in her car waving to me as I made my way to the front door. I waved back.

Yes, it was a very good day.

Truth Comes With the Telling

I'D JUST COME IN from walking Maizie when my phone rang. Jordan had news. The truckload of furniture was on the move again, this time in little pieces.

"A crew arrived and started unloading the container in the ware-house," he said. "We'd already planted cameras and were watching the whole thing. The guys almost missed what was happening."

Periodically a piece of furniture was opened—either a panel from the back or simply a drawer—and several small parcels had been removed and taken to the panel van that had brought the crew. The furniture was piled helter-skelter beside the container. They had blown up pictures from the tape and discovered approximately what was in the smaller packages.

"It's compact disks," Jordan said. "We haven't identified what's on them yet. We're not moving in on the panel van until we see where it goes. It has to be bootleg music CDs, movies or possibly software. In any case, when that van arrives at its destination, we are moving in for a huge bust. You forget these days that drugs aren't the only thing that is a big money-maker."

"That's great news, Jordan. Anything else I can do to help?"

"All right, wise guy. That was meant as a thank you. The fact that they weren't shipping humans in freight containers is just a bonus. It was your tip that got me down on that particular ship." Jordan paused and I was about to brush off the thanks when he continued. "Now that you mention it, though, maybe you could do a little investigating on where and how they are intending to get rid of this stuff. I know it's just 'guess work' on your part." Jordan was letting me off the hook regarding any possible evidence I might have that wasn't obtained according to proper search and seizure warrants. "But if you and your lovely assistant put your mind to it, I'm sure you can come up with some ideas."

"Uh, one thing you should know, Jordan," I said a little hesitantly. "Off-hand I'd say that BKL doesn't actually have that many assets that you could seize. There's been a major sell-off."

"Why aren't we hearing about it through normal channels, then?" he asked.

"Well, it's a privately held company, and it's a holiday weekend. US markets were only open for three hours this morning. I'd guess that some of the partners don't even know about it yet," I said.

"That's why you were holed up with Simon Barnett for three days?" Jordan asked. "I should have known. Look, old friend, there had better be no tracks that lead back to you."

"That sounds accusatory, Jordan. I can't think of any reason tracks would lead to me."

"Later," Jordan ended the conversation. "Our truck is on the move."

I'd done Simon one last favor when I dissolved the business. I'd done it in Bradley's name. There was no evidence of anything that would lead back to Simon. I did think, however, that it merited a little investigation to see if I could tell how they were planning to move the pirated CDs. That kind of a job took some forethought.

I was still sitting at the kitchen table with my laptop open when Riley knocked on the door at 2:00.

"Hey! I thought you might want to grab a bite before the movie," she said when I answered the door. I invited her in. Food seemed like a good idea.

"What are you working on?" she asked when she saw my open laptop. I recapped the conversation I'd had with Jordan.

"So what do you think?" I asked. "What's the most effective way to quickly convert several thousand bootleg CDs to cash?" When Riley starts thinking you can almost see the wheels turning in her mind. She shook her head.

"Nothing comes to mind that would be profitable on such a big scale," she said. "Not in this country. You'd think that they would have kept and distributed the stuff in Asia, not import it from Asia." I agreed and we headed out for a bite at Ralph's before we crossed the street for the movie at the Cinerama. It was easy to escape for a while from real life outside the theater into the fantastical world of a secret agent. But really, what did he have that I didn't have? In the past three-and-a-half weeks I'd been undercover in a private club that catered to the whims of rich and important businessmen. I'd been knocked unconscious by a jealous boyfriend. I'd been thrown into the Chicago River by a thug. I'd even had a one-day affair with a beautiful woman. I had followed a woman on a train, was taken on a private jet ride with my ex-wife's husband, and I'd moved two billion dollars in assets. I'd survived another heart attack, and Thanksgiving Dinner. Now I was out on a movie date with my extraordinarily beautiful partner. And of all, only one of my contacts had actually died. I was definitely secret agent caliber.

The fact that I spent most of my time analyzing computer data didn't seem to matter.

I was in a great mood when we left the movie theater. I'd only missed one short segment when I had to get up for the bathroom. And I was feeling sharp. My mind was working well and I still felt—if not as grand as yesterday—reasonably well. I could lick this thing. I would survive.

And during the movie, I'd figured out part of the clue to moving the money that Bradley must be using.

We were talking about the crowds that were out on the day after Thanksgiving and how much money would be pushed into the local economy today when Riley surprised me and asked, "What do you want for Christmas, Dag?"

"All I want for Christmas is a brand new heart, a brand new heart, a brand new heart," I sang in my best "Two Front Teeth" style. Then I realized that I hadn't actually told Riley that I was waiting for a transplant.

175

"What do you mean, Dag? You're getting better now, right?" .

"My heart is not going to get better, Riley. I'm on the transplant list."

"Dag! Were you ever going to tell me?"

"I didn't want you to be worried unnecessarily," I said. "There's really nothing you can do to help it more than you already do." She lapsed into silence and I decided we needed a little more time this evening.

When she got me home, Riley was shocked that I invited her up to stick around and watch TV for a while. The holiday fare on the tube was bleak, so we sat and talked. I started to explain my theory of money movement.

"The big problem with a movie like that is that you can't dispose of a hundred million dollars easily. You have to get it into circulation and convert it into something that can be used easily. So, let's say the bad guys in the movie gave the investor $100 million. Each million if it were in $100 bills would take up four-tenths of a cubic foot, so we would have a total of forty-two cubic feet of money. That is a 4x4 palette stacked roughly three feet high. It would weigh about one-and-a-quarter tons. That's what the fellow loaded into the back of his panel van in three suitcases."

"Did you work that all out in your head just now?" Riley asked.

"No. I was playing with the numbers while I was transferring Simon's money. I was trying to figure out what half a billion dollars looked like. Believe me, you need a forklift. The point is that moving that much cash is no easy problem. So how can you move it more efficiently?"

"Well," Riley said, "if that was the case, moving CDs would only be more complex. If every CD was worth $100 then a million dollars would take up six-tenths of a square foot. They are heavier than a hundred dollar bill, too, and what CD is worth $100?" I was almost into my next sentence when I realized the calculations that Riley had just made in her head on the spur of the moment. Damn she was good.

"True," I said. "The only difference is that all kinds of retail stores will pay for the CDs with checks that can be deposited. So, they convert cash to CDs and CDs to checks. Instant legitimate income."

"It would make a lot more sense if they put data on CDs that was worth a million dollars. Then they could carry a million on a CD, pop it into a computer, and have instant credit."

"Like putting all the records of cash cards sold in a certain store on a CD, then packing it in a suitcase and taking it to Switzerland with you. Riley, that's brilliant! I love you."

"Do you Dag?" she asked.

I realized I'd said this rather often this month. It was all in good humor. She was brilliant and a great help in everything I did. What was not to love?

"Sorry, Dag," she broke in before I could answer. Somewhere in our banter I'd struck a nerve that I knew nothing about. "Nobody does," she continued. "Nobody ever will. I'm a freak of nature and that's just the way it's going to be."

"Riley," I said moving over beside her on the sofa. Our conversation had been so spirited and intense for the past hour and a half I hadn't noticed any effect it was having on Riley. "Why do you think that?" I asked putting my hands on her shoulders and turning her to face me. "You are funny, charming, brilliant, and beautiful. Any guy in his right mind would be in love with you. Including me. Why do you put yourself down? Why don't you tell Santa what you'd like for Christmas?"

I looked at her as a tear began to run from her eye. Then she slowly reached up and dragged the wig off her head—her perfectly smooth, bald head. She pulled one of my unbelieving hands up to her head.

"Nobody wants a freak," she said. She started to get up, but I pulled her down in my arms and held her, softly stroking the silky smooth skin on her perfectly shaped head.

"Tell me about it," I said softly. "Are you in chemotherapy?"

"I wish it were that easy an explanation," she said. "Though, believe me, I wouldn't trade places. I don't have a fatal disease. It's called Alopecia. It's a hair loss syndrome that is not as rare as you might think and is most common among women. For some it is temporary and the hair grows back. Mine hit at adolescence and all the hair on my body fell out. None has ever grown back." She held up her arm and pulled back her sleeve. Her arm was perfectly smooth and hairless.

"Men are plenty interested when they see me, but not one has been able to see a future with a bald freak. And now you're disgusted, too."

She was crying freely now and I just continued to hold her in my arms and stroke her head. She seemed to love having me touch the now-exposed skin. Well, why not. We all love to have our head's stroked.

"You have never disgusted me, Riley," I said. "I've always loved you, and I always will."

That seemed to make things worse. At least she was crying more.

"My Dad always said that," she choked out. She hugged me more tightly and I finally began to see what she really got out of our relationship.

"Is that what you have nightmares about?" I asked. She probably didn't realize that I knew about the nightmares. I'd found out one night on the long drive back to Seattle after my Las Vegas heart attack. She looked up at me, blinking the tears out of her eyes.

"I haven't had a nightmare for months now. Probably because I didn't sleep at all last week, but still… They stopped a while back." I smiled. That was good.

"My mother was an alcoholic," Riley continued. "An abusive alcoholic. From the time I started losing my hair she ridiculed me. She said I should join the circus because I was a clown. My father had to work to support us, but he protected me as much as he could. He defended me to my mother and was always the parent that went to school to deal with the situations I got myself into. He's the one who took me out to buy my first real wig."

"She gave me a fright wig to wear. Told me it was the right thing for a clown. The thing is I was so ashamed of my head that I wore it. When Dad got called to school he was furious. He took me out right then and got me a real hair wig. He and Mom had a terrible to-do that night."

"That sounds awful," I said.

She wiped her eyes on the back of her hand and leaned into my shoulder. I've always been a little stiff around women. I've been told more than once that I had wooden hugs. I just let her fit where she wanted, and it was somehow comfortable.

"All through high school it was like that," Riley continued. "Growing six inches in a year didn't help either. Clothes and wigs put a huge strain on our family budget."

"What happened to your Mom and Dad?" I asked. "I've never met them or heard you mention them."

"There was an accident soon after my twenty-first birthday. I was so glad to leave home and go to college, and yet so afraid to live any-where else. It was terrifying, but I didn't have to wake up to my mother yelling 'hey Baldy!' every morning. My Dad called me one Friday while he was still at work to see how I was doing. I loved him so much for all he'd done for me when I was growing up, and I hated him so much for keeping us with an abusive witch of a woman."

"Why didn't they divorce?" I asked.

"Laws or no laws, it is almost impossible for a father to prove that he is a fitter parent than a mother. I heard them talk about divorce, and I heard my mother threaten that he would never see me again. I suppose he figured that it was better to stay together where he could protect me part of the time. But I hated it all the same."

"And when he called?" I prompted.

"I told him I was fine and happy. I was on my own. I'd made friends. No one at school knew I was bald. As long as it stayed that way, I was safe. It kind of limited my potential romances, but it was worth it. We talked about nothing important and he said he just wanted to hear my voice again. That night he and mom went to one of the casinos up on I-5. Apparently they both got pretty blitzed. He headed north on I-5 when they left instead of south. About ten miles later, he drove off the bridge into the Stillaguamish River at 110 miles per hour. The autopsies said they were both in excess of 1% blood alcohol."

"That's terrible," I said holding her more tightly. "You poor, poor baby."

"The thing is, Dag, I never saw my father drink a drop in my life. He always thought that one parent should be sober. I think he did it on purpose, and I've been so afraid I'd end up the same way." Now Riley was sobbing so hard that I could barely contain my own tears.

I just held her and rocked back and forth, petted her poor hairless head, and whispered "You never have to be afraid with me." The sobs subsided after an eternity.

After another eternity, I realized she was sleeping in my arms. It was midnight.

I gently laid her down on the sofa and covered her with a blanket.

I settled myself into my chair and took a last look at the picture in front of me. That picture has traveled with me for nearly forty years, and I still can't figure it out. I fell asleep with the image in my mind.

Walking Into the Light

THE CLOSE CONTACT with Riley sent me back to my own adolescence and I had painful dreams.

There is something I believe only happens once in your life. This blanket statement is based on the exhaustive research of my fifty-seven years. For me it happened the fall of my sophomore year in high school. Rhonda and I were high school sweethearts and dated (on and off) for three years. We'd started talking to each other in the hall at school because I'd lost an assignment and asked her if she had it. But we kept talking. And talking. We met for lunch and talked. We met at football games and sat together. And talked.

At homecoming that fall, I asked her to go to the dance with me. We were both just old enough to date at school events and nothing more. We talked until the music got so loud we couldn't hear anymore, and then we got up and danced until we were sweaty and exhausted.

The dance ended and I walked Rhonda home. It was after 11:00 and we had midnight curfews, so we weren't talking much as we walked through the Ballard neighborhood where we lived.

Then it happened.

The backs of our hands touched as we walked along. Once. Twice. The third time they seemed to stick together and we walked with just the backs of our hands touching for nearly two blocks.

And we didn't say a word.

I'm not even sure I breathed in that whole time.

A sixteen-year-old boy can transfer every nerve ending in his body to a single square inch of skin that is touching a girl for the first time. Not that we'd never touched each other before. But for those two blocks, there was no other reason to be touching each other than that we wanted to.

And it completely took my breath away.

For forty years after that night, every time I thought of it everything around me stood still and I lived in that square inch of contact. It is the single moment in a lifetime that you realize that someone outside your own skin can become so important that the rest of the world disappears. And that first realization happens only once.

There is never a second first time.

Two weeks later we went into the football stadium and took seats next to our friends Randy and Kay. Kay and Rhonda sat between Randy and me which was okay because both of us guys were more interested in the girls than in each other. As we got settled, I reached over and Rhonda took my hand in hers. We sat there holding hands.

"That was fast!" Kay said. I looked at her with complete lack of comprehension until I saw the disappointed look on Randy's face as he held his hand palm up on his knee, being ignored by Kay. To us, it was where our hands belonged. On the other hand, Randy and Kay married right out of high school, had three kids, and lived happily ever after.

That first experience isn't necessarily an omen of the future.

I was a good student in math and science. Rhonda was an artist. She was, in fact, a very good artist and it was her skill at design and art that kept her active in everything from decorating for the prom to editing the school newspaper. I loved to look at what she painted, even though I couldn't tell her that the colors she described to me as she painted were no more real to me than the numbers in the national debt. There were a lot more of them than I would ever see.

In the fall of our senior year, we went with friends up to Whidbey Island and climbed to the top of Goose Rock. Rhonda wanted to look at the sunset so she could paint it someday, and we managed in the process to get separated from our friends. It turned out that we liked it up there, and the sun was moving westward over the Straits of Juan de Fuca. We sat up there watching the sunset, holding hands on the rock. I couldn't remember ever watching a sunset like that. There are pretty ones in Seattle, but looking out to sea and seeing the sun sink into it was a breath-taking experience.

I didn't know what I'd missed until about nine months later.

It was the week before high school graduation and for all practical purposes seniors had cut out of school. We were meeting for parties and making general fools of ourselves. I wasn't too surprised when Rhonda invited me over to her house one afternoon. In fact, I had hopes that this might be a sign that we were going to consummate our relationship. We'd had some rocky patches during the year, but everything was great now as far as I could tell.

The surprise she gave me wasn't sex.

She had me sit on her sofa in the living room while she went to get my surprise. I closed my eyes as she instructed and when she told me to open them she was standing in front of me holding a painting. It took me a few minutes to recognize it as the sunset on Goose Rock.

"This is a going away present," she said. I had already enlisted in the navy and would have about thirty days after graduation before I reported for duty. You might think it was crazy for me to enlist right out of school, but I didn't have the money to go to college, and if I didn't enlist I was sure to be drafted. I figured the Navy was a good place because North Viet Nam didn't have one.

"It's nice," I said. "But I'd rather have you." Neither subtlety nor tact was my strong suit. She looked at me steadily, but I could see a glistening in her eyes. I was afraid I'd really hurt her feelings.

"It's also a good-bye present," she said. That totally didn't sink in. She sat down beside me on the sofa and held the picture in front of the two of us, almost in the position that I remembered looking at the sunset from Goose Rock. She really captured it, I had to admit. I could almost feel that same awe and tug that I felt watching the sun fall into the sea.

"I'm not going to be here when you get out of the service, Dag," she said. "I'm going away to college and we are going to start living different lives. Someday you'll find the perfect woman for you, and you'll live happily ever after like a fairy tale. But she's not me. I realized it the day we sat up on this rock."

"But… I don't get it," I said. "I thought we were, you know… that we would… How did you know then?"

"Remember what we did?" she asked. I nodded. "Everybody else headed down off the rock to get to the cars, but I kept you there to watch the sunset. That wasn't actually what I wanted. I wanted you to show passion and smother me with kisses when we were alone. I wanted to make love. I wanted it to be magic." Now that was a shock to me. She'd wanted that? Then?

"Instead," she continued, "you held my hand like a perfect gentleman and stared out at the sunset. Then you were worried that we'd get in trouble if we didn't get back down and you carefully led me back to the group. I appreciate you being a gentleman, Dag, but it just wasn't magic. I want something more in my life, and I realized up there that you want something more, too." She called my attention back to the painting that I found was a little blurry due to an abundance of water in my eyes.

"See that?" she asked.

"The sunset?" I responded.

"No, down here." I looked and on the beach there was a tiny figure.

"It's someone on the beach."

"It's you."

"I was up on Goose Rock. I was never on that beach."

"Yes you were. I was holding your hand up on that rock and you were a mile away looking out at the ocean. I could see you on the beach as clearly as if I had a telescope. And when I painted the picture, I couldn't stop until I'd put you out there on the beach where you belonged. I knew that even though I'd always love you, we weren't connected in the kind of way that we wanted."

"But we are, Rhonda," I began. "I've never wanted anyone but you."

"Shhh," she said. She kissed me a long lingering kiss that I tried to push a little further, but I knew one thing for sure, I would never force myself on her. I could taste her tears when our lips parted.

Or maybe they were mine.

I didn't understand then, or at any time after. I thought at first that if I sat and stared at the painting, it would all come clear to me. I left it at home when I went into the Navy, but two years later, it was still there, hanging on my bedroom wall. I took it with me to college and hung it in my dorm room. I hung it in my first home with Brenda and would still sit in front of it while I played music, trying to discover if I had found what I was looking for out there.

Perhaps if I could really see the colors in the sunset, I'd know what it was that she was trying to tell me. I just knew that I'd never feel what I felt when the backs of our hands touched that first time.

Then, it seemed, I was suddenly old, and I touched the top of Riley's head. And all the nerves in my body were transferred into that square inch of contact. It was different, but I knew that I'd never loved anyone like that before.

Desperate Attempts

SOMETIME BEFORE DAWN my phone jangled me awake and I fumbled to answer it. What I heard didn't make sense.

"…see her again… …laptop and back-ups… Wait for our call…" None of it made sense. Then…

"Dag, it's Riley. I'm so sorry." Then the line was dead.

Riley? She was asleep in the living room on the sofa. I must have moved to the bedroom sometime in the middle of the night because I distinctly remember holding her and her falling asleep. I covered her up.

I got up and pulled on a robe. What time was it? 5:30 a.m.? I wandered into the living room, expecting to see Riley stretched out on the sofa.

It was all neat and clean. No blanket. No pillow. Even my chair was upright and the afghan that I keep there was folded neatly on the side table.

This was surreal. There was no sign that Riley had been at my house at all. What happened to the Chinese food containers that we had eaten from? I went to the kitchen and checked the garbage, but it was empty with a new bag in the garbage pail.

I automatically put water on to boil. I needed a cup of coffee.

No. Wait a minute. I was on the program. I needed a new heart.

I felt my chest. It felt fine. Maybe I just imagined it all.

How much? Simon? Brenda? Angel?

Riley?

I felt suddenly alone and afraid. I began to worry. Maybe I was dead. I went back to the bedroom and looked at my bed to see if I was still in it. The bedclothes were rumpled where I'd just gotten out of it. Maizie looked up at me from her basket beside the bed and then jumped up and stretched. She padded over to me and snuffled against my leg.

No, I wasn't dead. I wouldn't have a wet cold nose pressed against my leg if I was dead. If I was dead, a little mutt wouldn't be running to the door to be taken out.

I pulled on trousers and a jacket and grabbed my umbrella before taking Maizie out into the early morning rain. Something just wasn't right.

After we had walked, I fixed breakfast, showered, and dressed for the office. Program or no program, I was stopping at Tovoni's this morning. I needed a cup of coffee. They open at 7:00 even on Saturday, so Maizie and I put on our jackets and headed out. I figured that by the time I got to the office my head would be clear and I'd be able to sort out whatever was happening.

Tovoni's was closed.

Damn.

I looked at my watch again. 7:15. I looked at the hours on the door. Monday-Friday 7:00 a.m.–9:00 p.m. Saturday 7:00 a.m.-7:00 p.m. Closed Sundays. I glanced down at the headlines on the newspaper in the paper box by the door. "Seattle moves to forefront in battle to save lives." "Loyalists seize Iraqi TV station."

I stared at the paper for several minutes trying to figure out what was out of place. The huge words at the top of the newspaper finally sank in—**Sunday Edition.**

When did it become Sunday? Friday night Riley and I had talked late into the night and she fell asleep crying in my arms. Now it was Sunday morning? Did I sleep through all of Saturday? How could that be?

Maizie was getting impatient so we continued on toward the office.

"Well, girl, I'm not supposed to have coffee anyway," I said as we walked along. "Would you let me know what happened yesterday?"

At the office I toweled Maizie off and sat down at my desk while she curled up in her bed by the window. I opened my computer and tried to rebuild what I knew was planned for Saturday to try to jog my memory. What were my plans?

"Eat and sleep. That's all you have to do, isn't it girl?" I said casually. "And poop."

Okay. That was first. Maizie goes with Mrs. Prior on Saturday to get her grooming done. I looked over at the slightly soggy pink bow attached to her collar. She had been to the groomer. Check.

I usually play cards in the afternoon at the Swedish American Center. It would be easy enough to check with a friend about that, but I wasn't going to call anyone at 8:00 on Sunday morning.

And Riley. Riley hadn't intended to spend the night Friday, but fell asleep on my sofa. She was going to take me to the SA Center Saturday afternoon and then go to a party Saturday night with Cinnamon and some of the girls at the condo. I wasn't enthused about that, but Riley insisted that it would be okay. She had become friends with Cinnamon, and even though my identity was out, Riley was still playing at being my girlfriend. The condo was closed for a "girls' night" holiday party. I flipped open my phone and pressed her speed-dial number. The phone rolled immediately over to voicemail. Either the phone was off, or she was on it.

I went to my window and stared out at the Elliott Bay. God, I love that view. On a clear day I can see Mount Rainier from here. Today wasn't clear. But I could imagine where its dominant shape would rise, just over the stadiums down there, if it were clear.

A ferry left the terminal, and traffic was beginning to pick up. I turned my eyes uphill toward the Market and looked at some of the newer high-rise apartments and condos between my office and the Harbor Steps.

It's funny. I had never noticed before that I could see the building where the party condo occupied the top floor. Of course not. Why would I notice it before I'd actually been there? Nonetheless, I went to my desk and got out a pair of binoculars from the drawer. Usually I use them to watch for orcas and dolphins in the Sound. This time I trained them on the top of that building.

I didn't recognize the condo at first. The roof seemed bare of any gardens that I could see. Then I realized that there was a lower roof with glass doors leading inside. On this rooftop deck, there were, indeed, a few plantings, and I assumed if I had a better angle I'd be able to see the hot tub. That could have made for some interesting nighttime viewing, I thought.

My curiosity sated, I was about to lower the glasses when I saw a flash of movement. I refocused in time to see a woman run to the edge of the roof and look over. A huge block of a man grabbed her from behind and dragged her back from the edge. She fought him, but the fellow swung and connected with her face. I watched in horror as I first thought her head had flown off the building and then realized that the floating object was a wig.

I fell back into my chair gasping for breath as if I'd been the one struck. Riley was in trouble. My head was too fuzzy this morning. I couldn't work out why she would be at the condo in the morning. I couldn't imagine who had called me. And Riley had said what? She was sorry?

The phone rang, moving me into action. It wasn't a dream. What did they want, and who besides the refrigerator man, Oksamma, was holding her?

"Do you have the disks?" the voice demanded. I already had a good idea who it was, even though he was trying to disguise his voice. I had the presence of mind to snatch a press-on mic and push the record button on my laptop.

"What disks?" I asked. "I didn't understand anything you said this morning. You woke me up."

"Well, get this straight then," he said. "I want Simon Barnett's computer and the backup disks. You get them to me and I'll give you back your bald little freak." God, I hoped Riley wasn't in hearing distance. I would wring that coward's scrawny neck with my bare hands. I kept my voice under control as I answered.

"None of that will do you any good, Bradley," I said. "The money is all gone."

"All what money?" Bradley dropped all pretense of disguising his voice.

"All the money," I said. "All the BKL assets were liquidated over the weekend. By tomorrow morning there won't be anything left. Just give up and turn yourself in."

"Who cares about BKL? It was nothing," he dug in. "Simon is trying to pin all his dirty little tricks on me and I'm not going to stand for it."

"Your thug already killed Simon. Didn't he tell you?"

"You think he's mine? You're some hotshot dick. I don't want to be next, understand? I need that computer. Either you bring it, or your little bald-headed girlfriend suffers a permanent accident. She just couldn't live looking like such a goddam freak. It's that simple." That was twice, Bradley. I looked through my binoculars at the condo garden. A ladder led from the rooftop down to the patio. The boxy shape of a roof-access stair enclosure poked up from the roof. I wondered how far I would have to climb to get to Bradley. He was really pissing me off.

"Fine Bradley. Don't hurt her. Where do you want me to bring the laptop?" I didn't want to let him know that I knew where Riley was held. Bradley might not be there. There was a pause. I had the feeling that he hadn't prepared this very well. He was improvising.

"Wrap it in plastic and take it to the market. Slip it under the haddock at the fish stall—the one with the "Low Flying Fish" sign. Have it there in one hour. I'll have my contact pick it up."

"It will be there," I said. "How do I know Riley is okay?" I heard him yell at Riley and the phone was pushed close enough to her that she could speak.

"Dag," she gasped. "Don't give them anything. Don't give them the disks." The phone was snatched away and I heard a smack and cry.

"Loyal bitch," Bradley said. "If that computer and the backup disks aren't at the fish market in sixty minutes, she'll be the one on ice." The phone went dead. I looked at the recent calls list and saved the number. I might need it. What was important now was that I act quickly.

I dialed Jordan's number and got his answering machine. I told him Riley was at the condo and played my recording of the phone conversation into the open receiver onto Jordan's answering machine. Then I hung up.

I opened the vault and pulled out Simon's computer and the two copies I had made of the hard drive. There wasn't enough time to make another backup, but it was pretty well worthless now anyway. Just for good measure, I removed the jump-drive and left it in the vault. There is always bubble-wrap in the office from drives that have been delivered. I taped a makeshift bag around the laptop and the two disk drives, and headed toward Pike Place Market. I went in through the lower parking garage and took the elevator up seven floors to the skybridge across to the Market. As soon as I was out of the concrete structure I opened my cell phone and tried Jordan again. He was either out of range or couldn't get to his phone.

I came across the sky-bridge directly toward the fish market, a Seattle landmark where they throw the fish when the workers fill people's orders. I checked my watch. It was close to 9:30—twenty-five minutes since I got Bradley's call. I was panting. The merchants had just dumped a fresh load of crushed ice in the bins that would be filled with fish by 10:00. As they moved to the back of the market to wheel out the racks of fish, I frantically dug in the ice at the near corner and shoved the computer under it. I really didn't care if anyone saw me doing it. Bradley hadn't said to be subtle, and had chosen a ridiculously public place to stow his precious goods. As long as no one dug it out before he got there, I really didn't care.

I retraced my footsteps to the stairway down a level in the market. This quiet area had less traffic, and if Bradley or Oksamma was on his way, I didn't want to run into him. I surfaced at the north end of the

Market on Western and headed for the condo. It was nearly 10:00 on Sunday morning. I was betting that there was no one but the two kidnappers with Riley at the condo. I entered through the garage, practically collapsing from lack of breath. My heart was thudding in my chest like it would burst at any moment. I didn't have time for that. I fumbled for my pills and swallowed two, then opened my eyes and focused on the surroundings. The standard elevator was where I remembered, but I looked further and found a loading dock with access to a service elevator. It was key-locked it took a few minutes to pick it with my pocket knife. I entered and jammed my finger onto the button for the next to top floor. I didn't want to take the chance of having the doors open only to be staring directly into the face of the Refrigerator. I was going to have to climb the last two flights to the roof.

Standing at the open stairwell and looking up, I almost gave up. It was too much. I could no more climb those flights of stairs than Mt. Everest. Who was I kidding?

Damn!

I struggled forward and up to the first landing before I had to stop to rest. A few minutes later I had made it to the second landing. Stop. Breathe. Climb. Stop. Breathe. Climb. Stop. It seemed like an eternity. I cleared my eyes and looked at the crash-bar on the door ahead of me. There were no more stairs. Somehow I'd reached the top. I slammed through the door and was almost blown from the roof by the gusts of wind that whipped across the tops of the buildings. The gusts brought stinging bites of fine wet snow. I hadn't worn a coat or gloves when I left the office. I still wasn't sure I could finish this.

If my footsteps on the roof didn't alert the kidnappers below me of my presence, I felt sure my gasping breath and pounding heart would. The first edge of the roof I stumbled toward was the wrong one, and I found myself staring down onto First Avenue. I reeled back and regained my bearings. There was the escape ladder to the penthouse patio. From there, a network of ladders led down the waterside of the building. This was one of the few buildings in central Seattle that still had an outdoor fire escape. I knew now that was where Riley was headed when I'd seen her subdued by Oksamma an hour-and-a-half ago.

I surveyed the patio from above before lowering myself over the side and dropping down quietly behind the hot tub. A vinyl cover was over the water, but I could feel heat radiating from the tub anyway. I turned to my left and ducked back into a corner by the tub and a potted plant. I was directly next to a window that I hadn't noticed before. Had there not been a light on, I would not have been able to see through the silvered glass into the room beyond. It was an office space, and standing with his back to me was Oksamma. Beyond him, Riley was tied to a desk chair with her own scarf. She was wearing that same incredible cocktail dress that was one of my most vivid memories of my first heart attack.

But she was bareheaded.

I couldn't see well enough through what was clearly intended to be one-way glass to tell how badly she was hurt. I knew she had taken at least one nasty blow to the face. I didn't see Bradley in the room, so I assumed he must be on the errand to retrieve the laptop.

Staying low and as sheltered as I could, I made my way across the exposed patio to the sliding doors into the living room. They were unlocked, much to my relief. Who would lock doors onto a private patio twelve stories above the street? I glanced behind and thought I still saw Oksamma's back through the window, but I was at a bad angle now and picking up huge reflections of the potted trees. I was going to need a weapon and a way to get Oksamma out of the office. I would cut Riley free and we'd escape down the main elevator. That sounded simple.

I rushed toward the bar and slid to a stop just before slamming headlong into the ex-marine Davy Jones, Angel's jealous boyfriend. I had no time to think. I could see him reacting to my sudden appearance already. Before he could deck me this time, I felt my hand close around an object on the bar. I swung it hard and fast and felt the very satisfying thunk of a champagne bottle meeting the side of Davy's head. His simultaneous blow glanced off my jaw, but was enough to shake me just the same. He stood facing me and I could see his hand drawing back for a second try as he crumpled to the floor, unconscious.

That was too close. I was already surprised that the racket hadn't brought Oksamma running, but apparently the noise was nothing out of the ordinary for the kitchen. I couldn't just leave him there, though. I had no idea how long he would be out. I couldn't afford to have him wake up and alert anyone. I stripped off my belt and strapped his hands together behind his back. Then I tied his shoelaces together to hold his feet. I dragged him into the living room by the windows and used his own belt to tie his hands to his feet. Finally, I ran into the kitchen, grabbed a couple of dish towels, stuffed one in his mouth, and used the other to tie it in place.

I stood back and surveyed my work, panting with my head spinning. There was one more thing. I pushed the heavy leather sofa back, pinning him between it and the windows. I would like to have done more, but at that point I heard Bradley slam through the front entrance and I ducked down so he couldn't see me as he stormed through the condo and into the office swearing. I wasn't sure what his problem was; he should have had the computer by now. I still needed a knife to try to cut Riley loose. I needed to get them out of that room.

As I got closer, I heard Bradley ranting.

"The disks aren't here, bitch!" he yelled. "He doesn't care that much about you, does he? He packaged up the computer with two hard drives. Where are the disks?"

"If you had listened to me when you started, you'd know he doesn't even know about the disks," Riley spat back. "I stole them and didn't tell him."

"You couldn't do anything without him knowing about it," Bradley spat back. "If you know where they are, you are going to tell me."

"Never." I heard the sound of flesh slapping flesh. If I ran in there now, Oksamma would simply pummel me and we'd both be goners. I flipped open my cell phone and pulled up Bradley's number that I'd saved earlier. He answered on the first ring.

"Who is it?" he snapped.

"Touch her again and I'll kill you where you stand, Bradley." There was a sudden silence.

"Where are you?"

"Where I can see you and the lummox you are with standing in the office. You should really patrol your perimeter more frequently."

"Davy!" he yelled. "Get out on the deck and find Hamar!"

"Davy is indisposed," I spoke quietly. "I don't think he'll be looking for me. You'd better come yourself, Bradley." I heard Riley squeal and could tell that she'd been grabbed. "Let go of her Bradley. You can't get her between us."

I saw from the kitchen Oksamma suddenly come rushing from the office and out the patio doors. I disconnected from Bradley and followed the refrigerator as quickly as I could, slid the door shut and locked it. There was a safety pole standing at the frame and I dropped it into the track. Even if he succeeded in getting the lock opened, the pole would stop the door from sliding in its track. Now to deal with Bradley.

I moved to where I could see the open door of the office. Bradley was cowering in a corner of the office that appeared somewhat shielded from the outside window by the desk. As far as I could tell, the only weapon in his hands was the cell phone. I grabbed a knife and a sharpening steel from the counter. Then I crept into the study. Bradley was intent on the window where I could see Oksamma gesturing that he'd found nothing and motioning Bradley to the locked door.

Sometimes a headlong rush is not the best idea. I decided to sneak into the room and try to get to Riley as quietly as possible. I knew we'd stand a better chance if she was free. I wasn't counting on Oksamma's frantic gesturing at me through the window to alert Bradley. I was behind Riley when he turned and saw me. I couldn't free her, but I put the knife in her hand before I leapt for Bradley, brandishing my steel.

He frantically jerked a drawer out of the desk so hard that it scattered its contents on the floor and he dove for the gun that fell. I didn't have much time. Oksamma had moved back to the patio doors and was slamming into them with all his massive weight. It wouldn't take long for us to be pinned down.

I cracked Bradley's wrist with the steel just as his hand closed around the gun. He howled in pain and I whacked it again. The gun went skittering across the floor as I heard a crash from the direction of the patio doors. Bradley was diving for the gun with his other hand and I grabbed him. We wrestled in front of the window. I knew that I had only moments before Oksamma would slam into me and end it all. I knew I had to drop Bradley fast, but my hands weren't working with my mind. I couldn't move them to hit him. I couldn't make them work.

My sudden limp state was what saved my life. Oksamma rushed through the door and Riley, who had managed to free herself, moved to intercept him. Bradley grabbed the gun. I dropped and Riley propelled the giant using his own momentum across the room.

Oksamma crashed into Bradley as the gun went off. Bradley, borne backward by Oksamma's weight crashed into and through the window onto the patio. Oksamma howled and rolled over clutching his leg. Riley had her hands under my arms and was hauling me out of the room before I knew what happened.

"Go!" I croaked. "Leave me and get to Jordan."

"Not on your life, partner," she growled back. As we stumbled out into the foyer, I could see Oksamma crawling toward the abandoned gun. Fortunately the elevator was still at the floor from Bradley's arrival only minutes before. We fell into it and Riley punched the floor button. As the doors closed three rapid shots slammed into them. Riley fell back on top of me.

"No!" I screeched. I cradled her in my arms as blood blossomed from her side. When the doors of the elevator slid apart in the lobby, I scooped her up and out into the foyer. We stumbled through the huge front doors just as Oksamma came crashing through the escape stair door onto the street. He waved the gun in my direction and I heard the shot ring out. But instead of feeling the pain or sudden death, I watched as Oksamma fell to the ground. I turned and fell forward, directly into the arms of Jordan Grant and a stampede of officers piling out of cars that were still screeching to a stop.

He caught Riley from me and in the sudden release of her weight from my arms everything gave out. I could feel my heart pounding in my ears. My vision went from slightly fuzzy to reddened as blood swam in my eyes. I could not draw a breath. My legs folded under me and I knew that this was the one I'd been waiting for. I saw Riley turn her head in Jordan's arms. She looked at me with her penetrating blue eyes and I fell into them.

Drifting

THEY SAY WHEN YOU DIE there is a white light at the end of a tunnel and you go toward the light. I could see the light, but it didn't get any closer. I couldn't figure out how to move toward it. Nothing seemed to work. I couldn't walk. I didn't know how to fly. I just drifted there seeing the light.

I was keeping time by counting my heartbeats. Somewhere around a thousand I lost track. How long is a thousand heartbeats?

Assuming I had a heart rate of around seventy beats per minute, I'd knock out a thousand pumps of my heart every fifteen minutes. I could still do math.

After the third thousand, I realized that being a human clock was a tedious thing.

I shut down and slept.

The light was back. Someone should tell hospitals that the beep that the machine sitting by your bed makes is not conducive to sound sleeping. But as the incessant beeping penetrated my mind, I realized what it meant. I was alive.

For all I knew, Bradley had escaped and was at this very moment getting ready to kill us all again. How did such an inept dolt get in the middle of all this? Bradley, who was laundering half a billion dollars for the mob, who had me put a laptop computer under a pile of ice in a public market. He really wasn't smart enough for this job.

Who was? Riley could figure it out. Was she alive? I heard the beeps on the machine speed up with my heart rate. She had to be alive.

I promised her. She wouldn't have to be afraid when she was with me. I promised.

Angel. She was funneling money through her travel agency, but so were dozens of others, probably without even knowing what was happening. Angel just wanted to be with a rich, powerful man. So why did she bother with Davy Jones? Because he was strong?

Brenda. She owned the condo. Did she know? She collected pictures of herself with powerful people. Did she collect the rent from them as well?

Simon. Smart enough. Smarter than all of them. Smarter than me. Simon could manage that kind of money—change its form—put it into the economy under a legitimate guise. Simon was dead; wasn't he?

I went back to sleep.

It was better than light the next time I woke up. Something soft and lingering touched my parched lips. Even through the cracked dryness the touch was arousing. My eyes flicked open of their own accord. Riley's blonde mop was next to my face and her lips were caressing mine. She realized suddenly that I was awake and pulled away.

"Hey you," I said with my best effort at a smile. Woken from death by a beautiful woman. This was becoming a cliché.

"Hey Sleeping Beauty," she answered.

"Wakened by Princess Charming's kiss," I responded. "I didn't know where I was for a while. Are you all right?"

"Me?" she asked. "I'm going to have a nice little scar under my arm, but it's hardly more than a bandaid job."

I raised my hand to her face. It was bruised almost black on one side, no matter how much foundation makeup she put over it. Her eye was swollen and her lip was cut. I gently drew my fingers across her cheek and her eyes fluttered closed in the stillness as I touched her.

"I let you down," I said. "I let them hurt you."

"You couldn't have done more than you did, Dag," she said. "I brought it on myself when I stole the disks from Brenda's house."

"You did what?"

"I broke into Brenda's house a few days ago, while you were flying home from Atlanta. I searched the office for backup disks for Simon's computer. There was too much information missing that should have been there when we examined the hard drive. I thought they might have backed it up before they erased it. So I went looking for backups and I found them. That's how I found out that Brenda owned the condo."

"That's why you went to the party there Saturday night," I said. "You were hoping to gather more evidence about what was going on."

"You said Simon had outsmarted himself when he encrypted the jump-drive," Riley said. "It looks like I was too smart for myself when I decided to wade into the condo. I slipped away from the other girls while they were playing a drinking game on pretense of going to the bathroom. I slipped into the office to look for records. I was too intent on what I was looking for to notice someone was already in the room. I didn't realize it until I was falling face first into a vase of lilacs after being cracked on the back of the head."

"Bradley hit you?" I said. "He's got a lot to account for."

"His accounting is over," Riley said. "Jordan was here most of the night. He says that when the Refrigerator fell on Bradley and knocked him through the window, Bradley fell on the cut glass and was stabbed through the back. He was dead before the police got up to the condo. I'm sorry, Dag. It was my actions that killed him."

"No, Riley," I said straightening a lock of hair that jutted out from her head. You might as well say that he killed himself. He brought it all down on himself. What about the Refrigerator?"

"Jordan shot him," Riley said simply. "There was no question that he was going to shoot you."

"Dead?" I asked. She nodded her head. Poor Jordan. He wasn't the kind of man to take killing even a criminal like Oksamma lightly. "What day is it?" I asked.

"It's Monday night," Riley said. "You've been mostly out of it for about thirty hours. I was discharged this morning. Stevie brought me a wig she was cleaning for me and Teri stopped by my apartment to bring me clothes. I ran to the office to make sure Mrs. Prior had picked up Maizie and grabbed your computer. I needed something to do while I sat here."

"How did you get into my computer?"

"Same as last time," she said. "You only have so many fingers, you know."

I took the computer from her and opened up a "new user" screen. I reached over and took her hand and placed her index finger on the scanner, then logged out.

"There," I said, "now I have ten more to choose from."

She looked at me and bent over the bed to kiss me again. Not passionate, but soft.

"Dag, I was so afraid," she said.

"Those guys would scare anybody, kiddo."

"I wasn't scared of them. I was afraid I'd lost you. What would I do without you?"

There were a lot of things I could have told her. A lot I wanted to say. But overwhelming lethargy was taking its toll on me again. All I could say was, "Don't worry. We're safe now." Then I drifted off to sleep again.

Payoffs

I SWAM UP OUT OF MY SLEEP more easily this morning. Either the painkillers they had me on were working or I was feeling better. I opened my eyes and they focused slowly on the red hair and freckled face of Jordan Grant.

"Damn," I said. "I was getting used to beautiful women waking me up."

"You're welcome," he said. "I assume that was a thank you for saving your wretched hide Sunday."

"It was," I moaned. "And for saving Riley."

"That was an unexpected bonus. She is one hot…" he broke off. "Sorry. Strictly business. I thought you'd like to know what was in the truck."

"Do tell," I said. "We had theories."

"Well did any of them have to do with the upcoming release of a major computer operating system?" he asked. We'd definitely been a little slow on that one. "There was, at first calculation, twenty-two million dollars worth of counterfeit software in that truck. It became obvious that they weren't taking it anywhere. They just drove back and forth from Seattle to Spokane. The one time they actually unloaded, it was at an interstate rest area where they transferred goods from one truck to another. We finally pulled both trucks over because if they kept splitting it up, we'd never have enough people to follow all of them. The drivers were very cooperative. They hadn't received orders

202

yet as to where to take the stuff. Apparently they were intending to keep it moving until just before stores got the official software in, and then start delivering theirs."

"The joys of never knowing when a product is going to ship," I said. "Bradley's timing sucked on everything."

"Well it would have been enough to convict him if he wasn't dead already. We've moved on BKL to confiscate everything in the offices. Everyone at headquarters is a little ticked that there's no one to convict."

Thoughts started rolling around in my head faster than lightning. No one to convict. Bradley was just as scared of Oksamma as Simon was. Oksamma didn't work for him, he was there representing someone else's interest. Someone who was still in the shadows.

"What about Davy Jones?" I asked.

"Hired help. He was security chief for the condo, he says. He thought Deb was being held because she had tried to steal something. That's what they told him. Said as soon as they knew who she was working for, they were going to turn her over to the police." Jordan sighed. "He was a Marine. He's used to following orders, and having served in Iraq, he's used to some of them not sounding entirely legal when they are given. I think he really thought he was acting in the best interests of his employer. What did you hit him with, by the way? He was out most of Sunday afternoon."

"A bottle of champagne," I said. That means I'd wasted precious minutes tying up a non-threat. When I got out of the hospital, I was through with being a detective. Riley was much better suited to the business than I was.

"He thought you'd hit him with your fist," Jordan laughed. "He has a tremendous amount of respect for you now."

"Well, don't tell him otherwise, will you?" I chuckled. A true pack animal. You respect the one who is more powerful. I decked him, I'm the alpha male. How simple. "By the way, did you find out exactly who he worked for? The condo isn't a business in and of itself is it?"

"No. His payment, he says, always came from BKL. Apparently it was one of the businesses they were in. We hope that the records will show a flow of money from certain high profile men in this city in the form of bribes and blackmail." Jordan broke off when his phone rang. He snapped it open and listened quietly. "Thanks," he said and broke off the call.

"It appears that I should make myself scarce," he said to me. "That was Deb in the lobby. She says that Brenda Barnett just asked for your room number at the front desk." My hand moved of its own volition and grabbed Jordan's arm. BKL. It wasn't Barnett, Keane, and Lamb. It was Brenda Katherine Lamb. Chances are that Bradley didn't even know he was being manipulated by the silent partner of the firm, his erstwhile lover, Brenda Barnett. Riley told me that she had found records indicating that it was Brenda who owned the condo.

"I hate to put you in the closet, Jordan," I said. "But I'd like you to stay close and out of sight for this."

"You think she's…?" he questioned. I nodded. Without another word, Jordan stepped into the closet and pulled the door closed. I didn't think she was personally dangerous, but it crossed my mind that she might be coming to close my final chapter. I breathed out to relax my suddenly tensing muscles and struggled to prop myself more upright in bed. This was not a good meeting ground for an encounter with Brenda. I heard her heels in the hallway long before she got to my door. The waft of her lilac perfume preceded her through the door.

"Dagget, sweety," she said, coming through the door. "I think I owe you hazard pay. I had no idea this little job would be so dangerous for you." She swept across the room and bent to kiss my forehead.

I sneezed.

"You never could stand my perfume," she said jumping back and grabbing a tissue to mop herself off.

"What brings you up on this visit, Brenda?" I asked. "I can hardly believe you were concerned about my health."

"Dag, we've always been concerned about you, Simon and me." She sat in the chair beside my bed, where so recently I'd seen Riley sitting. "Simon pushed me toward you in college. He always said you needed someone to look out for you. And now you've caught his killer.

How can I say thank you Dag?" She pulled out a checkbook. I let her write the check. She handed it over to me and I counted the zeros.

"It's a little more than we agreed to," I said.

"Just a small token of my appreciation for all you've done and all you've been through, Dag," she said.

"Yes. Let's see, what did I accomplish? I tracked down your husband for you so you could send a hired thug to wire the plane and kill him. I'll bet you were even mad that Oksamma tried to kill me before I found Simon—doubly so when you found there was nothing on my computer. Then Riley acquired the backup disks for Simon's computer that you made before you erased his files. Since she already knew you owned the condo, you knew she couldn't resist an invitation to see it. You arranged to have a party for the girls and get her invited up. You kidnapped her and called Bradley in to recover the property. But it was you who hit her. It's your office, after all. Riley saw the lilacs there. You sent Oksamma to see that Bradley stayed motivated. It was all a convenience to you that both Bradley and Oksamma got killed in the process. Now there are no witnesses that can tie you to your part in blackmailing area businessmen and laundering the money through cash card sales at a franchise you had Simon create." I'd spilled everything. It was all conjecture, but I knew that Jordan had heard it all.

"Simon always said you were the best," Brenda said. "I never particularly believed him. I always thought Simon was the best. But he turned out to be such a disappointment. He could never make the really hard calls. He had a juvenile sense of ethics. He even felt guilty about sleeping with me when you and I were married. And here you are, with such a fabulous theory and no proof. And there is none on those backup disks, either. Nothing that will tie me to anything that has happened. Good theory though, smarty."

"Why, Brenda?" I asked. "Why did you kill Simon? You had everything."

"I have everything, Dag," she said standing up. It was going to fail. "I was married to Simon for thirty years. I loved him to death." Her smile reminded me of a predator's open mouth after a kill. She leaned in close to me. The scent of lilacs was bringing tears to my eyes and I thought I might sneeze on her again. But what she said chilled me to the bone.

"I didn't kill Simon, Dag," she whispered. "You did. You with the help of that stupid blonde twit he thought the world of. I told you where the trigger was for the explosives on his plane. She spelled it out for you. F-8-e-d-2-d-1-e. When you sent the signal, the plane went poof." She stood and turned to leave, then turned back to me.

"Spend your money fast, Dag," she said. "I hear you're not long for this world." I saw Jordan slip out of the closet behind her and when she turned he had his ID out and his sidearm drawn. She screamed and I saw Riley fill the door blocking any entrance or exit to the room.

"Brenda Barnett," Jordan intoned. "You are under arrest on suspicion of murder, attempted murder, racketeering, embezzlement, money laundering, blackmail, and running a house of prostitution." He snapped handcuffs onto her wrists, perhaps more tightly than was strictly necessary.

"You have no proof of any of that," she spat. "Do you think that I will sit for a day in any prison? When my lawyers get finished with you, you won't even have a badge left."

"Then let's add this one," I said from the bed. "As sole surviving partner and majority holder of Barnett, Keane, and Lamb Ltd., you can also be charged for counterfeiting of computer software and smuggling it into the country for illegal gain." The instant look of loathing on her face was not directed at me.

"That idiot!" she exclaimed. It seemed she didn't know about Bradley's own endeavor to make money in the black market. Jordan turned Brenda and headed for the door. Riley stepped in. I couldn't resist one last dig at Brenda.

"Brenda," I called after her. Jordan stopped and turned her to face me. "How does it feel to get rid of two lovers in a week?" She paused and snarled at me.

"I'm hoping for a hat-trick, Dag," she said and jerked forward out of the room with Jordan holding her arm.

I hate hockey.

Riley came to me and hugged me.

"That was brilliant," she said.

"You only heard the end," I answered.

"Oh, I heard it all," she responded. I looked up at her she pulled back the hair from her ear and I saw a tiny earbud inserted there. She pointed to the lamp beside my bed. Tucked up under the shade was a tiny transmitter. I knew that someplace nearby she had also concealed an amplifier for the low-wattage signal that the little device would put out.

"You are very sneaky," I said.

"Well, you showed me how to open the vault," she answered. When I went to get your laptop, I saw the mic on your desk. I picked up the transmitter and earbud out of the vault before I came back. I wanted to be sure I could hear you if you needed me."

"I need you Riley. You know that." She perched up on the edge of my bed and I could see her smooth bare legs sticking out from beneath her skirt. She heard the beeping of my monitor speed up slightly and glanced at it in alarm, then turned and smiled back at me.

"So I do have some affect on you," she said smugly. "What do you need me for right now?" I handed her the check for $100,000 that Brenda had written.

"I need you to get this to the bank right away," I said. "Let's hope it clears before Brenda thinks to stop payment on it."

"You'd take money from her?" Riley said in disbelief.

"Can you think of a muffin-top more deserving of having money taken from her?" I asked. We both laughed. Doc Roberts appeared in the doorway.

"I need to speak with Mr. Hamar, for a few minutes, Miss," he said.

"Yes, Doctor," she answered. "I'll be back in a flash," she said to me. She took the check and headed out the door.

"How am I doing, Doc?" I asked. I had to admit that I was feeling a little tired now, but other than that, I didn't seem too much the worse for wear.

"You know the story, Dag," he answered. "You were in cardiac arrest when they brought you in Sunday morning. No one counted on your heart restarting." He opened my gown and examined my chest where there were two burn marks from the defibrillator. I noticed my meager chest hair was all gone and I was painted orange.

"What's all that?" I asked.

"Well, they brought an organ donor in right on your heels. I had you rolled into the operating room and prepped for the transplant before we found out the heart was no good. The guy had fallen on broken glass and a sliver was driven right up under his scapula and into his heart. An inch higher and the bone would have stopped it. Of course, he wouldn't have been donating then. We transplanted a lot of his other organs to recipients though. Too bad about the heart."

Bradley had done some good in his death then. He just hadn't done me any good. It's okay. I don't think I could have lived with part of him in me.

"A second body came in at the same time with a perfectly good heart, but no donor card. We can't just harvest organs without the donor's consent. We're keeping you prepped though. We came through the holiday without as much activity as we often have, but we've got time. The ventricle chamber wall has grown extremely thin. A tear could be the last of it, so quit bringing business into the hospital with you, would you?"

"You've got it Doc," I said. "It's not giving me any pain right now."

"Well, we've got you on ARBs, Beta-Blockers, and Diuretics to expand your blood vessels and slow your heart. It takes the pressure off the heart and makes it so it doesn't have to work so hard. But it also gives you low blood pressure. That's why you've got everything you need in bed. We don't want to be getting you up and down a lot with this. So just lie back and relax and try not to aggravate the condition until we can get a donor through the door, okay?"

I agreed to Doc's conditions and he left. It was getting pretty serious. I closed my eyes for what seemed like only a few seconds. When I opened them, I had another visitor. If this kept up they'd put me in a locked ward. Angel stood beside my bed with her lower lip clenched between her teeth.

"Are you all right, Dag?" she whispered. She glanced toward the door.

"Mmmm. Yes," I said taking inventory. The machine next to me was still beeping along. I must be alive. "What did they tell you?"

"Just that you weren't allowed any visitors now. I came up the back stairs and sneaked in."

"Just to visit me, Angel?" I asked. "What's on your mind?"

"You are a kind man, Dag," she answered. "Simon trusted you. I trust you." A tear was beginning to form in her eye. I wasn't sure if I could trust my judgment that it was real or not. "Can you help Davy?" Ah there, it was out.

"What's the problem?" I asked.

"They are holding him for kidnapping your girlfriend. He didn't know. None of us knew. I wasn't even going to go to the party Saturday night, but Cinnamon called and said she'd invited Debbie. I like her and I thought that it would be fun. And I still hoped that she was going to say by some miracle that Simon was alive and it was all a big mistake."

"What happened?" I prompted.

"She disappeared. We're all so used to each other walking in and out that we didn't think anything of it for a while. Then Davy came out. He's always there because he's the security person, you know. He came out a little after midnight and said that we all had to go. He'd just gotten orders that he was to lock up the condo until further notice. He collected all our security cards from us and ushered us to the elevator."

"How many are all of you?" I asked.

"There were about twenty of us there at the time. We didn't really get started until 9:00 or so. We thought it was pretty rude for them to kick us out so early. But that's when Cinnamon noticed that Debbie was gone. I asked Davy and he said she had left earlier—didn't I know? I thought that it was strange that she didn't say anything to us, but we were all a little tipsy and I thought she might have gotten sick. I grabbed my cell phone out of the basket and called her as we got on the elevator. I heard a phone ringing as the doors closed. It gave me a little chill, but we didn't know what to do. She didn't answer, and I knew she was still in the condo. I should have done something.

"Then Davy called me last night and said he was in jail. I went to visit him this afternoon and he said they'd kidnapped and hurt Deb and he was in trouble for it. He was just doing his job, Dag. He didn't know they kidnapped her. They told him she was trying to steal something and they were going to hold her till morning and then call the police. He couldn't believe the way you came busting in Sunday morning and decked him. He said you were like a berserker." She paused and reached out to touch my cheek.

"He's a good guy," she pled. "He really didn't know. Can't you help him?"

"Angel," I said, breaking the mesmerizing stroking of her fingers against my cheek. "I'm sure things will be all right."

"If there is anything I can do for you that would help," she said. I saw her unzip her short fur jacket and knew what she was attempting. Get real. I've got a fucking catheter in.

"Angel," I said, "the thing that will help Davy is for him to come absolutely clean with the police, including agreeing to testify against Brenda Barnett. I'm pretty sure he knew who his boss was, just as I'm sure you knew that it was her and not Simon and Bradley that ran the condo. And you can help by agreeing to testify as well. No one knows what you really did up there except those who were involved. We can't expect any of the men who were there to come forward, especially if they think Brenda has something on them."

"I'll do it," she said. "I don't care anymore. I'll talk to the other girls. Most of them believe their jobs will be in jeopardy if they talk, but I can convince some of them to testify, I'm sure. Thank you, Dag." She leaned in and kissed my forehead again.

"Angel," I said, suddenly curious about something. "There is one thing you could do for me personally." She looked at me and smiled.

"You told me that you and Simon and Bradley all had tattoos. What does yours say?"

I will never, ever, understand women. All she had to do was tell me. Instead she kept that slightly sensuous smile on her lips as she stared into my eyes. Then she reached for her waist, unfastened the button, and lowered the zipper on her skin tight low riders. I stared in amazement as she slowly pulled them down. I kept expecting her to turn and show me her buttocks as the anticipated place for a tattoo. Instead the jeans crept lower and lower from her waist.

If Angel didn't shave, I wouldn't have been able to see the tattoo. When I saw it, I couldn't believe she'd tolerated a tattoo needle on that sensitive flesh. When I read it, I knew she hadn't chosen the tattoo herself. This was more of Simon's work. "36DB00BS." The Os had been artfully transformed into nipples on either side of the cleavage, with shoulders drawn above.

I tore my gaze away from the offered sight and looked back into her eyes. The sardonic smile was still in place and she pulled up the jeans and refastened them.

Damn.

No consideration for my ailing heart.

"Angel," I said. "Why do you waste your time with older men? Why don't you satisfy yourself with Davy, go to the house in Croatia, and be happy?"

"Davy is nice, and I love him in a way. But already he looks at younger girls at the condo instead of me," she said. "He sees me getting old. I'll be thirty next month, and he's right. When I'm with a man who is fifty or sixty, he sees me as young and beautiful. And as long as we are together I'm still twenty or thirty years younger. He keeps looking at me. When he's seventy, fifty is going to look young. And even if he sees someone younger and prettier, he still knows he's got a young beautiful woman that other men his age envy him for. And if he happens to be rich and kind, then there are all kinds of bonuses. I'll be waiting for you when you get out of here if you say so."

"I'm not rich, Angel," I laughed.

"But you are kind," she said. "Call me when you get out." She zipped up her jacket and left. She looked down the hall both ways before she stepped through the door, then turned and waved good-bye as she left.

Legs, and Other Things You Miss When You Don't Have Them

I WOKE UP with tubes in my nose and other orifices and a weight on my chest that was unfamiliar. I was getting oxygen through the tubes, but my breathing was shallow.

The weight on my chest was Riley's head.

Apparently she'd crawled up on the bed during the night and went to sleep with her head on my chest. Boney pillow if you ask me. She was wearing a white silk blouse that in her present position gaped open showing rather more than she usually exposed.

All right. A lot more.

I could see the bandage above her right breast and under her arm, where Oksamma's bullet had struck. The bastard. If he weren't dead, I'd get out of this bed and go kill him. To harm that beautiful woman. She was lucky it had hit at the angle it did.

I know that you want me to say that I covered her and restored her modesty, and that is just what I did.

After about ten minutes.

I wasn't dead yet.

I couldn't tear my eyes away from her soft smooth skin until I felt tears running from them and down my cheeks. Afraid that I would sob and wake her, I gently reached over and pulled her blouse closed.

Damn.

What a lousy time to be old. I just wanted to hold her and protect her. The bruises on her cheek had changed to that horrid yellow color that, in spite of how bad it looks, signifies healing. I wanted to kiss that cheek, but settled for letting my fingers glide softly across her skin.

She fluttered her eyelids open and smiled at me. She reached for my hand and held the palm against her cheek and closed her eyes gently again. We stayed that way for several minutes.

All night I'd had dreams filled with memories. Simon and Brenda and me in college. My marriage and her betrayal. The years I'd missed with them and the different people they had become. What drove people who have it all to think they don't have enough? Maybe it was me who changed. What was Brenda really peddling? Sex? Influence? Ways to wealth? The secret had to be on Simon's jump-drive, if there was only a way to crack the encryption code on it.

The more I thought about it, the more I became convinced that the tattooed words on Simon and Angel held a key. F8ed2d1e36DB00Bs. It was suddenly looking a lot more feasible. I reached for the piece of paper on which I'd written Angel's tattooed message and in so doing wakened Riley. She stretched luxuriously, threatening to undo the modest covering that I'd put in place a few minutes ago. A sudden wince as she reached the point of flexion where it pulled on her wound stopped the stretch with a stab of pain. Yes, that would take a while to heal.

"Good morning, partner," she said. "Sorry I borrowed a corner of your bed last night."

"Anytime you want, Riley," I said.

"I'm going to count on that," she replied.

We were interrupted by a small voice from the door. "Excuse me; is this Mr. Hamar's room?" We looked over at the door and little Billie was sitting there in a wheelchair pushed by her mother.

"If it's not convenient, we'll come back some other time," Wanda said.

"No, no," I answered. "Come in. Billie, this is my partner, Deb Riley. Deb, this is Billie and Wanda Martin. It's good to see you Billie."

"Nice to meet you, Billie," Riley said extending a hand to her.

"Wow! You're beautiful!" was Billie's spontaneous response.

"It's nice to meet you Miss Riley," Wanda said as they shook hands. "We heard Mr. Hamar was in the hospital and Billie wanted to come to see him."

"I've got a new heart, Mr. Hamar." Billie said smiling. "I'm getting better now. Have you moved into the hospital so you can get yours?"

"Yes, Billie. It's best to be prepared, don't you think?"

"Are you a private investigator, too?" Billie asked Riley. She nodded. "That's what I'm going to be when I grow up. I'm going to investigate things and solve mysteries."

"You've made a big impression on my daughter," Wanda said to me. "I know we aren't supposed to know this, but I saw you talking to the same lawyer that told us about Billie's trust. Whatever part you played, I wanted to say thank you."

"I don't know that I played a very big part," I answered. "Sometimes when there is a flood, you just need to dig a little channel and the water will flow where it belongs."

"Thank you anyway," she said. "And good luck."

"Thank you," I said, "and thank you, Billie, for being such a great inspiration to me to get my new heart and get well."

"Honey," Wanda said to Billie, "we don't want to tire Mr. Hamar out. I'll bring you back to see him tomorrow."

"I'm going home next week," Billie said. "I hope you get to go home soon!"

I waved and Riley and I watched them leave. We sat in silence for a few minutes.

"Riley," I said.

"I'm not leaving," she answered quickly.

"You can't stay here forever, kiddo," I replied.

"Dag, I can't. I won't say goodbye." I could see tears in her eyes and I could feel them building again in my own. Billie's visit had brought the reality of my situation home for both of us. That beeping machine next to me was a constant reminder that my life was holding on by a thread.

Even the little conversation I'd had in the past few minutes was tiring.

"I'm not asking you to say good-bye, Riley," I said. She fell on me—gently—and hugged me as well as she could. I stroked her back and patted her. This wasn't going to get easier. "You know what I need?" I asked.

"What Dag?"

"I need a pair of legs."

"You can have mine anytime you want them," she said, and brought them up onto the bed beside me. So help me, I let my hand fall on the perfect smooth skin of one of her legs and just rest there. My catheter suddenly felt uncomfortable. I removed my hand and reached for the pad of paper by my bedside. I handed the paper to Riley. She looked at it and then at me.

"36DB00BS," she said. "You are obviously not referring to me."

"Angel told me in Atlanta that she and Simon and Bradley had gotten drunk one night and had tattoos done. All three of them. Simon's was F8ed2d1e. Angel told me hers was 36DB00BS," I lied just a little. She hadn't actually told me. "I think if we had Bradley's tattoo, we might have the final pieces to the puzzle. Simon found out Brenda was blackmailing a lot of people. He put the necessary information on his jump-drive and encrypted it. I'm betting that with the three of these together, we'd have the 24 characters of an encryption code. What we don't have is Bradley's tattoo."

"You want me to go to the morgue, examine the dead body of the man who kidnapped and beat me, and copy down his tattoo?" she said to me in a threatening tone.

"Well, if it wouldn't be too much trouble," I said. "Only, I'm guessing that either the body is here where they harvested the organs, or the police have it sealed at the morgue and you won't be allowed to see it. I don't know what to tell you."

"Don't tell me anything more," Riley said. Now I was definitely seeing a vengeful glint in her eye. "I know how to get to the body. And if there is a scalpel handy when I get there, I'll cut the tattoo off and bring it to you."

"Uh just copying down the word should be adequate, Riley," I said. I had a feeling that if she started cutting at Bradley's body there wouldn't be anything recognizable left of it in the morning.

"You got it, Dag." She slid off the bed and gathered her things.

"I love you, Riley," I said softly as she prepared to go. She turned and looked at me.

"You'd damned well better mean that," she said. She kissed me and left the room. She didn't turn back or she'd have seen the tears rolling down my cheek. I had a heartache of a kind I'd never had. I looked down the front of the hospital gown at my bare chest under it with the two diodes connected to the heart monitor. Beneath the orange stain of iodine, I thought I saw a darker area. My heart had begun to leak.

I napped. It was afternoon when I woke up again. My meals were coming in a bottle this week. I was feeling edgy. I looked at my surroundings. Did I mention that I hate hospitals? The constant beeping of the heart monitor had almost become a background white noise over the three days I'd been here. But now it was an irritating reminder of my weakening heart.

I took my time—used the controls on the bed to change my position. This was going to be hard. I assessed the things I was attached to.

First, the drip. That was the least likely to create problems. I loosened the tape and pulled the needle out of my arm. I quickly slapped a piece of the tape back over the hole and clamped my arm shut. That wasn't so bad. I rested a few minutes and reached under the covers. I didn't even want to look at what I was doing. I untaped the tube from my leg and slowly inched the catheter out of my penis. Oh God! The beeps sped up slightly, but I focused on my breathing and in a minute it was out. It was a strange feeling. If I had the opportunity, I was going to pee sometime soon, just for the pleasure of it. I left the oxygen tubes in my nose for as long as I could. It helped to steady my breathing.

Now I had to deal with the heart monitor. A heart monitor is a computer with a network connection. It beeps in the room, but on the monitor at the nurses' station, it just shows the constant wave and signals an audible alert only if the patient is in distress. There was no way I could learn enough about it to hack it in the time I had before nurses would be prowling the halls again. But Riley had left my laptop and it would only take a few minutes to jury-rig an intercept program to record the signal from the machine. All I needed was a surveillance toolkit that was on the network at the office. I checked the connections and plugged my laptop into an open network port. I set it to record and waited. I didn't dare wait too long, but if I set too short a cycle, it might be spotted before I was safely away. I forced myself to wait five minutes before I disconnected the computer and set it to play back what it had recorded in a continuous loop. Then I set it on top of the monitor and quickly unplugged the network connection from the monitor and put it into my computer. The signal was instantly picked up and continued the playback. I turned off the heart monitor and tore the contacts off my skin. I could see that the dark spot had spread and was darker. There just wasn't much time.

I was free, but naked. Remembering what Doc Roberts had told me about light-headedness, I rose very slowly from the bed until I was upright. Finally, I had to leave the oxygen behind in order to walk to the closet. Once there I dressed. Riley brought me clean clothes yesterday to lift my spirits. She'd even brought a new shirt she said was lavender, but registered to me as blue. I loaded my pockets with my wallet and checked to be sure my money was there. I was wearing down. I slipped my shoes on without bothering with socks or to stop and tie them, took my coat and hat from the closet, and shuffled out the door.

I had no choice but to go slowly, but I walked steadily upright down the hall to the elevators. Once inside I breathed a sigh of relief. I was free. A hospital is a terrible place to die.

I was in for a shock when I stepped out the hospital door to the taxi stand. No one had bothered to tell me it had snowed while I was inside. I hadn't seen snow in Seattle in five years. I made it to a cab and gave the driver the address I wanted.

Ten minutes later we pulled up in front of Tovoni's. It was open this time. I showed the driver a hundred dollar bill and tore it in half. I handed him half and told him he'd get the other half if he waited for me while I had a cup of coffee, and to keep the meter running. This wasn't to pay for the cab fare. I made my way to Tovoni's door and was pleased to see the driver settle back in his seat to snooze.

Jackie greeted me when I walked in the door.

"Dag! We haven't seen you in a while. Everything okay?"

"Thanks, Jackie. I was out of town for a while. Just back now."

"Want the usual?"

"Yes, please."

In a moment she had placed a small mug of perfect espresso and water in my hand. I hovered over it just inhaling the intoxicating scent. Just breathing. I lifted the cup to my lips and sipped at the crème.

Damn.

Everything made me cry these days. If there is a heaven, Tovoni's coffee is there. It was so good.

I left a generous tip and went back to the cab. I handed the driver the other half of the bill and gave him my address. A few minutes later we arrived at my home. I paid him and made my way to the door. Inside our common entry, I saw that Mrs. Prior's door was ajar.

"Maizie," I called quietly. "Here girl." I heard the jingle of her collar and she came rushing out of the door, tail wagging. "Hey there. You really are glad to see me, aren't you?"

Maizie was up and down the stairs three times in the time that it took me to make it to my door. My breathing was labored now. I was beginning to hear the buzzing in my ears that always preceded an attack. I checked my pocket automatically and discovered I had remembered to pocket my pills from the drawer in my hospital room. I popped two into my mouth just inside the door. My chair was only a few steps away, but it seemed like an eternity before I reached it. I left the door open so that Maizie could go back to Mrs. Prior if she got tired of sitting with me.

I settled in my chair and reclined it. As soon as I had spread the afghan over my legs, Maizie jumped up and settled herself on my lap. I reached for the remote control and pressed play. Brahms leapt from the speakers in an instant, all-encompassing moment of ecstasy. A single picture light that I always left on was burning over the seascape hanging on the wall in front of me. I turned my head toward the window and saw mixed rain and snow had begun to fall. By morning it would wash the snow all away.

What did I care?

I was home.

My Third Year in Kindergarten, I Learned That All Stories Have a Good Ending

BEFORE YOU GO THINKING that I was a really dumb little shit, let me set the record straight about why I was three years in kindergarten.

Back then, in those olden days fifty plus years ago, there wasn't an organized nursery school or preschool program, and kindergartens were taught mostly by volunteers in church basements. That was what got my mother into the classroom. She had been a campaigner for teaching the children of Swedish immigrants how to speak proper English and putting them on the road to success. When Pastor Olmquist called on her with a proposal to start a kindergarten at the local Swedish Lutheran church, she couldn't really say no, even though she was nominally Catholic and publicly an atheist. She believed that religion kept the masses down, and she ran her family as a good socialist would.

But she also knew a good thing when she saw it. Having a podium to advance the education of Swedish children in America was all it took to get her to say yes.

I was four years old—too young for regular admittance into kindergarten, but because mother was the teacher, I was permitted to attend.

I learned how to make snakes out of clay and to weave the snakes together to make little clay baskets.

The next year I was five and eligible to attend kindergarten. I had already learned how to make snakes out of clay, so I allowed my curiosity to get the best of me and started looking at books. They were mysterious things, these books. When mother opened them, they had wonderful stories in them. When I opened them, they were filled with secret scribbles that meant nothing. I even attempted to put my own stories in them with scribbles, but mother disapproved and said that my marks made it hard to read the words. So, she began to teach me to read.

By the end of that year, I could read simple books to myself or out loud. It was wonderful.

A silly rule was implemented by the school district that year. The school board decided that they would move the cut-off date for the age of being admitted into school. It went from September 15—my birthday—to September 1. You had to be six by the first of September to be admitted into first grade. Mother protested, and when the school principal learned that I could already read, he was willing to admit me to school.

Then the illness came. According to the doctors, I'd had an untreated strep throat condition during the summer and less than a month later, I contracted Rheumatic Fever. It was pretty severe, and for a while mother thought I was dying. I fought through it, and recovered. But by this time school was six weeks in session and the principal was adamant that he would not allow me to start at such a disadvantage at such a young age. So at six years old, I found myself under my mother's tutelage again in kindergarten. I spent my days reading. I had little care for anything else that was being taught to the kindergartners because mother had insisted on only English being spoken in our home, and I'd long since mastered the art of making clay snakes. I emerged from my cocoon in the reading area only for arithmetic lessons. I hoarded the books. I drove away smaller children who wanted to read them.

But I couldn't protect them all, all the time. I sat one day to read a book that had interested me only to find that the last dozen or so pages had been torn out by an enraged five-year-old some weeks before. I was furious. I cried. I stormed. I kicked my feet. I was six and I would never find out the ending of the story.

My mother weathered the storm. She sat down beside me and told me that it was indeed a terrible thing that pages had been torn from a book, but that children who did not know the secrets of books often did not value them as I did. And, she revealed, I had not yet learned all the secrets of books myself.

I was shocked. I read well above my age-level for all that I was stuck back in kindergarten again. My first grade contemporaries were still struggling with "see Spot run" and I was deep in Hardy Boys Mysteries. What did I have to learn about books?

My mother told me that true masters of books often did not need to read the ending. They were quite content to put down a book without finishing it because they could tell the ending themselves. A true master of reading knew that all stories have a good ending. So they could simply close the book before the last chapter and imagine what that ending would be. Often, if they went back to read the ending of a book they had previously skipped, they were disappointed that it did not end as well as they had imagined.

She encouraged me to read the book again and when I reached the torn out pages to close my eyes and imagine the ending of the story. It was liberating for a six-year-old. I often closed books before the ending from that day onward and let my imagination tell me what came next.

Of course, later I learned that my imagined ending might not be the same or anywhere near as good as what the author had written. But I often closed books before the last chapter to let my imagination complete them before I read what the author had written. And I often found that mother was right—my endings were better.

I learned fifty years later what rheumatic fever had done to my heart. It wasn't until I had a battle with strep throat just a year ago that left me back in the throes of rheumatic fever. It was a short-lived battle. With the help of modern antibiotics, I came through quickly. But after my heart attack eight months ago, I learned that the damage done to my heart by the disease was irreversible. It was weakening daily.

I denied it as much as I could. I continued to walk to work, even when Maizie and I had to stop three or four times in the mile to rest. I suffered increasing chest pains and shortness of breath over the months following the attack. I would have phases when for days everything would seem completely normal, and then weeks at a time when it seemed like I would never draw a deep breath again.

The spreading dark stain on my chest tells me that my heart is leaking. The valves and chamber walls are disintegrating, and I just don't want to die in a hospital.

So I came home. I thought I'd just rest for a while in my chair, but now I find that with Maizie on my lap, I really don't want to waste the effort of getting up. Besides, sitting here, I can see the picture that Rhonda painted for me all those years ago. I never noticed how vivid the colors are in a sunset. Do you see the way the reds and oranges blend into each other, and the incredible streaks of pink that radiate out from the center of the yellow-white orb? It captures my senses and transports me to that very beach. I can almost feel myself standing down there watching the sunset with the fresh salt spray in my face. I wonder what it was that I was contemplating, and how Rhonda that knew I was there.

Numbers keep going through my mind. I should have told Riley that the tattoos were hexadecimal codes. Put them together and with twenty-four characters you have a what? 384 bit encryption code. That can't be right. No one makes 384 bit codes. It would have to just need two of the three to have a 256-bit code. Maybe the secret is to find which of the two codes out of the three go together. There are only six possible combinations.

Riley will figure out that the "S" in Angel's tattoo is a 5 won't she?

Dear, sweet Riley. I want so badly to be thirty years younger. Idiots who can't see what an incredible woman she is! Why would they care if she has hair? She is beautiful inside and out.

I wandered off-subject there for a minute. Sorry. I find that has happened more and more lately. I start thinking about something and my mind just wanders from subject to subject. That is probably how I came up with a missing day Saturday. I hope nothing important happened that day.

I should have stopped at the office and tagged the jump-drive. I'd like to know what is on the backups that Riley picked up from Brenda's house. If I had this all to do over again, I'd break a few more rules, like she does. I should have disconnected all the disk drives so that they weren't damaged if someone...

No.

My partner will take care of the office. Riley will be there. Won't she be surprised when she finds out what I left her? She'll get her master's in January. She's done a good job. I wonder if she'll get a PhD.

I was telling you a story. I don't remember where I was. I wanted to finish it for you. And I wanted to tell you the answer to life, the universe, and everything. But I never found the question.

Sorry. I'm wandering again.

I'm so tired now. It must be past midnight. Brahms is still playing on my stereo. I'm feeling awfully sleepy.

I could just walk into that painting; it seems so real to me.

Do me a favor, would you?

Tell Riley my story had a good ending.

Printed in Great Britain
by Amazon

34074696R00136